DOUBTING THOMAS

ROBERT REEVES

DOUBTING THOMAS

CROWN PUBLISHERS, INC.

NEW YORK

This is a work of fiction. The characters, incidents, and dialogues are products of the author's imagination and are not to be construed as real. The author's use of names of actual persons, living or dead, and actual places are incidental to the purposes of the plot and are not intended to change the entirely fictional character of the work.

Manufactured in the United States of America

Library of Congress Cataloging in Publication Data

Reeves, Robert N.
Doubting Thomas.

I. Title.
PS3568.E472D6   1985   813'.54   84-23107
ISBN 0-517-55616-2

BOOK DESIGN BY LESLEY BLAKENEY

10 9 8 7 6 5 4 3 2 1

First Edition

FOR BIG BOB

PART I
<u>THEY</u>

═══ONE═══

I LEFT THE OLD MAN lying there, curled around a commode in the men's room at Suffolk Downs, nuzzling with his cheek an empty bottle of Black & White. Experience had taught me not to help drunks to their feet. Upright, they flailed like drowning swimmers and clutched wildly at anything within reach. But supine, they enjoyed the blissful security of the floor, where balance was effortless and equilibrium foolproof.

After the feature race, I had left Cleve Dickey in the Paddock Bar, cashed my second straight winning ticket, entered the men's room, and discovered the old drunk in the second stall on the left. His eyes were open but glazed, and his arms twitched slightly, like a dog running in its dream.

"Jesus . . ." the old man muttered. Even though he lay at my feet, I could smell the digested alcohol on his breath.

"Easy does it, sport," I said. Not wanting to add to his humiliation, I turned toward the next stall. He reached out with a spastic movement and caught my ankle. The empty bottle of B&W rolled loudly across the tile. "Jesus . . . saves," he sputtered.

I smiled. "Looks like you've been backsliding," I said.

He released my ankle and tried to get up. His arms reached into the air and then fell back.

"Relax," I said. "Stay down."

I hesitated over him. To be honest, I felt a strange bond between us, a peculiar sort of camaraderie. Yes, I was a little drunk myself, and yes, I was undeniably a sinner, but it was more than that. In him I saw an image of every gambler who had ever lived, myself included. He tenaciously clung to hope—for Jesus, for a winner, for some future happiness—despite the deflating lessons of experience.

Which was why I had come to the track twice a week for the past three years: to watch with fascination and dread and even with love as the sorry horseflesh struggled around the mile oval, carrying on their heaving backs the hopes of the sorry humanflesh who assembled there to bet on them. The air of desperation tugged at me, kept pulling me out of my own deadening academic routine, out of the collegiate calm where no risks were taken, where tenured futures were monotonously secure, and where I was Assistant Professor of American Civilization, Thomas C. Theron. At Suffolk, I was just another schmuck fingering a *Racing Form.* Here I was caught, like everyone else, in a punishing cycle that with each race knocked me back and forth between hope and despair. The only difference between me and the drunk at my feet was racing luck.

The tile beneath the old man's head was wet with urine. I took a section of my *Racing Form,* gently lifted his gray head, and rested it on the newsprint. "Relax," I said, leaning over him. "Stay down."

Suddenly he grabbed my tie and held on for all he was worth. His eyes focused momentarily, and he sputtered again, urgently, "Jesus saves! Jesus . . ." From this close, his breath made me wince.

Uncurling his bony fingers from my tie, I managed to tell him cheerfully that I hoped so, for his sake. His head sank back onto the *Racing Form.* I left the men's room and headed back to the Paddock Bar and Cleve Dickey.

Cleve was sipping ginger ale at the same table he had occupied for the last eighteen years, right above the box seats, precisely on the dividing line between grandstand and clubhouse, providing him a rare and undistorted view of the finish line. His face carried an habitual expression of sourness, in great part because he wasn't permitted to bet on the races. Cleve was the track handicapper, which meant that he established the morning betting line and assigned the amount of weight that each horse carried in each race. The better horses carried more weight, the inferior horses less, the theory being that the distributed weight gave each horse roughly the same opportunity to win the race. But the fact was, Cleve and I and just about everyone else knew, half the horses at Suffolk were so infirm that they couldn't hit the wire first had they been weighted with helium balloons.

"That's four out of six races, teach," Cleve observed. "Not bad for someone with your limited handicapping skills." His diminutives for me—"teach," "T.T.," "Tommy"—had been conceived months ago as insults. Sometime thereafter, when he learned that I was not among the casual, slumming professionals whom he despised, the nicknames came to serve as rough endearments. "How much you up?"

"Five hundred," I said. I was up $420. Like most bettors, I tended to exaggerate my winnings and understate my losses.

"Quit while you're ahead. The ninth is a twenty-five-hundred-dollar maiden race. There's no future in it."

In response, I ordered another Old Forester, and instead of water on the side, I asked for a Miller. "No way. I'm feeling bullish." I grabbed my crotch for emphasis. "I'm investing in the future of my children." I had the feeling I was slurring my words.

"You don't have children."

"If I keep winning, I'm going to buy some."

Cleve frowned. "That's what I like about you, Tommy. I see you, and I don't feel so bad about not going to college." He had watched me self-destruct before. Today was among the five or six times in the past three years that I hadn't found a way to lose. I had been winning, drinking, betting recklessly, and still winning. But there was still a race left; failing that, there was still tomorrow.

Cleve turned his eyes wearily to the *Racing Form* spread out in front of him. On his head sat a jet-black toupee that fit like a Sears catalogue purchase. Whenever he bent his head, a two-inch gap grew between the rug and the gray bristles on the back of his neck. He wore the powder-blue side of a reversible vest and contrasting, navy-blue, sans-belt slacks. Eighteen years at the track were enough to make anyone lose sartorial perspective. Even so, given the competition, Cleve remained more or less at the cutting edge of Suffolk fashion.

Of course, I was no one to talk. I still arrived at my lectures all tweedy up top, all blue jeans and hiking boots down below, halfway between the sixties and the seventies. I intended no statement, except perhaps a general one of disinterest. The future corporate giants in my classes didn't trust anything not in pinstripes. For that matter, I didn't trust them back.

I folded the *Racing Form* to the ninth race and scanned the field of horses. Halfway down I saw a name that made me cough into my bourbon. The alcohol in my mouth started creeping up to my nose.

"Watch it!" Cleve said, frowning at the flecks of liquid spattered on his *Form.*

I looked again and there it was. Coming out of the fifth position was a three-year-old filly, dun-colored with white markings, named Jesus Saves.

"The hairball was trying to give me a tip!" I half shouted, half laughed. "He was trying to give me a horse!"

"What?" Cleve said irritably.

"This guy, this old man was on the floor in the bathroom. Dead drunk. He was slobbering and pawing the air and saying "Jesus Saves" over and over. Hell, I thought he was talking to me sinner-to-sinner, and he's giving me a horse." I raised the tumbler of bourbon in a toast. "He was a goddam tout!"

"Fascinating," Cleve said. He looked down at the *Form* and found the horse named Jesus Saves. An expression came across his face as though someone had farted. "If the creep has been betting horses like this," he observed dryly, "then it's no big secret why he's sleeping with his head next to a toilet. The only thing keeping Jesus Saves out of a can of dogfood can is the FDA."

I studied the filly's past performances. Cleve was not exaggerating. Rarely had I seen a thoroughbred with so little to recommend it. In the last year, Jesus Saves had raced nineteen times without losing her maiden. She had run mostly at Willington and Hopworth—both third-rate tracks in New Jersey—and she had yet to win a dime. The brief commentary on her races read like a catalogue of insults. Trailed. Ran green. Stopped. Eased. No threat. Her best finish had come ten months ago when she placed sixth in a field of eight, sixteen lengths back. No excuse. Today marked her seemingly pointless debut at Suffolk.

"And she's in against colts," Cleve continued, "which is a losing proposition to begin with."

"Have you been listening to the backstretch sexists?"

"Don't look at *me*. It's Mother Nature. A filly gets the lead against colts, she slows down, waves her butt, and hopes something will mount her."

"Ah, Cleve." I shook my head sadly. "Forget that. Isn't a name like Jesus Saves illegal? Wouldn't someone find it offensive?"

"The Jockey Club approves names. Can't duplicate a name used in the last fifteen years. Can't be obscene. Other than that, most anything goes. There was a nag at Rockingham, maybe five years ago, named Scumbag. I still don't know how they slipped that one by."

Lots of horses at Suffolk were bad, but Jesus Saves was outstandingly bad. Intriguingly bad. "Who in their right mind would still be trying to win with a horse like this? They have to be losing money."

"Who knows? Could be anything. Some guy needs a little extra in the way of a tax shelter. Or somebody buys it for their daughter and she thinks it's a pet. Or some meatpacker from Woburn thinks it's a great kick to own a racehorse, hoping for a winner's-circle photo for his den. Or maybe it's just a badger."

"A what?"

"A badge horse. Some guys stable a cheap horse so they can get owner's privileges at the track. Impress their friends." Cleve paused and chuckled. "I'll be damned. Jacob Bloomberg."

"Who?"

"Says here that the trainer is Jake Bloomberg," he replied, his lips turning up in a rare, halfhearted smile.

"What's so amusing about that?"

"I met Bloomberg this morning in the press box. Kind of skittish, not real friendly. Petey knew him a little back in New Jersey. Not much of a trainer, Petey said. Said he mostly scrounges around, works a few horses on the northeast circuit. His daughter just quit some finishing school outside of Boston. I don't know which one. Has some woodsy name. Piney something."

"Pine Manor," I assisted. In my college days I had often climbed the brick walls there after hours. "Pretty ritzy."

"Yeah, that's the one."

"What's the amusing part?"

"Well, Petey said she dropped out of school a couple of months ago and took a job in the Combat Zone."

"Hooking?"

"No, shedding her clothes."

I perked up. Unfortunately, this was the sort of thing that interested me. And I found it a more imaginative response to the high cost of tuition than selling magazine subscriptions. "An all-college-girl revue?" I asked.

"That's what Petey said." Cleve shot me a look that said he knew what I was thinking. "No, I don't know which club. But," he teased, "Petey hears that the girl is very shapely. Anyway, the word is that Bloomberg shipped a couple of horses to Suffolk so he could come up here and drag her home, straighten her out, whatever."

It was eight minutes to post. I finished my bourbon and ordered another one, trying to disperse the vaporous image of Bloomberg's daughter that had coalesced in my mind. The ninth was virtually impossible to handicap—a group of inept maidens, none any better or any worse than the rest—with the conspicuous exception of Jesus Saves. Maidens were racehorses that had never won a race, did not know how to win, and, because of the herd instinct, were too frightened to win. A few months of training had yet to obliterate their primordial desire to run in a pack.

The toteboard flashed. A colt named Sultan was getting most of the action. I glanced at my *Form*. The money being bet on him seemed absurdly out of proportion to his ability.

"They're getting on Sultan," Cleve observed. "In the last minute they've knocked him down from 8 to 1 to even money. They like Sultan."

I asked Cleve a question I had asked him a hundred times before. Each time it annoyed him. "Who are 'they,' Cleve?"

He snorted. "You know damn well. The smart money. The people with a tie to the backstretch. The insiders."

"But Cleveland," I said, feigning shock, "all these months I've been thinking you were an insider."

"Laugh if you want," he replied stubbornly, "but when a horse is going down in odds like Sultan, somebody is pulling the strings."

I shook my head. "The bettors have the same herd mentality as the horses. Somebody puts a little money on a decent horse, and all the ten-dollar bettors get on the bandwagon and knock the odds way down. It's all momentum. There's no 'they.' There are only lemmings."

The toteboard flashed again and Sultan dropped to 4–5. "They like Sultan," Cleve insisted.

I smiled self-righteously, swallowed what was left of the Old Forester, and headed for the betting windows. Cleve, like every horseplayer I had ever known, believed in *They* with the same fervor that other people believed in God. No matter how unpredictable thoroughbred racing was, no matter how chaotic and absurd, Cleve needed to believe in some unseen force pulling the strings, in some privileged, all-knowing group of bettors who knew *a priori* the outcome of a race. Whether out of insecurity or fear or paranoia, horseplayers needed to believe that some invisible power—whether God or *They*—made sense of the chaos and gave form to the void. I felt like an heretic. Or a doubting Thomas.

At five minutes to post, I stood in the betting lines, looking around, feeling giddy from the bourbon. As frantic as the grandstand was during the day, the atmosphere was even more desperate for the last race. The intelligent bettors usually left after the feature allowance, their last opportunity to wager on, by Suffolk standards, sound horses. The gamblers who stayed on were of two kinds: those who were losing, drinking heavily, and betting wildly to catch up. And those, like myself, who were winning, drinking heavily, and betting wildly with their winnings.

Everyone else—mostly nonbettors who compensated with noise and motion—fell into more obscure categories. Geriatrics ran about aimlessly, clutching day-old *Racing Forms,* babbling and cursing in obscure dialects; here and there the Stoopers, perpetually bent over, searched with insane purpose among the debris in hopes of uncovering a winning ticket. And beneath all of the mindless activity lay my favorites, the Mystics: supine, genderless, pee- and saliva-stained beings, who, untugged by human desire, tucked their heads beneath coats or newspapers, and curled up by the escalators or concessions. Or around the commodes, calling Jesus' name.

Of all the varied, roughly humanoid species at the track, I felt closest to the Mystics. They did not believe in *They.* They did not rebel against the chaos. And their wounds, like mine, were self-inflicted.

At two minutes to post, I reached the window.

"What'll it be, Mr. Theron?" Gus said.

The bills in my hand felt as insubstantial as air. I hesitated and glanced back at the toteboard.

A fat lady behind me poked me in the ribs. "Get off the pot, mister!" Glancing back, I saw her wild, matted hair, eyes even wilder.

I stood there in a kind of stupor. I was thinking of Bloomberg and wondering what his daughter looked like. I was wondering if at that very moment she was in the Zone, pulling her dress over her head. And mostly I was thinking of the Mystic slobbering on the men's room floor. I pushed the bills toward Gus. They rested on the counter like an offering on the altar of chaos. I cast my lot with the Mystic.

"Give me Jesus Saves to win," I told Gus.

Usually poker-faced, Gus turned a skeptical stare toward the toteboard, where Jesus Saves, without benefit of divine intervention, remained at 99–1. The odds might have been higher, but the board was not equipped to record it.

"You know something I don't?" Gus asked.

"I got religion," I replied mildly. The fat lady was pushing me out of the way. I turned, feeling slightly exhilarated. I heard the fat lady put two dollars on Jesus Saves. Lemmings, I thought.

"Cleve," I announced, "order me another bourbon and beer. I'm going to need it."

"Who'd you go for?"

I told him.

"That's suicide."

"Don't be melodramatic. I prefer to think of it as charmingly self-destructive." My stupor was fading; in its place was a growing embarrassment about the expensive gesture I had just made.

"For how much?"

"I'm not really sure." I wasn't. I checked my wallet and found the pari-mutuel ticket. Right below the sweaty thumbprint I saw the amount. "Two hundred-fifty." I added defensively, "Hell, I was up twice that."

Cleve shook his head slowly in exasperation and disappointment. By no means, I thought, the first time I'd provoked a rebuking shake of the head. My mother had started the trend well over a decade ago, when I told her I planned to bypass law school and write novels. More recently, Elizabeth had picked it up . . .

The ninth began like a hundred cheap maiden claimers I had seen before. The colts broke in a pack, and over the first furlong they remained in a pack. After three furlongs they were not fighting for the lead so much as they were hellbent on seeking the comfortable security of the middle of the herd.

The exception was the filly. Jesus Saves stumbled out of the gate, finally managed to catch stride, and settled behind the other maidens, which were grouped like frightened cattle ten lengths in front of her. Her jockey, an apprentice named Kevin Rourke, virtually stood up in the irons.

They hit the half-mile pole in forty-seven seconds, an appropriately bovine pace. Three colts, Sultan among them, ran shoulder-to-shoulder at the front, each delicately abstaining from the lead.

Turning for the stretch, Sultan got a strong whip and elected himself dominant male. I noticed for the first time that Sultan was blinkered, which protected him from the terrible knowledge of his isolation, two lengths in front. The blinkers, I supposed, accounted for the odds.

Cleve made a noise something like a grunt. I followed his eyes to the rear of the pack. Jesus Saves was making a wide turn, dangerously wide, taking her into the deep muck near the fence. But maidens often made wide turns; that's not what made Cleve grunt.

Speed made him grunt. The filly had exploded forward as though stung in some tender, lathered crevice by a swarm of hornets. Rourke rose in the irons, yanking savagely on the reigns to straighten her. Jesus Saves not only straightened, but veered radically back toward the rail. Despite her erratic path, she might have been on the Mass Turnpike and the colts on a Vineyard sand dune.

With a good 150 yards to go, Jesus Saves bolted past Sultan, who seemed only too happy to relinquish the lead. As she neared the wire, Rourke pulled her head so fiercely to the side that her nose was pointed at the grandstand where Cleve and I sat stunned. She zigzagged again. Rourke lost his irons, then his balance. He finished the race draped on the filly's neck like a wounded cowboy.

The following day's *Racing Form* would read, "Ran green. Won going away." It would not mention that chaos had prevailed.

I heard Cleve whispering, "Mother of God. Mother of holy effing God in heaven."

The grandstand crowd, having cheered the freakiness of the ride, turned sullen and angry with the growing realization that few tickets were to be cashed. Men around me were flinging their *Racing Forms* to the ground, or in the air, shouting "Fix!" and "Take him down!" Occasionally, a shriek of joy erupted from the bettors who always put two dollars on the long shot, no matter how long.

I sat speechless, feeling my veins dilate and the bourbon surge through them. My hands trembled and couldn't put a flame to my cigarette. The bottle of Miller looked easier to handle than the tumbler of bourbon, so I put that to my mouth. The glass clicked against my teeth.

My voice finally returned. "Praise the Lord," I said, mimicking the North Carolina twang that made Billy Graham famous.

"Goddam fix," a burly man snarled at no one in particular. "Goddam them. I don't know why I keep coming here."

The toteboard had not yet flashed Official. I sat thinking of things that could go wrong. I looked at Cleve, who was again calm. He'd seen too much over the years to stay excited for very long.

"That was some Wild West ride," I said. "Could they have doped her?" I caught myself as I said it.

"Who's 'they,' teach?" Cleve asked pointedly.

"Okay, I give. But what do you think?"

"Doubt it. You don't dope a horse to win, you dope a horse to lose. A drug can slow a fast horse down, but it can't speed up a plodder. You give a slow horse a pep pill, all you'll get for certain is a slow horse with its eyes bugging out."

"So it wasn't fishy?" I asked hopefully.

"I don't see how," he answered. "The odds were too high. If it was a fix, somebody would be laying a lot of money down, trying to cash a bet, which would knock the odds down. Maybe if the filly had gone off at 30–1, even 40–1, something might be screwy. But nobody goes to the trouble of fixing a race, then lets the horse come out of the gate at"—the toteboard flashed Official and the prices appeared—"my God. 127–1."

My hands shook wildly as I did the math. My numbers were as illegible as a prescription. But I made out three-one-seven-five-oh.

And on this day, I thought, the lame shall enter first. I had won $31,750. Half again what I earned in a year. Wesley College, according to its own smug formula, paid part in money and part in prestige.

The adrenaline was still making my heart flutter, but my hands were quiet enough to grip the tumbler. I finished the bourbon and Cleve went with me to collect.

"Nice little score," Gus said, trying to maintain a professional demeanor. Then he confessed with a guilty smile, "Put down a five myself. Realized a neat six-fifty. Thanks for the tip."

So Gus, too, was a lemming, I thought. "Happy to spread it

around," I said. "But don't thank me. I got the horse from a drunk doing an Australian crawl in the toilet."

"No kidding." Gus gave me a form to fill out, which signed over ten percent to the IRS.

"That," I said, putting my name to the document, "is the only absolute certainty in horseracing." The federal government took a percentage of any single-bet winnings over a thousand dollars. And out of each betting pool, no matter the outcome of the race, Suffolk Downs took an ostentatious nineteen percent off the top, a fourth of which they gave to the state of Massachusetts. "That's the smart money."

"You can pick up the check anytime tomorrow afternoon," Gus said.

"What? I can't have any cash?" I heard my voice rise to a whine. But Gus was taking the fun out of winning.

"Sorry."

"Not even a lousy grand?" I couldn't believe how the win was making me talk. I hated people who said "a lousy grand." All I needed now was a money clip, white shoes, and a big belly.

"I tell you what I can do, Mr. Theron. I can give you four hundred now, and you can pick up the check for the rest tomorrow."

"Perfect." I had something in mind for the cash.

The grandstand was almost deserted. Cleve started toward the gate, but I stopped him.

"Come with me to the men's room," I said. "I've got a debt to pay."

"You giving the concession back their beer?"

"The old man. If the government gets a percentage, so does he."

"Think he's still there?"

"He didn't look like he was going to get his land legs anytime soon."

"You feeling generous?"

"What's a lousy two hundred?" I laughed, and we went in.

Just inside stood a tiny bald man with his forefingers stuck into his ears, humming loudly to himself. I knew instantly what he was doing. He was drowning out the track loudspeaker and the conversation of the bettors so that he couldn't hear the results of the ninth race. He wanted to extend as long as possible the moment of hope, the exhilarating oasis of possibility.

Cleve winked at me, then stuck a *Racing Form* in front of the man's face and pointed to Jesus Saves. The man unplugged his ears and looked as though he were going to cry.

"You're a cruel man, Mr. Dickey."

Cleve shrugged, dropped the *Racing Form* to the floor, and went to the sink to wash his face.

The tile floor looked as though few of the patrons had bothered aiming at the urinals. I opened the second stall and found the evangelical where I had left him. He looked the same, except his head had slipped off the *Racing Form,* and he had vomited.

"Rise and shine," I announced amiably. "Today is the first day of the rest of your life." I held four fifties in my hand, and I began to wonder if the money would tempt him to begin the struggle for respectability all over again. Would it put the nagging fear—or hope—in his mind that perhaps things mattered after all?

Nonsense, I decided reasonably, pulling him away from the commode and rolling him onto his back.

The laxness of his body startled me.

I flushed the toilet, wet my hand with the clear water at the center of the bowl, and sprinkled his face. The old man did not move. He did not appear to be breathing. I searched around on his neck for a pulse, aping the gesture of a TV cop. I had no idea what I was doing.

"Cleve, come here. This geezer's not moving."

"If you poured that much whiskey down your gullet," he said, "you wouldn't move either. Just tuck the two hundred in his shirt and let's go."

"Look at him," I said.

Cleve peered over my shoulder. His voice wavered at a queer pitch I had never heard before. "That's no hairball," he said. "That's Jake Bloomberg."

═══*TWO*═══

FOR MOST OF THE NIGHT, an horrific image of Bloomberg's face floated in my dreams. But when I awoke, I found myself peering into the avuncular eyes of Captain Kangaroo. I had fallen asleep—or passed out—with the TV on. The residue of the Old Forester throbbed in my brain in perfect rhythm with my heartbeat. My mouth tasted as though I'd been licking the inside of a shoe. I gave myself a brief temperance lecture, the moral authority of which, I knew, would vanish with the headache.

A half-empty bottle of Bass ale and a pair of pliers rested on top of the TV, which in turn rested on an empty fruit crate next to the bed. While I gargled with the beer, I tried to steady my hands enough to coax the nose of the pliers onto the on-off spur of the TV. The nineteen-inch black-and-white Philco had been a rare bargain, even for a used set, because the control knobs were missing. I was vaguely aware of Captain Kangaroo conversing with a puppet in the shape of an ear of corn. The pliers finally gripped and turned the spur. Captain Kangaroo shrank to a tiny point of light and disappeared. In his place the image of Jake Bloomberg reappeared in my mind.

Cleve and I had waited at the track while an ambulance arrived, and after that two police officers. The medics made a perfunctory effort at resuscitation, which yielded only a sick hollow sound as they pounded Bloomberg's bony chest. The policemen seemed only slightly less bored. A cop with an enormous paunch and no rear end took a statement from me.

"Name, occupation?" he asked.

"Thomas Theron. I'm a teacher."

"Yeah?" He lifted his eyebrows skeptically. "Wheredaya teach?"

"At a local institution of higher learning," I replied evenly.

His eyes had come to rest on my hiking boots. "Higher than what?"

We weren't hitting it off. "Higher than O. Henry," I replied, "but lower than, say, *Gravity's Rainbow.*"

"What's that suppose to mean?"

The cop's nose impressed me a lot more than his mouth. The size of a tulip bulb, mottled with the purplish residue of burst capillaries, his nose was a trophy earned with a lifetime of dedicated drinking. "Forget it," I said, and told him the little I knew about the dead man in the toilet.

The second officer came over. "The old shitbox probably aspirated on his own vomit," he said.

Behind me, the medics zipped Bloomberg's urine-soaked corpse into a bag, handling him as fastidiously as if he were a used Kleenex. They wheeled him out, and with him any aspirations I had for a night of uncomplicated revelry with the largest amount of money I had ever had at one time. Instead, I said good-bye to Cleve and spent the night sipping Bass ale and bourbon in front of the TV.

I crawled out of bed at nine-thirty. By ten I had showered and dressed and was feeling better. No classes on Mondays. But mostly what cheered me up was the thought of three-one-seven-five oh. When Gus brought the check to the cashier's window, I would be there to greet him.

I dialed Elizabeth's number, thinking I might catch her before she left for work. She worked at a very high-toned mental health clinic in the suburbs, which kept banker's hours. Beth was an ex-student of mine who in two months would also be my ex-wife.

A male voice answered, but a second later I heard Beth say hello.

"Beth, it's Thomas. How's every little thing?" I gathered that every little thing was just fine. Her Back Bay apartment had housed both of us for two years, and the only telephone was right next to the bed. And Beth had always liked the mornings better than I did.

"I thought we had agreed not to talk," she said impatiently. I listened for the slight breathlessness of *coitus interruptus.*

"I know, I know," I said. "But this is an unusual circumstance. I've come into a little money. I'll be able to repay that loan sooner than expected."

"Listen, Thomas." Whatever breathlessness was in her voice was gone now. "How many times do I have to tell you that you don't owe me anything? Whatever you feel you owe me, I'm happy to write off to experience. Can't you just leave it at that?" This was not, I thought, the speech of a twenty-four-year-old. Living with me had aged her.

"No, I can't. Whether you call it a loan or not, you made the car payments for a year, and you shouldered the rent those months I was short. So I figure I owe you twenty-three hundred dollars, which I happen to have just now free and clear. We both know if given the chance, I'll just piss it away."

"Well, piss it away. I don't want it."

"Listen, take it. It'll make me feel better." Just don't make me beg.

"I have absolutely no interest in making you feel better. Not after—"

"Can we please not go into that? Forget how it will make me feel. It's your money. You deserve it."

"What's the catch, Thomas?"

"There's no catch."

"Don't be a shithook. I don't believe you." She hung up before I had a chance to ask her where she had picked up a word like *shithook.* From the man who answered the phone? Well, I didn't blame her for refusing the money. I hadn't really expected her to accept. I took an envelope from my desk, addressed it, and wrote a check. Like it or not, she would get the money in the mail.

By eleven-fifteen I was halfway through a pack of Lucky Strikes, halfway through another bottle of Bass ale, and halfway through the Callahan Tunnel on the way to Suffolk Downs. My Volkswagen Beetle, one of the few left on the road, lurched out of the tunnel at an insect's pace. In ten years the only traffic violation I had committed was not making minimum speed on the freeway. The parking lot at Suffolk was already filling up. I entered the front gates while a green bus dropped off a load of senior citizens, eyes uniformly bright with optimism. Today was the first Monday in April, and I hoped that they hadn't just cashed their social security checks. I found Cleve upstairs in the press box, assigning weights for next Friday's field of horses. He was wearing the plaid side of his vest today.

"What's the word on Bloomberg?" I asked. "The thrill of racing make his heart give out?"

"Whiskey and Quaaludes," Cleve replied quietly, pushing away from his desk.

"My God. Did he do it on purpose or by accident?"

"Neither. The police think someone did it for him."

"Taking sedatives with alcohol is a sign of stupidity, Cleve. Possibly suicide. Not murder." The word felt strange in my mouth. Outside the context of a newscast or a joke, it took on a surreal quality.

"He didn't take them. They found the drug dissolved in the whiskey bottle next to him. Someone mixed him a highball." Cleve paused to rub the dark circles that had formed beneath his eyes; dead trainers weren't good for business. "Which is not even the peculiar part. The police also found a healthy dose of Bute in the bottle."

Bute, or Butazolidin, was an anti-inflammatory drug that enabled trainers to run thoroughbreds that otherwise would have to be rested. Hard times forced trainers to race horses so frequently that half the stock at Suffolk had sore or injured leg joints. Bute relieved the pain and allowed the horses to run freely. But its presence in the whiskey bottle, I thought, didn't make sense, unless Bloomberg was treating himself for one hell of a swollen ankle. "Bute's not lethal, is it?" I asked Cleve. "Even if someone did, uh ... murder him ... Bute?"

"How the hell should I know?" he said irritably. "Maybe someone just wanted to make him sick to his stomach before they killed him. Hell, the coroner said the Bute almost saved him."

"How's that?"

"The Bute made him puke up the alcohol and Quaaludes. He just didn't puke soon enough. He'd digested too much."

"Do the police have any ideas?"

"They're not saying. But I guarantee you they're a lot less bored with it today. Three detectives were here all morning, along with a half-dozen uniforms, which is more than they'd send out if somebody killed the mayor." Cleve checked his watch. "You pick up your check yet?"

"In ten minutes. Gus said noon. You don't think there'll be a problem?"

"Uh-uh. All bets final. No matter who gets killed."

"You think the race might have been a fix after all?"

"I watched the replay about a dozen times this morning. If it was, it was the most pitiful fix I've ever seen. Rourke almost fell off the goddam horse. Well, shit. Lots of rumors flying around the press box."

"Such as?"

"Jesus Saves has a pretty checkered past. Nothing damning, but lots of weird associations. I picked up a few screwy details here and there."

I found this to be a more congenial topic than the contents of Bloomberg's stomach. Cleve, too, seemed relieved to change the subject. I lit another cigarette and listened.

"From what I can make out, about two years ago some guy from New Hampshire bought the filly at a yearling sale. He was pretty well set, owned a lot of land, a ski resort up near Waterville Valley."

"Doesn't sound like a shrewd investment."

"All yearlings are a gamble. Some horses won't run for shit no matter what their bloodlines. But anyway, this guy, his name was Briarly or Beardly or something, got religion about a year back. A group of religious nuts living in a big commune near Waterville converted him."

I remembered something. "Were these fanatics called Adamites, by any chance?"

"Yeah. How'd you know?"

"An article in the *Globe* a few months back." The Adamites, I remembered, were causing a political stink in New Hampshire because of their tax-exempt status. The article stuck in my mind by virtue of one detail: in the summer, the disciples cavorted in the nude.

"So," Cleve continued, "this rich guy gives all of his money, his possessions, the ski resort, everything, including the yearling, to these Holy Rollers."

"And that's why the name Jesus Saves," I concluded.

"That's what I figured. These Jesus freaks place the horse with Viceroy Stables. And they start her running as a two-year-old, and nineteen races later she ain't done shit—until yesterday. The way I see it, the creeps are swimming in money, don't know a fetlock from fettuccini, so they keep the filly in oats even though she's not paying her keep."

"Possibly," I said. "But that doesn't explain the race. Unless Jesus Saves's dramatic improvement was the result of fasting and praying."

Cleve shrugged. "I'm going to talk to Kevin Rourke this afternoon and find out. After Bloomberg bought it, the stewards got a little more suspicious of Rourke's ride. They gave his mounts to the house jockey for the time being. The police already talked to him this morning."

"Mind if I come?"

"Why not? Let me finish up here. You can pick up your check and meet me in the parking lot." Cleve smiled. "We'll take my car. I'd like to get there sometime today." I left for the cashier's window.

Gus got to the window a couple of minutes after I did. "You been waiting here all night?" He grinned, sliding the envelope toward me. Inside was a check for $28,175. The validating signatures were in ink, not stamped. I held the check by the edges, like a Polaroid photograph. Gus saw that my hands were trembling.

"Nice piece of change, Mr. Theron. Bet at my window anytime."

I turned away and Gus called me back. "Did that fellow find you?"

"Did who find me?"

"Some young guy said he works for the *Herald,* I think. Wants to do a story. You know, a turn-two-dollars-into-a-fortune kind of thing. I thought it would be good publicity for the track—bring the suckers in—so I gave him your name. Maybe it's not such a good idea since that trainer croaked."

"That's all right, Gus. He won't get any bad PR from me. I'll just make something up, tell him I always bet on the last horse to take a crap in warmups." I walked outside thinking of a possible headline: AC-ADEMIC DEVELOPS CRAP THEORY, WINS PILE.

Cleve was waiting by his Buick just as the bettors started pouring in the gates. We found a deadspot in the crowd and nosed out of the lot.

"These horses don't care who bets on 'em," Cleve said, frowning at the multinational mob that surged toward the entrances. "Makes you think the track's got a little Statue of Liberty parked out front."

I decided against a joke about Cleve's own pedigree. Instead, I smiled and said, "If it weren't for the unwashed masses, you'd be out of a job."

"Maybe so, Tommy. Maybe so."

I'd pieced together Cleve's past mostly from the stories he told—some of them mythical, I guessed, and some contradictory, but with enough truth mingled in so that a coherent narrative had gradually emerged. A transplanted Southerner, Cleve had appeared at Suffolk one morning two decades ago, wiry and bowlegged and wearing a cowboy hat. "What I knew about thoroughbreds," he'd told me, "would fit up a rat's ass. But I was jockey size, and I made sure to muck up my boots so I smelled the part, too." So, with a Louisiana drawl, more pro-nounced then, he had slow-talked his way into a stable job. "And the crazy thing was," he'd said, "I had a gift for it." That much I knew was true; the veteran horsemen at Suffolk had long since accepted him without question. Cleve had learned quickly, eventually moving out of the stables to the front offices above the grandstand. And somewhere in the process, he had given up his cowboy hat and jeans for mix-and-match suits.

On Route 1A, the going was easier. Cleve got in the left lane and kept the Buick at sixty-five. Like a lot of jockeys, Rourke lived in Re-vere, a suburb north of Boston and adjacent to the track.

"There's one rumor about Jesus Saves that I didn't tell you," he said.

"Yeah?" I was debating whether to tell him to slow down. My right foot was pressing hard on an imaginary brake pedal.

"You ever heard of Vincent Ciullo?" He pronounced the name "Chew-low."

"Who hasn't?" I said. Ciullo was the classic newspaper underworld personality, perpetually linked to this and that, but never charged or convicted of anything.

"The rumor is that he has an interest in Viceroy Stables. Nothing on paper, but—"

"Dammit, Cleve. Do you really believe that?"

"I don't know. That's just what I heard. That's what Petey said."

"Well, Petey has his head up his ass," I said. Every time something went wrong in Boston—hell, in New England—somebody dragged in the name of Vincent Ciullo. Whether murder, or pederasty, or jaywalking, somebody always suggested that Ciullo was behind it. Another *They* theory, I thought: someone has to be responsible for the evil. That events should happen—or not happen—arbitrarily was impossible for most people to accept. In Ciullo's case, he played the role, not of God, but of Satan. I found it laughable. One newspaper story had mentioned his nickname, "Vinnie the Book." Hardly a name to inspire fear. I imagined him to be a media creation, little more than a mythologized bookie.

"Well, Petey was right about one thing," Cleve said defensively. The Buick left Route 1A for the Winthrop Parkway, which ran the length of Revere Beach. "He was right about Bloomberg's daughter. She was at the track this morning to pick up some of her old man's stuff."

Cleve knew he had recaptured my interest. "She almost caused a riot," he continued. "She was wearing these pants made out of some kind of stretchy stuff. Fit like a second skin." Spandex, I thought, among the few genuine achievements of the synthetic age. "From the rear she looked like she was hiding a couple a hardboiled eggs. And it was so tight in the crotch that you could—" Cleve stopped, a little red in the face.

"Could what, Cleveland? Read her lips?"

"Never mind. Let's just say she didn't leave much to the imagination."

"Pretty?"

"Yeah, and tough looking. Big head of black hair. But nobody was looking upstairs too much."

Kevin Rourke lived in an apartment building called Chateau Lodge. The façade looked out of place this near the ocean, an uninspired design that might have been copied from a package of Swiss Miss cocoa. Kitsch and overpriced. Even an apprenticed jockey earned more in a year than I did. Then again, did he know that Walt Whitman published a little-known temperance novel in 1842?

"What's Rourke like?" I asked as we mounted the outside steps to apartment 22.

"Never had dealings with him. Can't ride for shit, I know that. He gets in tight quarters, he'd rather lose ground than take a little mud in the face. Sanitary rides, we call 'em. Taking the scenic route. Other than that, he's just a creep. Used to bop around the tackroom with one of those big portable stereos, jumping around like he was on a pogo stick. Except he didn't have a pogo stick. Sorry goddam excuse for music. Sounded like somebody hitting a garbage can with a stick."

"The times, they are a-changing, Cleve."

"Not if I can help it. I told Rourke to get an earplug for the noise-maker or I'd make him eat it."

"Did he?"

Cleve looked insulted. "Damn straight. I said he was crazy. I didn't say he was stupid."

Rourke didn't open the door when Cleve knocked.

"Who is it?" a voice asked from the other side.

"Cleve Dickey." Cleve brought his face in range of the peephole, bringing himself full height, stiffening slightly, preparing for official business.

"What do you want?" The voice sounded belligerent.

"What the hell do you think, Kevin? The stewards have a few questions about the ninth yesterday."

"Who's that with you?"

"A friend of mine. He came along for the ride. He's got nothing to do with it." Cleve's patience was giving out. "Open the door, you little pissant. You have to talk sometime."

"I ain't saying nothing to nobody."

"Tell you what, son. Two things are going to happen. First, the stewards are going to make your temporary suspension permanent. Second, you are going to get me personally annoyed."

"Since when do I get suspended for winning a race?"

"Since Jake Bloomberg drank a half-pint of Bute and Quaaludes. Not to mention that you rode that filly like a goddam epileptic."

Rourke fell silent, and I could hear him thinking. After a minute the door opened and he said, "You can come the hell in, but I ain't saying nothing. I already talked to the police a couple of hours ago." Behind the door and the tough voice was a thin-faced boy who looked like a punk reincarnation of Huckleberry Finn. He couldn't have been taller than five feet five inches, and his reddish hair was cut short enough for boot camp, a fashion that disguised a prematurely receding hairline. Rourke was trying hard to look menacing, but without much success. What made him appear vulnerable was a right eye swollen shut and an upper lip that needed a half-dozen stitches. I noticed dried blood on his neck that could only have trickled from his left ear.

"Godamighty," Cleve said. "What got ahold of you?"

"Do you want a doctor?" I asked.

"I'm all right. I'm all right." Rourke sat on his sofa, silently nursing his lip. Above him was a poster of David Bowie wearing a spacesuit. Rourke sipped a can of Budweiser and I saw his hand shake. His open eye had fear in it and he said, "Don't call no damn doctor."

Cleve asked him again what happened.

"I been slamdancing, man," he snarled. His voice cracked midsentence and he fell into a sullen silence.

Cleve looked at me. "What's this boy trying to say?"

After a short silence I tried to find a basis for conversation. "Listen, Kevin," I began amiably, "that was a terrific ride yesterday. It might not have been pretty"—I stopped myself short of 'aesthetically pleasing'—"but it got the job done. You made me a bundle. Thanks."

Rourke leaped off the sofa and, with his open eye on me, started pacing around the far side of the room like a trapped animal. "Shit, Dickey!" he screamed. "I thought you said this asshole didn't have anything to do with this!"

"I don't," I started, "I—"

"Did you cash a bet on that fucking horse?" Rourke yelled.

"Yeah, but—"

"Are you a goddam professor?"

"Yes . . ."

"I got to be insane to be anywhere near you, man," he shouted, his voice an odd mixture of panic and anger. "I'm putting a goddam gun to my head." He stopped in front of the poster and hit David Bowie with his fist.

"Kevin," Cleve finally interrupted. "if you don't calm down and mind your manners, I'm gonna have to—"

I waved Cleve off with my eyes. As much as Rourke was annoying me, there was no point in antagonizing him. I wanted to know what the hell he was talking about.

The jockey was back on the sofa, rocking back and forth from his waist. I noticed that his feet barely touched the floor. He was saying shit shit shit shit. He stopped rocking and finished the Budweiser. He glared at Cleve. Then he turned his good eye on me and laughed. His puffy cut lip curled in a sneer that conveyed to me, roughly, that I was not a credit to my profession. "You, professor, have royally screwed yourself. You don't know what the hell you're in for."

My reply was mild. "That's what I'd like to find out, Kevin." I didn't particularly mind effacing myself in exchange for information about my future welfare. I went to the refrigerator and got him another Budweiser and one for myself. "If you're talking about the bet I made yesterday," I explained in a reasonable tone, "it was just a matter of dumb, blind luck. Just tell me what's going on."

Rourke began to talk, not so much because I had pacified him, but because he was getting some pleasure out of his role as bearer of bad tidings. "Lookit, man. I don't *know* what's going on. But I'll tell you this, just so's when you go down for the count, you'll know what hit you." His hands were still quivering while he held the beer can. "Look at it from their point of view. They have Jake B. setting up this filly for I don't know how long—maybe a year now—spending a lot of money, moving the horse around to these shitty little tracks, making damn sure nobody in his right mind will put more than two dollars on her."

At this point Cleve shot me a look that identified me as someone not in his right mind.

"Then one day Jake B. goes to the john and winds up dead, and the last person to see him alive goes to the window and cashes a bet. I mean, if you were them, what would you think?"

Whoever they were, I imagined they were not thinking what a lucky fellow I was. "What did you tell them," I asked, "when they came to, uh, talk with you?" I couldn't take my eyes off the blood on his neck. I kept wondering how hard you have to hit someone to make his ears bleed.

"I told them what happened, man. They didn't have to hit me to get me to spill my guts. These fuckers don't play games. They hit me afterwards, when they didn't like what they heard."

"And what was that?" I asked, my voice still calm, pleasant, innocuous.

"That the fucking horse just got away. I couldn't hold her. Jesus Saves is wicked fast, man. Loves to run. Could win allowance races, except they won't let her. But Jake wanders off an hour to post and doesn't come back. The stableboy says he's just nervous and sneaks off for some juice. But he doesn't come back and I got no instructions on how to hold the filly. I never been up on her." Rourke nervously poked his cut lip with his tongue. I kept wondering about his ears. "You saw me. I got her to stumble and lose stride out of the gate, and I'm high in the irons the whole backstretch, choking her for all I'm worth. Her damn eyes were about to pop. But we hit the last turn, the horse just says 'Fuck this' and takes off. She just got away. You saw me. I had her nose pulled back so far she could of bit her own rump. The only way I could have kept her from winning that race was if I had reached down with a butcher knife and cut her goddam throat. I wish I had. I don't even know if that would have worked. But Jake didn't give me no instructions." Rourke sat back down, exhausted by his confession, but he stared defiantly at Cleve. "I'll take a suspension," he said, "and be damn happy with it."

"When you told them this," I asked with feigned calmness, "did they believe you?"

"Enough not to kill me, man. But they don't believe nothing and they don't trust nobody. They kept asking me if I knew some professor, some guy who had scored on the race, and I said no, I didn't know no goddam professor."

"Do you think they believed that?"

"How the fuck would I know? But they ain't in no rush. They're just sitting back, giving everybody a little room, waiting to see what turns up. And what turns up?"

I turned up, I thought.

"You. The professor who I been swearing I don't know. The man who cashed a bet. And you know what they figure now?"

I wasn't sure, but I could guess.

"They figure you're in here right now paying me off for letting the filly run."

"One last question, Kevin. Did they kill Bloomberg?"

"What are you? Deaf? They think you killed him. Jacked him out of his share." Rourke smiled through his puffy lip, his open eye gleaming. Despite his own precarious position, he was still enjoying my predicament. "Face it, schoolmarm," he spat contemptuously. "You're in over your head. They got you by the short hairs. If I was you, I'd be hiding in some library."

I asked him another question, one that I really wasn't certain that I wanted him to answer. "Who are 'they'?"

"Just get the hell away, man."

We left Rourke alone with his bleeding ears. While Cleve drove me back to my car, I kept trying to think of the whole episode as a joke, but my mental laughter had a nervous quality to it. I felt the same helplessness I had felt the day before when I'd tried to find a pulse on

Bloomberg's neck. I had no idea what to do. I couldn't decide whether I should call the police or write a letter to "60 Minutes."

Cleve pulled up to the Volkswagen. "I can put you up if you need a place."

"No thanks, I'm fine."

"I don't think there's anything to worry about," he said.

"Me either," I replied without much conviction.

Cleve shrugged. "I told you he was a creep." After I'd climbed into my car, Cleve rolled down his window and asked, "What you doing this weekend?"

"I don't know. Unless Rourke is completely hallucinating, I think I'll keep a low profile." Then I remembered the check, which perked me up. "Stay home and count my money."

"What you got planned for it?"

"You know the old saying. I'll spend half of it on wine, horses, and women. Then I'll just piss the other half away."

"Well," Cleve said, smiling, "I may be taking a trip to New Hampshire this Saturday. The stewards are going to want me to talk to the filly's owners and see what the hell gives. Want to come with me?"

I thought for a second and shook my head. "I think I'll stay out of it."

"If you change your mind, let me know." Then he teased, "Didn't you say these Adamites were a bunch of crazy nudists? No telling what we might get a peek of."

"Such pleasures are to me as chaff and straw," I intoned solemnly. "They are an abomination in the eyes of the holy."

"What?"

"Just nerves," I said.

I had one drink at four different bars and puttered around Boston in between. By nine-thirty, I made a decision. I drove down Commonwealth, took a left and then another left onto Marlboro. After six blocks I parked in front of an old brownstone, got out, and climbed the steps of number 336. I rang the doorbell five or six times before I got a response.

"I knew there was a catch," Elizabeth said when she answered the door. Her fine blond hair was disheveled, and she clutched around her a burgundy silk robe that I had given her. At the open neck of the robe her chest was red and flushed in a way that I recognized. She glanced nervously back into the apartment. I resisted the impulse to ask her if she ever took a breather.

"There's no catch, Beth. This has nothing to do with the money. I mean, it has something to do with the money, but nothing to do with my repaying you. I need a place to stay. I know this may sound melodramatic, but somebody may be trying to harm me."

"Who? The father of one of your more attractive coeds? He didn't understand that seduction was an academic fringe benefit?"

You never complained, I thought. Well, she was right, of course, and anyway, I had brought it on myself. She never came around in the middle of the night, asking for a place to stay. To be honest, I wished she would.

Elizabeth had fallen in love with me because my cynical classroom performance appealed to her collegiate rebelliousness. I fell in love with her because she was the most beautiful woman I had ever seen, much less been invited to bed with. But when her memory of college faded, she decided that success was not contemptible. She wanted to help people, but she also wanted the good life. It didn't take her long to discover that my nihilism ran deeper than a charming social eccentricity. She didn't want to be married to an academic who scheduled his classes only after consulting the Red Sox calendar and *TV Guide*. For my part, I didn't want to be married to a psychologist who didn't have a sense of humor about the self-cultivated neuroses of her wealthy clientele.

With separation, we both got what we wanted. On Sunday mornings she was free to have brunch at Casablanca and read *The New York Times;* I was free to get an Egg McMuffin and watch professional wrestling on Channel 25.

"I'm serious, Beth," I said. As clearly and calmly as I could, I told her everything.

"If all that's true," she said, "has it occurred to you that you might be endangering me by staying here?"

It hadn't. "Of course it has," I said.

"But you decided to risk it."

"No, of course not. I'm trying not to get paranoid about this thing." I was also trying not to think about Rourke's ears. "I still can't believe any of this is serious."

She wavered, then let me in. "I can let you have the couch for tonight."

"The couch is fine." Hell, it's my couch, I thought.

"Breck is not going to like it."

"Who or what is Breck?" I asked, already knowing.

"The man I'm involved with."

"What kind of name is that?"

When she didn't answer, I shut up.

I didn't see a sign of a Breck in the living room. But after Beth handed me a blanket and returned to the bedroom, Breck made his presence known. Elizabeth's love-noises were coming through the bedroom door and down the hall—louder noises than any I had ever elicited from her. I tried to go to sleep out of spite, but couldn't.

Then I remembered the other man I had seen in the toilet at Suffolk yesterday. The bald man. I stuck my forefingers into my ears and hummed to myself. One thought consoled me: perhaps Beth's noises were for me after all. Indirectly.

═══ *THREE* ═══

THE NEXT MORNING I slipped out of the apartment at a little past seven, before Breck roused himself and forced me to put my fingers back into my ears. At nine I had a conference class on the nineteenth-century novel—a class for which I had not prepared. I took the *Globe* from Beth's stoop and walked two blocks to the Greenhouse, a small corner cafe where I used to drink coffee when I lived in Back Bay. The proprietor, Mrs. Fuller, greeted me with surprise, but made a point of remembering my usual order. She brought a sausage roll and a cup of black coffee to the window table where I had always sat.

"Gracious, Mr. Theron, it's been a long time," she said, wiping the table with a red cloth. A roll of fat jiggled on the underside of her arm.

"It has. How's business?"

"Middling." She lowered her voice conspiratorily. "You're a little far from Cambridge. You and Beth aren't getting back together, are you?"

"No."

"Well, I didn't think so," she announced.

I looked up at her.

"She comes in here with that new fellow. Good-looking man. Like the kids say, a real hulk."

"Hunk," I corrected sourly.

"What? Mercy yes! And loaded. Him and Beth come in here a lot of mornings. He always tips me three dollars."

Another customer finally distracted her. "Thank you, Mrs. Fuller," I sighed.

While I sipped the coffee, I jotted down a quick outline for that morning's lecture. I had finished Fenimore Cooper last Thursday, which brought me to Hawthorne. I vaguely remembered having put *The Blithedale Romance,* a seldom-read novel that I liked, next on the reading list. The outline came easily enough. When pressed for time, I always resorted to the *People* magazine formula for lecturing—lots of authorial anecdotes, heavy on gossip and sex. Put a little sugar on the bitter pill of knowledge. After a few minutes I slipped the notepad back into my pocket and checked my watch. I still had time for the sports page.

The Celtics had to wait. A headline in the Metro Region section caught my eye: NEW HAMPSHIRE SECT LINKED TO SUFFOLK INVESTIGATION. I read the article quickly. Most of Cleve's rumors turned out to be correct, although I had imagined the Adamites more in the role of innocent, perhaps foolish bystanders. It wasn't hard to figure out why Bloomberg's death had attracted half of the homicide squad. The Adamites, under the leadership of a bare-assed, self-appointed guru—named Adam, of course—in less than two years had blossomed from a commune of skinny-dipping hippies to an institution with all of the characteristics of a large corporation. All, that is, except their tax-exempt status, which the courts were trying to take away.

If material prosperity was a sign of spiritual well-being, the Adamites were getting closer to God by the minute. Headquartered, according to the article, at the Waterville ski resort donated by a Frank Beardsley, the sect had attracted several wealthy converts. Some had apparently later lost their religious zeal and tried without success to repossess their homes, cars, land, and money. All of which, I knew, would stick in the craw of the rural folk of Waterville Valley, New Hampshire, where the license plates still carried the forbiddingly conservative motto "Live Free or Die." From political expediency as much as anything else, I concluded, it would be a coup to lay a murder—not to mention a race fix—at the bare and holy feet of Adam.

But I didn't have time to think about it now. I finished the coffee and resisted the impulse to tip Mrs. Fuller three dollars. I left a dollar at the table just as I always had. When I paid my bill at the register, Mrs. Fuller said, "It's funny, you know?"

"What's that?"

She pointed to where I had been sitting. "That new fellow. He likes to sit at the same window table as you."

And ride in the same saddle, I knew she was thinking. I wished I had my dollar back.

The Volkswagen crept toward Cambridge and got me to Wesley College only ten minutes late. On the top floor of Emerson Hall I found thirty-four sluggish students huddled in the back rows of the conference room. As usual, the thirty-fifth, Roger Potter, sat by himself front-row center, trying to affect the pose of an empty vessel waiting to be filled with learning. Potter was the only student who took issue with what I poured into him.

The events of the past two days had given me a reservoir of adrenaline that I tapped with good results. I worked myself up to some fine introductory anecdotes gleaned from Hawthorne's life. A bit off the cuff, but inspired. I moved quickly to Hawthorne's participation in the Brook Farm experiment, a Transcendental commune on which *The Blithedale Romance* was based. That got me to Margaret Fuller and the parts of Hawthorne's journals that his wife had expurgated. I even managed a lengthy digression on free love, utopian communes, and Oneida. For controversy's sake, I worked toward the view that the hero of the novel, Myles Coverdale, was, in spirit, if not in fact, a homosexual.

After thirty minutes, all I was getting were looks of sleepy noncomprehension and some rustling in chairs. Whatever they had been doing the night before, I thought, it wasn't reading.

I plowed ahead for five more minutes, until Roger Potter began waving his hand in the air like a grade-schooler anxious to pee.

"What's on your mind, Mr. Potter?" I finally asked.

"I don't mean to interrupt, Professor Theron," he began coyly. "But I don't see that at all. It just doesn't make sense. I don't understand."

"I just provide the ideas, Potter, not the understanding of them. Has it ever occurred to you that Coverdale's final, lame declaration of love for Priscilla simply underscores his inability to pursue an adult hetero-sexual relationship?"

"No, it hasn't," he mewed.

Snide little turd, I thought. "But isn't it rather obvious that—"

"No sir, it isn't," he jumped in. His coyness was gone.

"May I ask why not?" I said, studying him.

Potter looked at me triumphantly. "Because Coverdale is in *The Blithedale Romance,* and the novel we're suppose to read for today is *The House of Seven Gables.*" He began waving the reading list at me.

I cut my losses and dismissed class. "Be prepared for a quiz next time," I said as I walked out the door.

I stopped on the steps outside Emerson Hall, smoked a cigarette, and cursed myself. Above me, two white clouds drifted with imperceptible motion across a luminous blue sky. Presently I was aware of a young man approaching me.

"Professor Theron," he began. "I was hoping I might have a word with you. I'm Alex Cavanaugh." He offered his hand with a boyish, diffident gesture, and I shook it. He was not much older than the students I had just left, but he was not dressed like a student. He wore a stylish, European-cut suit, fitted shirt, maroon knit tie. "Gus Albritton told me about your good fortune at Suffolk," he continued. "I'm very much interested in doing a story about you. That is, if you're agree-able."

He seemed too ingenuous for a reporter, I thought, and clearly too well dressed. But I was still trying not to be paranoid. "What paper do you work for—Alex?" I hoped he wasn't going to tell me the *Adamite Times.*

"The *Herald.* I'm just getting started there. I thought your gambling success might make a good human-interest story. A kind of king-for-a-day piece. And when the trainer died, well, I figured no telling where it might lead. I could use the chance to do some investigative reporting. You know, prove myself."

While he talked, I noticed another man—larger, uglier, and older—ten yards away on the steps, watching us. His suit didn't fit nearly so well as the fellow's next to me. His biceps were ruining the line of his jacket, and his thighs were taking most of the crease out of his polyester slacks. His physique reminded me of Lou Groza's, an unsightly stump of a man who used to kick field goals for the Cleveland Browns. His face looked like what Lou Groza had been kicking.

I looked at Alex and then nodded in the direction of the second man. "Another cub reporter?"

He actually blushed. "I . . . a colleague," he stammered.

"Well," I said, grinding my cigarette nervously into the granite step, "you may be Bob Woodward, but there's no way in hell that he's Carl Bernstein. Would you mind very much if I had a look at your press card?"

The request confused him. He took his wallet out of his breast pocket and then put it back. "I don't have one," he announced, avoiding my eyes.

The human stump quit watching and walked over to stand silently next to us. He casually placed his hands in his pockets, which pushed back his lapels and revealed a leather strap at his right shoulder. His biceps, I concluded, weren't the only thing messing up the line of his jacket.

I pried my eyes off the holster and looked at Alex. "May I ask a silly question?"

"Of course," he said. For whatever reason, he insisted on appearing disarmingly sincere.

"I'm not really king for a day, am I? Journalists are not in the habit of bringing a gunman along to shoot people who don't give them a good story."

"Actually, no, Professor Theron," he confessed sheepishly. "I suppose you've caught me in an inept deception. I came here to escort you to someone who wants very much to meet you."

"Do I have a choice?"

"Well, not really." He nodded toward the stump. "Whatever his faults, Gerald is entirely competent to elicit your compliance." I watched while an oddly humble smile appeared on Gerald's ugly face. He looked as though a huge disembodied hand had just scratched him behind the ears. "But there's nothing for you to be concerned about," Alex went on.

His voice seemed monotonously earnest, but I was not reassured. I kept thinking that his mildness might be a side effect of a religious conversion. "Would this someone I am to meet," I asked, "happen to be wearing long, flowing robes and a rapt, otherwordly expression?"

Alex grinned boyishly. "No, this man is very much of this world. I think you'll like him. In fact, you have a great deal in common with him. He's something of a literary scholar." Whatever else Alex knew about me, he wasn't aware of my professional habits. He made an elaborate ushering gesture with his right arm. "My car's parked on Mass Ave."

For two blocks I walked between them, until we stopped next to a Mercedes 500SEL. Gerald opened the rear door for us, then took the driver's seat. We pulled away from the curb and entered the traffic on Mass Ave.

"Mind another question?" I asked Alex.

"Not at all."

"Did God send his only son Jesus into the world to die on the cross in exchange for our collective sins?"

He studied me curiously, though his expression remained pleasant. "I like LaForgue's response to that."

"Pardon?"

"When Napoleon asked the great scientist LaForgue whether or not he believed in God, LaForgue answered, 'God is a theory of which I have no need.'"

Not the doctrine of a fundamentalist, I thought. Unitarian, maybe. In either case, it baffled me.

The Mercedes cruised along Storrow Drive, roughly in the direction of the expressway north. I sat quietly, steeling myself, preparing for a

great effort of concentration. I had determined to memorize every turn
we made during the trip, no matter what mazelike route we pursued,
even into the farthest reaches of New Hampshire forest.

I needn't have bothered. After five minutes we had passed the freeway ramps and were heading toward the center of Boston. We turned
down Tremont, took a left, then another left onto Washington, and
finally crossed some nameless side streets. Gaudy marquees displaying
triple X's popped up everywhere. The streets were so narrow that I
could make out the magazines in the storefronts, all promoting Girls
Who Like It this way or that way. No deceptive advertising here, I
thought. Other windows held the paraphernalia of rubber-stickler love:
exotically shaped dildos, every human orifice recast in supple pink
latex. We turned and passed two women on a corner, one black,
dressed in garish silver sequins, the other white, in candy-red lipstick
with matching slit-to-the-waist skirt.

I was surprised, but not disoriented. I knew the Combat Zone well.
In the daylight, though, and in my present state of mind, it looked
more dismal and hopeless than I usually thought of it. The Mercedes
parked in a tiny alley at the rear of a club called the Pink Lady.

"Professor," Alex said, "if you follow Gerald through that door, he'll
take you to see Mr. Ciullo."

So, I thought. Chew-low. Alex hadn't lied. He had brought me to a
man of this world. I had been expecting sacred, but I got profane.
What was the difference, after all? Both places trafficked in men's souls.

═══*FOUR*═══

GERALD GRUNTED and jerked his head. I got out of the Mercedes and followed him to the alley door.

"I'll be back later," Alex said, getting behind the wheel, "to take you wherever you wish." My mind latched hopefully on to his words. I would, after all, be coming back. And I would be in a condition to wish something.

Inside, after my eyes adjusted, a hallway appeared out of the pitch darkness. Gerald led me to a door at the end of the hall, knocked once, and we entered an office that was surprisingly spacious and well lit. My eyes adjusted again.

From ceiling to hardwood floor, the walls held as many shelves as a library, each packed with expensive-looking books. A vast mahogany desk sat in the middle of the room on an oriental rug. Bent over the desk was a middle-aged man wearing a gold-buttoned, navy-blue blazer and a small red bow tie. His small blue eyes peered up at me through a pair of steel-rimmed spectacles. His whitish jowls resembled a bulldog's. My mind flew back to stories I had heard about Vinnie "the Book" Ciullo. Bookworm? I thought incredulously.

The man rose and smiled but did not extend his hand. Gerald closed the door and stood by it.

"How do you do, Professor Theron. I'm Vincent Ciullo. I'm very happy you could come and see me."

Not happy enough to offer me a seat, I thought nervously. I said, "Attendance was compulsory."

"Yes, well, I trust my nephew didn't annoy you with his pose. He's a bit romantic about these things. He can't bring himself just to come out and say what's on his mind."

"Nephew?"

"Alex is my sister's son. A little inexperienced, but a fine young man. He graduated *summa cum laude* from Boston University two years ago. We weren't able to get him into Wesley."

I looked behind me. "If he had brought Gerald with him to the admissions office, I imagine something might have been arranged."

Ciullo smiled politely. "Good, yes, very good." He took a meerschaum pipe from a rack on his desk and filled the bowl. "Shall we get down to business? Then perhaps we can chat."

"Do you mind if I sit?"

"I would prefer that you stand," he said, blowing a cloud of smoke in front of his face. "Now, it is my understanding that on Sunday you experienced, let us say, a kind of religious vision. One that worked dramatically to your advantage?"

"Not all that dramatic," I said. "Just enough to stem the tide of atheism that was washing across my heart."

"Professor Theron," he said, tapping the bowl of his pipe on the ashtray, "if you are capable of a serious reply, I would like to ask you a serious question."

Anxiety made my mouth do funny things. To be safe, I clenched my teeth and nodded silently.

"Good," Ciullo said. "What precisely was your association with Jacob Bloomberg, and what motivated you to wager on such an unlikely horse as Jesus Saves?"

As unhumorously as possible, I told him why I bet the filly.

"So I am to understand that you wagered on this horse—thinking it was the selection of an alcoholic—out of perversity? Out of some self-destructive impulse?"

I shrugged apologetically. "I was up a few hundred at the time."

"Why did you visit Kevin Rourke?"

I told him, careful to leave Cleve's name out of it. I mentioned only an anonymous "friend."

"I would like you to convince me of the truthfulness of what you are telling me."

Anxiety was beginning to loosen my lips again. I got as far as "Cross my heart and hope to . . ." and immediately regretted it.

Ciullo looked past my face and toward the piece of muscle standing behind me by the door. His eyes made a subtle signal, as though he were bidding on a Renoir at Sotheby's. "Gerald," he said.

With his open palm, Gerald slapped the back of my head. I was too startled to really feel it, but I heard a loud kind of pop. Some instinct I didn't know I had made me turn and bristle. Gerald stood there passively. He shook his head firmly back and forth to say "No." The momentum of my turn carried me another step toward him.

His palm still open, he slapped me hard across the face. This time I felt it. Again he shook his head "No." I felt like a dog being trained to stay. Gerald then nodded in the direction of Ciullo. I turned around. I was prepared to roll over if need be.

"These are important matters, Professor Theron. I was hoping I would like you. I was hoping that I could believe and trust you. I was hoping that you would see fit to cooperate. One way or another, of course, you will cooperate."

The right side of my face had developed a fever. I glared at Ciullo. There was a little anger inside of me, and beneath that, humiliation. But neither was making much headway against the fear of pain.

"Please convince me that you are being forthright," Ciullo said. His blue eyes held an impersonal, appraising stare, as though I were an exotic insect that he contemplated stepping on.

I hadn't wanted to mention Cleve, but a little voice inside me kept asking what friends were for. "Cleve Dickey can vouch for everything I've—"

"Alex is interviewing Mr. Dickey at this moment," Ciullo interrupted. "I'm more interested in what you have to say."

My mind fumbled for some intricate, irrefutable logic that would satisfy him. Nothing came. I retreated to the obvious. "You must have read the newspapers. The police—not to mention half the population of New Hampshire—are falling all over themselves trying to implicate the Adamites. An officer took a statement from me, but no one's bothered to follow it up. They could care less about me." I studied his eyes to judge the effect of what I'd said. He remained unimpressed.

"I'm well aware of that," Ciullo sighed, sinking back into the depths of his chair. "Forget the police. They are creatures of convenience, victims of their own fallible logic. They think precisely what they're supposed to think." His fingers, stout and freshly manicured, fanned the air in front of his face as though he were being bothered by gnats. For a moment he seemed to forget me, and I noticed, behind the neutrality of his gaze, a deep weariness.

A long silence followed, during which Ciullo meticulously cleaned his pipe. "I'm inclined to believe you, Professor Theron," he said finally. "Not because of anything you've told me. As a matter of fact, you haven't told me anything that isn't painfully obvious." A faint smile crossed his lips, and he nodded toward the red leather wing chair to my right. "I think it's time you took a seat."

I perched stiffly on the edge of the cushion.

"Could Gerald get you anything? Something to drink?"

I thought of several things that Gerald could get me—including a cattle prod with which to fend him off—but I held my tongue. Stay sober and alert, I debated, or whiskey to lubricate the nerves? "Bourbon?" I managed. "Neat?"

"Fine. Certainly," Ciullo said, sending Gerald for the drink. Alone with me, Ciullo rose from his chair with careful dignity, circled his desk, and placed his hand on my left shoulder. I resisted the impulse to flinch. But the menace I had seen in his eyes was now replaced by a shyness, a diffident quality that left me bewildered. I became aware that he was inviting me to admire his collection of first editions. I touched my cheek to make sure I hadn't dreamed the slap. The skin still tingled.

"It's not often that I have the opportunity to display these volumes to someone who can appreciate them," he said, delicately fingering the worn leather bindings of his incunabula. His face expressed an odd mixture of pleasure and embarrassment—the unmistakable characteristic, I knew, of a self-taught man.

Gerald brought a generous tumbler of bourbon for me, and what appeared to be a glass of milk for Ciullo.

"Half-and-half," Ciullo sighed, regretfully patting his stomach.

For nearly an hour, Vinnie "the Book" spoke of his passion for literature—the "corrupt vitality," he said, of the Renaissance, the "searching intellect" of Milton, the "tortured resolutions" of Donne. He confessed a special obsession for modern poetry. I did my best to match his enthusiasm, interjecting shrewd-sounding literary judgments, hoping to foster whatever notion he had of me as an authority and kindred spirit: gangster—what else to call him?—and professor, bound together in mutual pursuit of beauty and truth.

Though his knowledge seemed prodigious, he insisted on deferring to my opinions. I had seen it before, but it always unsettled me when my academic status cowed others—more often than not, men more successful, more ambitious, and undeniably more intelligent than myself. So criminals, too, I thought, like doctors and bankers, suffered intellectual insecurities and craved the prestige of Art.

His expression rapt, his tone reverent, Ciullo discoursed. I listened and drank as many bourbons as Gerald would bring me. Ciullo seemed to imagine himself in terms of a time-worn, heroic cliché: a man of both culture and action, doomed to exist in an age that valued only passivity and abdication. There was something pathetic about him, as though he believed that some essential part of his being had been forever and tragically frustrated. I might have felt sorry for him if I hadn't been too busy feeling sorry for myself.

My face must have appeared grim, for Ciullo finally said, "I'm afraid I must be boring you."

"Not at all," I replied truthfully. As a rule, my palms didn't sweat when I was bored.

"Forgive me for indulging myself. We have other matters to discuss.

I imagine you are rather confused about the position in which you find yourself. Perhaps I can clarify some things." He returned to his desk, and as he did so, an unnerving stare of absolute authority returned to his eyes, as though in crossing the room he also crossed a mental boundary from my turf to his own.

Of all the questions I might have asked, only one or two mattered. "You seem to have known from the beginning that I wasn't involved," I said.

"I was reasonably certain."

"Then why am I here?" I tensed perceptibly, like someone anticipating a blow.

"I wanted to meet you. To see what kind of man you are."

"What kind of man am I?"

"Beneath your sometimes puerile sarcasm," Ciullo observed wryly, "I find a glimmer of intelligence."

"That's kind of you. But it doesn't clarify anything."

"I've brought you here, Professor Theron, to ask a favor. Consider it a business proposition if you like."

"Consider what a business proposition?"

"Simply this. I want to enlist your services as"—he paused thoughtfully—"as a collector of information. I want you to go to New Hampshire and visit the Adamites."

"You're not serious, of course."

"I do not share your compulsion to make jokes," he said, his expression increasingly austere. "If you would be patient, you might understand why I'm making this request. May I speak off the record?"

The question, I understood, was rhetorical. I had an uneasy feeling he was going to tell me something I didn't want to know.

Ciullo talked, and the outline of a complicated story unfolded— about Jesus Saves, about the Adamites, about Bloomberg and Kevin Rourke. My apprehensions had been justified; most of what he told me I'd rather not have known. The gist of it was this: a little more than a year ago, Ciullo, through Bloomberg, had arranged the race-fixing scheme. Bloomberg had led the jockeys who rode the filly to believe that the owners, the Adamites, had orchestrated the fix. Bloomberg's murder had prematurely aborted the conspiracy. "So," Ciullo concluded, "when Rourke talked to the police, he told them genuinely, sincerely—even, I imagine, with dramatic reluctance—that this so-called Adam had employed him. Mr. Rourke could pass a lie-detector test." Ciullo paused. "Is all of that reasonably clear, Professor Theron?"

"The only thing that's not clear," I said, "is why you want me to go to New Hampshire. How in God's name could that be a favor to you?"

"Yesterday," he said, "you visited Kevin Rourke with Cleve Dickey. Correct?"

I nodded cautiously, trying to anticipate whatever logical trap he might be laying.

"You accompanied Mr. Dickey because he is your friend?"

I nodded again.

"Well," Ciullo said, "I have reason to believe that Mr. Dickey will interview the owners of the filly, the Adamites, on behalf of the Suffolk stewards—for the same reason he talked to Rourke. The stewards have an investigative responsibility in this matter." Ciullo paused and looked at me. "Mr. Dickey may have already mentioned this trip to you?"

My face remained blank, but my eyes must have shifted.

"Good," Ciullo said. "Good. Now, Professor Theron, I simply want you to accompany Mr. Dickey to New Hampshire. In a spirit of friendship, let's say. While you're there, I want you to observe carefully, remember what you see and hear—"

"And then report to you," I said.

"Precisely."

"You want me to act as some half-assed informant?"

"There's no need to be melodramatic. I'm not asking for information that you wouldn't, in all likelihood, tell a stranger over a drink in a bar. If Mr. Dickey considered these matters confidential, he wouldn't be inviting you along in the first place. I merely want to be kept abreast of the investigation."

"I thought you said the Adamites were not aware"— I searched for a euphemism—"of how you and Bloomberg were using them."

"I still believe that. But," he conceded with chilling irony, "Mr. Bloomberg's corpse suggests that I might have been mistaken."

"Surely, you have other . . . uh . . . sources of information."

"I do. And I want to count you among them."

"But I'm not qualified for—"

"You are eminently qualified in my opinion. You are a man of intelligence, and the task I have in mind requires little more than perceptiveness and a good memory. Moreover," he added, "you are here, and you are in my debt."

"In your debt?"

"You owe me thirty-one thousand dollars. That's roughly my investment in holding back the filly this past year. Actually, it comes to a little more than that, but let's not quibble. What I'm offering you, Professor Theron, is the opportunity to keep the entire sum for services rendered. Think of it as a retainer."

"A retainer?" Astonishment sent the pitch of my voice a full octave higher. Did he seriously believe that I owed him thirty-one thousand dollars? "Mr. Ciullo," I started, "I don't even have the money anymore. At least not all of it." I thought of Beth. "I've paid off a couple of loans. Hell, the IRS already took three thousand."

"Professor Theron, if you choose frivolously to tithe the U.S. government, that is none of my concern."

The futility of arguing with him was beginning to hit me. Ciullo was obviously accustomed to having his way. I sat speechless.

Ciullo had come round his desk once more and placed his hand on my shoulder, signifying to him, at least, that everything was settled. "Frankly," he said, "I relish the notion of having a Wesley professor in my employ. If you like, think of it as the whimsy of an old man."

"And if I whimsically decline?"

"Really, I'm asking for very little. Just listen while Mr. Dickey talks to this Adam. And I expect he will want to speak with the fellow who originally owned the filly. Beardsley, I think. That's not so much, is it? And, I think it's fair to say, thirty-one thousand dollars is a generous remuneration. I hope you won't disappoint me."

My mind felt a peculiar sensation, as though it were sinking back into itself, assuming some mental equivalent of the fetal position. What were my options? I wasn't going to give him a nickel, and I didn't want Gerald to slap me silly. Or worse.

"Did Mr. Dickey mention when he might be going to New Hampshire?" Ciullo was saying.

"I don't know," I replied glumly. "He said something about Saturday."

"Saturday morning would be perfect," he said. "Then Monday evening you could stop by here to see me."

"Listen, if I start telling Cleve when we should go and who we should talk to, he's going to want to know what the hell's going on."

"You're a reasonable man," Ciullo said, smiling faintly. "Think of a reason."

When I rose to leave, Ciullo took my elbow and once again ushered me to the bookshelves. "There's one volume I neglected to show you earlier. I have a special love for the poetry of Ezra Pound," he said, handling with obvious pride a 1942 edition of Pound's *Cantos*. "I've spent a good part of the past five years pondering the meanings of these poems."

As far as I could tell, Ciullo had only one weak spot, however ludicrous, and I felt miserable enough to go for it. "You shouldn't have bothered. It's gibberish."

He looked at me evenly. "Your apparent contempt for ideas surprises me."

"I like ideas fine," I said. "It's just that Ezra Pound never had one. There's a standard illustration of the theory of probability: chain a monkey to a typewriter and keep him there long enough and he'll write *King Lear*. I consider Pound's *Cantos* the monkey's first draft."

I half expected Ciullo to explode in anger. Instead, he smiled benignly. "I see that you are repaying me for the slap Gerald gave you. For the demands I've made of you. We'll let this pass."

Feeling more than a little foolish, I followed Gerald outside.

Stepping out into the small gray alley, into the softening afternoon light, I no longer felt foolish. Instead, I felt the same disorientation, the same stupor I'd felt when I bet on Jesus Saves. I found myself re-membering with fresh sympathy the standard dramatic device of old movies: the hero, a battered victim of tragic circumstances, breaks into hysterical laughter that gradually metamorphoses into convulsive sobs. As I watched Alex pull the Mercedes up to the curb, I felt myself capa-ble of such a shameless reversal.

Alex looked annoyingly cheerful. "Did you accept Mr. Ciullo's prop-osition?"

"Only in the sense that I agreed to come here in the first place. I didn't have a choice."

"I think he intended to pay you a high compliment. He truly ad-mires—"

"No offense, Alex, but you realize that Uncle Vinnie is—"

He cut me off. "You don't understand his situation."

"You're right. And I don't particularly want to." I looked at him. "Why the hell do you call your uncle 'mister'?"

"Because I work for him."

Poor, harmless, dumb, inept Alex, I thought. Being Ciullo's nephew couldn't have been easy. Perpetually intimidated by the monumental example of a powerful uncle. An old story, really. The energy and deci-siveness of one generation dissipated in the next, transformed into self-consciousness.

Alex changed the subject. "Can I give you a ride to Cambridge?"

"No thanks. I'm staying here. I think I'll have a drink." The Combat Zone depressed everyone else, but it always seemed to cheer me up. And there was one detail of the past few days that, of its own accord, kept surfacing in my mind. "One thing you can tell me," I told Alex. "Bloomberg had a daughter who works in a club down here. A strip-per. You know which club?"

"I didn't even know he had a daughter. Where'd you hear that?"

"Just a rumor."

"Well, there's a pretty high turnover. Girls come and go. I could find her for you. What's she look like?"

"I've never seen her. Never mind, it was just a thought." A far-fetched thought. The thought was: Buy her a drink. Swap tales of woe.

More drinks. Commiserate. Eventually our hands, hidden beneath the table, tenderly and sorrowfully caress and explore.

Five minutes later I was seated in the darkest corner of the darkest bar in the Zone, the Cabaret, featuring THE WORLD FAMOUS ALL-COLLEGE-GIRL REVUE. An overpriced bourbon sat on the bar in front of me. Onstage, a tall blond named Monique was just beginning her routine, body sleek and firm, encased in a waterfall of red spangles. Eyes forbidding and experienced. At best, she was a very old graduate student.

I'd barely put the drink to my lips when I felt something soft press into my back.

I jumped.

"Hey, take it easy," said a throaty, feminine voice.

Turning, I looked into the face of a pretty, dark-haired girl wearing a white Danskin. She had been attempting to massage my back with her breasts. "Sorry," I said. "I guess I'm a little jumpy."

"No shit," she said, taking the barstool next to me. "Mind if I join you?" When they weren't onstage, the dancers hustled drinks. Drinks started at nine dollars, so I usually didn't buy. But there was nothing usual about today. I still had the hundred-dollar bills Gus had given me, and I took one out of my wallet.

"Hubba hubba," the girl said. "What's your name?"

"Thomas," I said. "Thomas More. I'm a saint."

Onstage, Monique slithered naked on a brown shag rug. "Floor work" it was called, offering the customers a climactic and unobstructed view. Monique lay on her stomach, her torso mimicking the motion of a slow wave.

The men whooped, of course, and catcalled and applauded. But a certain joylessness also invaded their eyes as they watched. They had been spoiled by accessibility and plenitude. I watched them watching, and I thought of Moses on Oreb. Would his joy have been tainted had the bush burned for him ten times in a single evening?

The bartender brought a champagne glass that carried a tiny cocktail straw. Probably ginger ale.

"Thanks, Tommy," the girl said, presenting her cigarette for me to light.

"I'd like to ask you something," I said.

"I bet you would," she grinned.

I grinned too. I was feeling better already. "But I'd like to ask you something else first. I'm looking for a dancer. She may not even work here. And I only know her last name."

"You've got my sympathy," she said. "Last names aren't real big around here. First names either, for that matter. You think my mother really named me Venus?"

"I guess not," I said. "Did she name you Bloomberg by any chance?"

"What?"

"Nothing. Just a shot in the dark. The girl I'm looking for is probably twenty. She just dropped out of college."

"Haven't you heard? We're all college girls here." Venus leaned over and put her mouth close to my ear. At the same time her fingers lightly brushed my crotch. Subtle, but unambiguous. "I'm majoring in Social Relations," she whispered.

"I bet you're the smartest one in your class," I said.

Venus giggled. I felt like giggling too. Two hours with Ciullo had left me yearning for the simple pleasures.

A couple of the men at the nearby tables, I noticed, were getting businessmen's specials. For the price of a double—eighteen dollars, soda water—some dancers would administer a quick once-over under the table, delicately referred to as a "manual release." Such liaisons were always consummated with discretion and taste. Obscured by the shadows, only the subtlest motion of the woman's arm could be detected, as though beneath the table she were kneading dough and didn't want anyone to know about it. The men, too, participated in the deceit, heroically trying to converse while they were being worked on.

Venus tilted back her head, blowing a lungful of blue smoke toward the ceiling. "Haven't I seen you in here before, uh ...Terry?"

"Tommy," I said. "Could be. Modern dance fascinates me."

"Yeah, I remember. You're usually in here with a little guy, wears a rug. Looks like he gets his suits from Sears. Paisley ties."

"Damn," I said, getting up. I'd forgotten Cleve.

"Hey, listen," Venus said. "There's no accounting for taste. I didn't mean—"

"It's not that. You reminded me of a phone call I have to make."

"Your wife wears suits from Sears?" she smiled.

"Not my wife." I excused myself and went to the pay phone. Alex was supposed to have talked with Cleve. Even though Ciullo's nephew appeared too inept to do any harm, I needed to make sure.

"What's up?" Cleve said when he heard my voice.

"Are you okay?" I asked.

"Why the hell shouldn't I be okay? I should be asking you. What's that noise I hear? Where are you?"

"The Cabaret."

"Sounds like you're okay too," he said sourly. "We're both okay. What's the problem?"

"Listen, did you have any visitors today?"

"What? Well, my brother-in-law came for supper. Dropped in out of the blue. The jerk's still here, running his mouth."

"No, I mean has anybody come round asking about me? About Jesus Saves?"

Cleve paused. "Oh yeah, him. Nice guy. Works at the *Herald*. He just wanted some details for a story he's doing. Looks like you're not only rich, you're gonna be famous too."

Jesus, I thought. "You didn't think he was dressed a little too spiffy for a goddam reporter?"

"What? Hell no. He wasn't dressed any better than me. What's eating you?"

"Okay," I said. "You've made your point. In fact, there's a stripper here who's been complimenting you on your suits."

"Yeah? What'd she say?"

I didn't tell him. I took a deep breath and prepared to reinvite myself to New Hampshire. "Listen, Cleve," I began offhandedly, "you remember that offer to go to New Hampshire with you?"

"Forget that a second," he said. "I got something important to tell you." A note of pride rang in his voice.

"What?" I asked patiently.

"I figured out how Bloomberg stiffed the filly," he announced.

"Already?" I silently revised my opinion of his gullibility. Insight into thoroughbreds, I supposed, didn't translate into the human realm.

"Can't put much by ol' Cleve," he said. "Gotta give Jake credit. I've never seen it done that way before."

"Yes?" I prompted.

"Drop by the track in the morning. Say seven. I'll show you."

"In the morning?"

"Most people's not like you," he said. "Most people got to get up early and go to work."

"What about New Hampshire?"

"In the morning. I got to get back to my brother-in-law. Stand guard on the 'frigerator."

He hung up, and I returned to the bar in serious need of company. Venus's barstool was vacant and her champagne glass had been cleared away. I finally spotted her across the room. She had another drink, and she was whispering intimately into the wrinkled ear of a very old Chinese man. She's probably switched her major, I thought glumly, to Foreign Relations. Maybe Geriatric Medicine. Well, I consoled myself, how was she to know I needed her? Business is business. For each drink she hustled, the bartender gave her a coupon. At the end of the night, she redeemed them for two dollars apiece.

Ah, the Combat Zone. It was no place for romantic temperaments, I knew. But for a cynic, for a man who believed himself without illusions, well, the Zone would pleasantly confirm his worst suspicions about mankind.

Suddenly exhausted, a weariness deeper than panic, I finished my drink and took the Red Line back to Cambridge. Of all the bad things that had happened that day, one tiny consolation presented itself. I could sleep in my own bed, without the rhythmic accompaniment of Beth's guttural love-noises.

═══*FIVE*═══

"H"ORSES GOT PERSONALITIES just like people," Cleve was explaining to me. "Lot of quirks a trainer's gotta deal with. Of course, the bettors don't understand that. They think all you got to do is stick a horse in the gate, let 'er rip. Then stand around, hold a stopwatch in one hand, your pecker in the other."

In the first hours after dawn, Suffolk Downs was startlingly peaceful—a serenity, I supposed, exaggerated by my knowledge of what would transpire that afternoon. I'd entered the grandstand that morning at seven-thirty, bleary-eyed, my shoes clicking loudly on the concrete, the hushed reverberations making me feel as though I'd arrived early for church. Not the doleful, watchful religion of the Combat Zone clubs. Here the believers would wrestle with their God, shout in tongues, implore, shriek, and, after each race, examine their tainted hearts, searching for the hidden sin that had corrupted them, had led them to bet the two horse rather than the three.

Passing through the grandstand, I had found Cleve outside, hunched over the chainlink fence that hugged the length of the homestretch. He held a cardboard cup of coffee in both hands, warming them, and looked out across the infield.

"Speed in a horse is like intelligence in a person. It'll only take you so far. I seen some pretty fast horses that got sold to the packing house for thirty-five cents a pound. Just like I seen some real smart people wake up in the gutter with an empty bottle of Ripple." Cleve paused, grinning, as though he might include me in his account of the insufficiency of intelligence. "When I used to work out here in the stables," he went on, "you wouldn't believe the crazy fucking animals we'd come across. This one colt I remember had it all. Big Sid I think his name was. Well put together, beautiful stride, good speed, everything. Except he liked to chase seagulls. I mean, he'd be cruising along as pretty as you please, and one of these birds would fly in here from the bay and he'd fucking start chasing it. Must of thought he was a goddam dog. Of course, blinkers fixed him right up. That don't always work." He finally turned his head toward me and said, "You hung over?"

"Sleepy."

A damp fog, laden with the tang of sea minerals, had settled on the grounds and obscured the backstretch. Here was a Suffolk Downs I'd never seen before. No human smells, no confined air superheated by desperation, no psychic urgency. Across the fence from us, soft clods of earth, deep hoofprints everywhere, and mounds of grainy dung, odorous and rich in my nostrils. Horses were already out on the track, working. Of the hundreds of races I'd watched, I couldn't remember having actually heard a horse gallop. An exercise boy shouted at Cleve in Spanish as he breezed past. A big roan was led back toward the barns, toe-dancing, returning from a workout. Steam rose from the slope of his back, steam clouds shot from his nostrils, more steam from between his hindquarters.

When Cleve had finished his coffee, we headed for the barns. He gestured briskly, enjoying his moment, emphasizing in detail the enormity of the problem he had solved. "I mean, Bloomberg stiffed a real gifted filly for nineteen races, and there wasn't even a hint that something was going on. No drugs. Different jockeys. What he did was pretty clever. Shitty maybe, but clever."

"Okay, Cleve," I yawned. "Okay. So how'd he manage it?"

"The gad," he announced with obvious satisfaction.

"Oh," I said.

"I'll show you."

The barns, six long rows of low-slung buildings with corrugated tin roofs, each held a series of tiny stalls as far as I could see. Quarters for fifteen hundred horses during the winter meet, I'd heard, and two thousand during the summer. Young girls were mucking the stalls; exercise boys were joking among themselves. Trainers watched silently while their thoroughbreds were groomed, bandaged, taken out for workouts, and led back. Other horses hot-walked on the carousels between the buildings.

"Watch where you step," Cleve said. "And no smoking."

He spoke to a stocky young woman wearing muddy jeans and a Boston College sweatshirt, a harness slung over her shoulder. "Suzy, bring Jesus Saves out here so we can have a look at her. Tell W.J. I said it's okay."

The girl left, and Cleve disappeared into a tackroom. He returned carrying a jockey's whip in his hand.

"This," he said, "is a gad."

"Oh." Less of a whip, I saw, than a leather-covered stick. Cleve reached behind him and slipped the gad in a rear belt loop, like a sword.

In a moment Suzy appeared from a small passage between two barns, leading behind her the filly that had vaulted me to a higher tax bracket. Jesus Saves did not come willingly, tossing her head with nervous fury, bouncing sideways with little mincing steps. I was too embarrassed to ask if her configuration signified Arabian ancestry. Head smallish, mounted on the large, ripe-looking barrel of her torso. A dark gray coat, almost black, the color of gunmetal. Closer, I watched her ears flicker rapidly. White showed all around her liquid brown eyes. I kept my distance.

"There, girl. There," Suzy said, handing the reins to Cleve. "She's a little rank, Mr. Dickey."

Cleve worked the reins and made hard kissing sounds through tightly pursed lips. The filly resisted the pressure, shaking her head from side to side. I thought of Gerald. "She won't bite?" I asked without thinking.

"Stick your hand over here," Cleve winked, "and let's see." I took another step back.

"I'd stay out the rear of her, too," he advised.

I moved again, and Cleve looked over at me, a bemused, country-boy wryness in his eyes.

"You ever actually been up on a horse, T.T.?" he asked.

"Sure," I said. "In front of the A&P. Cost my mother a quarter."

"Lord God," he grinned. "Somehow I just knew that. So, cowboy, you see anything unusual 'bout this filly?"

I shook my head. "She's a beautiful animal."

"Take a look at them scars on her butt."

A dozen little gray ridges, two and three inches in length, marred the hide of her muscled rump. A few of the ridges were not gray, but reddish, fresh-looking.

"And up here," Cleve pointed. "Base of her neck."

"Was that done with a whip?"

He nodded. "Don't mean much, of itself. Lots of horses running around with gad marks on their rumps. Trainers call 'em stick horses. Loafers. Won't finish a race 'less you take a switch to their ass."

Retrieving the whip from his belt loop, he said, "Watch this."

He held the gad near the filly's eyes, giving her a good look at it. She shied immediately and cocked her hind legs as if to rear, backing up with short, hopping steps. I retreated, sensing that she might bolt. But Cleve kept the whip in her face until eventually Jesus Saves gave in to the threat. Head low, ears flattened, she sagged, spiritless, almost quaking. I had watched her power and beauty contorted, reduced to an embarrassing posture of meekness and submission.

Cleve returned the whip to his belt. "I don't know just how Jake trained her that way. But it sure scares hell outta her. She sees that whip, she slinks back like a kicked dog. Ramone took her out and let her run a little yesterday. If he even looked like he was going for the whip, she stopped cold."

"Clever," I said. Gruesome, I thought.

"You see the beauty of it, don't you?" he went on. "The jocks had been whipping her and losing, and who the hell's going to question the ride? The stewards figure it's honest. And the bettors, hell, the bettors love to see a jock whip the shit out a horse that's losing their money."

It made sense. "And when Rourke felt her running away from him," I said, "he went for the reins, not the whip."

"Right," Cleve said. "Beautiful."

"What's going to happen to her?"

He cast a doubtful eye on Jesus Saves. "I don't know. She's got a good tail male. Good female line. If it turns out she's ruined for the track, she ought to make a good brood mare."

"Dropping foals should be a relief after this."

Suzy, who'd been murmuring to the filly, turned and aimed a sour laugh at me. "You kidding?" she said.

"What?"

"Mister, have you ever seen thoroughbreds mate?"

"Well, no," I conceded.

"I didn't think so. You should see it sometime. First, what they'll do is bind her foreleg up under her, so she's standing on three legs and can't move. You know, they wouldn't want her kicking an expensive stud in the groin. Then they put a twitch on her upper lip."

"A twitch?"

"That's a nasty little wire noose they jerk tight when she tries to turn her head. Then the stallion has a go at her."

"Why don't they use artificial insemination?"

"Breeding rules say it's got to be natural. What they do is about as natural as rape. A brood mare," she concluded with disgust, "is just a life-support system for a womb."

College girl, I thought, as I tried to appear shocked. "I suppose even that's better than having Bloomberg as a trainer."

Her eyes bright with anger, she asked, "What kind of bastard would do this to a horse?"

I confessed that I didn't know. The three of us contemplated the spiritless animal at her side.

"If you two bleeding hearts don't mind," Cleve interrupted, "I've got work to do."

We thanked Suzy, and—why, I don't know—I added a private glance of sympathy. Then Cleve and I walked quietly back to the grandstand, just as the sun burned away the last wisps of morning fog.

"Want some coffee?" he asked as we entered the press box.

"Sure. Thanks." I tried to put a casual tone in my voice. "Now, about that trip to New Hampshire. I thought I might tag along after all."

Cleve busied himself sorting the snarl of papers on his desk. "I got to get more organized—"

"New Hampshire?" I said.

"What? Oh yeah," he said, studying me. "I thought you were gonna— Wait a minute. You haven't shot that wad already?"

"No," I said. "I've just changed my mind. There's no reason I shouldn't come with you, is there?" I held my breath.

"Nope. No reason at all—" he started.

I breathed again.

"—except I'm not going. The stewards told me this morning. Too much official interest in Bloomberg's death. The police are handling everything. Suffolk's out of it."

"Shit."

"Yeah, shit," he commiserated. "I was kind of looking forward to it."

"Is there any chance the stewards will change their minds?"

"Nuh-uh. Don't think so. There's some assistant DA wants to handle it all. Wants to make sure everything is strictly by the book, nice and legal. He figures if somebody from the track goes up there, we might violate one of these Holy Rollers' rights."

"Aw Christ."

"What's it to you? You a rich man. You can see nekkid girls in the comfort of your own home. Buy you one of them VCRs. Hell, you can—"

"Jesus, it's not that," I said, flustered, my hope fading. "Any chance that maybe you and I could go up there unofficially?"

Cleve looked at his watch. "It's only a quarter to nine, T.T. You already drunk? I'd lose my job—" eyes squinted at me—"there something you ain't telling me, boy?"

I stared out an open window that overlooked the track below. A crisp breeze engulfed me.

"No," I sighed, suddenly shivering. "Forget it."

For the next two days I fell prey to brief seizures of panic, which, exhausting me, gave way to numbness and mental inertia. Stay alert, I cautioned myself as Saturday approached. Be prepared for any contingency. On Thursday I evaded the quiz I'd promised my class, instructing Jeanne, the department secretary, to post a sign on the classroom door claiming illness. That evening I drank less than usual, and then limited myself to Bass ale. On Friday I found myself on the floor, attempting sit-ups. After I'd touched elbow to knee a dozen times, a cough rose in my throat and got away from me. I lay back on the floor, sputtering. I reached for a cigarette and the phone and called Cleve for the second time that day.

For godsakes no, he told me, nothing had changed. He wasn't going to New Hampshire. And why the hell did I keep pestering him about it? he wanted to know. Just checking, I said, and hung up.

But mostly I sat alone in my apartment, staring at the Three Boxes. I often stared at them when wakened by a hangover, the flu, or, in this case, depressing circumstances. The Three Boxes were, literally, three cardboard boxes lined up against a wall in my apartment, filled to different levels with manuscript pages. Simply by pondering the contents of the boxes, it was possible to chart a graph of my life.

The first box contained 244 pages of an unfinished novel. Title: *Helpless Laughter.*

The second box held 385 pages of a completed work of criticism, conceived and executed in a wide-eyed fit of optimism. Published five years ago, the book had been well received and in great part responsible for my appointment at a college with Wesley's reputation. Title: *Voyeurism in the American Novel.*

The third box held 120 pages of the manuscript that I presently worked on, or more precisely, diddled with. Four years of work, at thirty pages a year, toward a biography of Edmund Lowell, an important early-twentieth-century American critic. Unfinished; likely to remain so. I'd had a two-year head start on a Yale scholar pursuing the same topic; he was already into galleys. My title, imaginatively: *The Achievement of Edmund Lowell.*

The pattern suggested by the Three Boxes was bleak. From a novel to a book about novels to a book about a man who wrote about novels. A gradual withdrawal from life. Primary, secondary, tertiary response.

I couldn't stare at the Three Boxes for long—at least not without an ironic twinge. I never really fooled myself, finally. There are few activities so smug as coldblooded self-appraisal.

=====*SIX*=====

SATURDAY ARRIVED. At a little past nine, I stood looking out my window, studying the street two floors below. When I checked again a half hour later, something had changed. There, parked in a space two cars behind my Beetle, I saw the Mercedes. One occupant, male, driver's side, taking up more than his share of space. Gerald, I decided grimly. Making sure I held up my side of the bargain.

I circled my living room a half-dozen times, then stopped abruptly. "Well, shit," I said aloud. "Here goes." Out of my apartment and down the stairs, not giving myself time to reconsider, I approached the Mercedes like a soldier who leaps into the breach more out of fear than courage. He's only hired help, I reminded myself. Don't show weakness. I squatted on the curb next to the driver's door.

Gerald rolled down the window, but he didn't turn his face toward me. His jaw, I noticed, wouldn't have looked out of proportion on a sperm whale.

"Hello," I said.

He still didn't look at me. Finally he said, "Yeah?"

"Gerald, isn't it?" I began familiarly. "Well, Gerald, something's come up. Mr. Dickey, the man I was supposed to accompany to New

Hampshire, isn't going after all. The stewards told him to stay out of it. So it's really out of my hands."

He didn't respond.

"Now I was going to explain this to Mr. Ciullo on Monday. But if you think it's best, we can go right now and tell him."

More silence.

"What I'm saying is, there's no point in my going to New Hampshire. If Mr. Dickey doesn't go, there won't be anything for me to listen to."

Gerald slowly shifted his heavy head toward me. His voice was deep, and there was a slight rasp at the bottom of it. "I don't know nothing about that," he said.

"You were there, remember? Mr. Ciullo said—"

"You're supposed to go to Waterville," he said without inflection, without any effort to persuade.

Probably why Ciullo hired him, I thought. Not quick on the uptake, a little slow to assimilate new facts, but he followed orders. Speaking slowly, distinctly, and with patience, I explained it over again, marshaling whatever classroom skills I possessed. My knees were beginning to hurt from squatting by the window. "So you see," I concluded again, "if Mr. Dickey doesn't go, then there's no reason for me to go. Do you understand?"

"I don't know nothing about that," he said. "Get in your car. We're wasting time."

An absurd image appeared in my mind. My Volkswagen puttering at thirty-five miles per hour on the expressway north, a Mercedes hugging my bumper.

"Listen, Gerald. Say everything were different, say there was a reason for me to go. You see that piece of junk parked two cars up the street? I own that. It won't even make it up Beacon Hill, much less the mountains near Waterville. I swear."

What he said next caught me totally by surprise. Gerald said, "Get in."

"What?"

"Stop whining and get in back. I'll drive."

"You're not getting the point," I said, my heart rate increasing. "I wouldn't know what to say when I got there—"

His eyes full of dull menace, Gerald opened the door of the Mercedes onto my kneecaps. I fell back heavily, watching him shift his massive legs toward the curb. The lapel of his windbreaker twisted back, exposing the brown leather strap at his armpit. "Know what to say?" he said, rising and staring down at me. "You don't never shut up."

I was in the back seat of the Mercedes before I bothered to rub my knees.

The White Mountains of New Hampshire comprise the final, descending range of the Appalachians, rolling ever more gently northward until they disappear into the flat expanses of Canadian forest. The Kancamagus Highway hugs the base of the range, curving and twisting among the valleys, connecting within a distance of seventy-five miles a half-dozen ski resorts: Woodstock, Loon, Franconia Notch, Wildcat, Tecumseh, and finally the resort for which we headed, Waterville. In the long off-season of spring and summer, the resorts promoted hiking, golf, and swimming, but most of all scenery. From the Kancamagus, the mountainscape was unquestionably spectacular, but something else was taking my breath away. Out the side window of the Mercedes, the morning sun raced with disturbing speed along the tops of the hardwoods. My shoulders were alternately thrown against, then pulled away from, the rear door.

I held on to the center armrest and studied Gerald from behind, feeling as though suddenly thrown into the cage of a trained but potentially dangerous animal. His shoulders bulged in an awkward, muscular curve above the seat, peaking in a thick neck that supported a large, thick skull. On his pepper-colored hair, short and carefully groomed, he wore a porkpie hat. On his neck, near his shirt collar, I saw traces of baby powder.

I decided to test my authority. "Keep it at forty, Gerald," I said. "Lot of curves here."

He eased his foot off the pedal.

"Thanks," I said encouragingly.

It relieved me that he responded to my—commands?—and it surprised me that he didn't find anything inappropriate about who was giving them. He must have had military training in his past, I concluded. Follow orders and don't question the source.

"Thirty-five would be even safer," I suggested.

Again he eased off the pedal.

After two hours in the car, my confidence grew. Gerald hadn't said much, but I found myself, almost against my will, feeling comforted by him. If his was a soldier's mentality, mine was that of a hostage; I accepted that my own well-being was joined to his. I didn't know what to expect when we arrived in Waterville, but if trouble lay ahead, there wasn't a nudist alive who could take him.

By noon we had reached the town of Waterville, a two-hundred-yard stretch of highway bordered on either side by small restaurants, a cafe, sports and clothing shops, a real-estate office, and a country inn. No signs for the ski resort. Gerald parked in front of the Snowden Cafe for directions.

"I don't mean to tell you your business," I said, getting out of the car with him, "but if nobody in here knows how to get there, for godsakes don't flash your gun. These people won't understand. We're not in the city." We're in NRA country, I thought nervously. "Some old guy is liable to go out to his pickup and pull a twelve-gauge down from the rifle rack."

"Farmers don't bother me," Gerald said.

A waitress who reminded me of Patricia Neal in *Hud* gave us directions. Six miles ahead on the Kancamagus, turn right onto a steeply graded mountain road. Two miles to the main lodge.

The waitress looked out the cafe window. "Is that your car?"

Gerald deferred to me. "Yes," I said.

"You sure you got the right place?"

"As far as I know. The Adamite community?"

"That's it." She smiled. I didn't ask why.

Twenty minutes later we arrived at the lodge, a handsome two-story structure of gray stone and cedar, its slate roof slanting toward an enormous central chimney. The lodge was set in a clearing, halfway up White Birch Mountain. Above the lodge, against a deep blue sky, the mountain peaked into a single white cloud. The ski trails bloomed in spring clover, twisting down the peak like purple, melting fingers.

The Adamites must have sworn off automobiles; the parking lot lay empty. I gently persuaded Gerald to stay by the Mercedes. "At least for now," I said. "There's no reason to . . . unsettle anyone at this point."

He looked at me skeptically. "What's your pitch?" he asked.

"My pitch?"

"Who you going to tell them you are?"

I'd spent most of the trip mentally rehearsing what to say when we arrived. "First," I said, "I'll tell them exactly who I am. Then I'll tell them I want to ask some questions."

"Yeah?" he said doubtfully, his tone full of disapproval.

"Well, sort of." Like most people's, my experience with lying had been limited more or less to its value as a social lubricant. But I had learned this much: avoid the gratuitous lie; be truthful about details; falsify only a crucial fact or two. The result, I hoped, would be something resembling sincerity, not to mention an ability to keep my stories straight.

I approached the large, double oak doors, noticing only one renovation from the lodge's former use. A twelve-foot-high green slat fence extended from either side of the building. To thwart, I supposed, the eyes of casual voyeurs.

I stepped inside. On the other side of the doors, a three-sided partition formed a small cubicle that cut off my view of the larger, high-ceilinged room behind it. On the floor was a white pillow, and on the pillow a young, very plain woman, turning the pages of a *Mother Jones* magazine. Her straight black hair spread onto shoulders only slightly smaller than Gerald's. Obese, sitting there as nearly cross-legged as she could manage, she made the cubicle appear even smaller.

"Welcome to our Edenic community," she said without enthusiasm.

"Hello," I said. "You must be Eve."

Easy, Thomas, I told myself. Easy. Fortunately she either missed or ignored my irony. "I'm Thomas Theron," I recouped. "I was hoping to ask a few questions, perhaps have a look around. I'm gathering information—"

She frowned. "We don't encourage the merely curious, Mr.—"

"Professor Theron. I understand, of course. I *am* curious, but my interest is purely academic." I took my faculty card out of my wallet and handed it to her. "I'm researching an article on New England utopian communities. Mostly nineteenth-century sects—the Shakers, the Perfectionists, and so forth—but I wanted to get a sense of a living, working commune." When I'd rehearsed it in my mind, the story had sounded plausible enough. Now, spoken, it sounded queer, uncomfortably close to Alex's cub-reporter routine. But there was no stopping now. "I was hoping to interview Adam."

She silently studied my faculty card.

I pressed on. "I know this can't be a very good time for me to come round. I've read the newspapers. But this is the only time I have."

She surprised me. "I see. Would you please wait here, Professor Theron?" With a great effort she hoisted herself off the pillow, then turned the corner of the partition. I glimpsed the action of her enormous buttocks beneath the flowing garment. If she were Eve, I thought unkindly, she appeared to have been fashioned from an entire rack of Adam's ribs.

In about five minutes she returned—without, I noticed, my ID card. "Someone will be down to talk to you in a moment," she said.

"Thank you."

"It may be a while," she added. "In the meantime, I'm sure that I can answer any questions you have."

"Well, anything will help. Just tell me what you can about your community."

She sat down again, and the pillow wheezed beneath her. She began a speech that sounded even more rehearsed than my own had been. Her voice carried the inflection and nuance of a recorded message. "We Adamites are united together—one hundred fifty men, women, and children—in the belief that God intended us to attain perfection on this earth, both spiritually and sensually. We believe that Jesus Christ returned to earth in A.D. 81 to set up God's kingdom. Ever since, it has been man's obligation to return to the Edenic life before the Fall—"

"Yes, but—" I began, looking for an opportunity to butt in.

She didn't miss a beat. "Love here, of all kinds, is given and received freely and selflessly. Jealousy, the symptom of the old clutching, selfish love, has no place here. We are bound together in a single marriage. All partners participate equally and freely, without respect to old notions of physical beauty. We—"

"What about gender?" I jumped in. Anything to take her out of the security of the set speech. "Isn't a woman's role in all of this rather limiting?"

"Excuse me?"

"What is a woman's role here?" Insert a little controversy, I thought. Get a rise out of her.

"God created woman as a helpmate to man. It is in that role that she discovers a fulfillment."

"That doesn't bother you?" I asked. "You don't find it . . . confining?"

"It is a joy to me," she answered. I realized that she had heard it all before, many times. "Freedom is not attained," she continued easily, "simply by putting oneself awash in a sea of possibilities. True freedom grows out of the knowledge of one's role and true purpose. Does the poet find the sonnet confining?"

"I guess not," I said. "But then again, does he find the limerick librating?"

"Excuse me?"

"Never mind," I said. It was absurd for me, I realized, to try to tap some reservoir of feminist guilt that she clearly didn't possess. What was her motivation to rebel? What you have here, Thomas, I told myself, is a very fat girl who is apparently getting her bacon rubbed morning, noon, and night.

Just then a man joined us. He was a couple of inches taller than I, lean and well-muscled. Beneath his longish, unkempt hair was a deeply tanned, remarkably handsome face. He wore only two squares of cotton cloth, front and back, attached to a cord waistband. He looked more like Tarzan than Adam.

"How do you do," I said.

"Professor Theron," he replied, accepting my hand. His manner was reserved, even formal, but his blue eyes were wary and alive. "What has brought you to us?" he asked. I had a feeling that he was used to sizing up strangers.

"I'm here to learn about your community," I said. "I was hoping especially to speak with Adam. Are you he?"

"I am Adam," he said. "All of the men in our community are Adams."

I knew better than to ask him what happened at mail call. Instead I said, "I had in mind the particular Adam who founded the commune."

"I see. Professor Theron," he began with a kind of self-assured benevolence, "our policy is to screen our guests. We disciples of Adam are united by our love of God and our love of our fellow man. At the same time, we do not feel obliged to hold ourselves up to derision or to provide thrills for those bored with their own lives."

"I promise you," I replied amiably, "I haven't been bored for a week."

"Nor," he said, detecting something in my tone, "do we encourage skeptics."

As soberly as possible, I said, "It's true that I'm not a potential convert, but I do come here with a serious purpose. I understand your reluctance. There have been some nasty stories in the press."

"It's true that we have been the victims of various misrepresentations. Such harassment is nothing new. We accept the challenge that such untruths present. You are an educated man," he continued. "You must know that the history of religion is equally the history of persecution."

I nodded solemnly. He took my elbow. "We welcome those whose hearts are sincere. We have nothing to hide. Our founder will see you. For only a moment, I'm afraid. He is old."

I followed Adam—Handsome Adam—around the partition and into

the main lodge. More partitions divided the room and restricted my view. But I didn't hear anything, certainly not the paradisiacal chatter of a hundred fifty men, women, and children. We crossed to a central stairwell.

"Academic salaries must have improved since I was in college," Handsome Adam said, mounting the steps.

"I beg your pardon?"

"I saw a Mercedes parked in front."

"Oh. That," I said. "Family money." Ciullo family, I thought. I changed the subject, thinking he might hit on me for a donation. "It was a lovely drive. Beautiful country up here."

"Beauty assists us in the contemplation of God," he said. I watched the back of his head as we came to the top of the stairs. His brown hair, though unkempt, was well and freshly cut.

The stairs opened onto a large, cedar-paneled room that had obviously been the lodge bar. To my left, a floor-to-ceiling window offered a view up to the summit of White Birch Mountain. A redwood deck just outside the window produced the first signs of life. A half-dozen people lay nude, sunning themselves. Another couple, both long-haired, sat on a picnic bench, facing away from me. Their buttocks hung off the edge of the bench, scalloped.

Handsome Adam led me to the other side of the room, past a large central fireplace, to a parquet floor where the skiers had once danced. A four-by-six-foot Persian rug was centered on the dance floor. Centered on the rug was a tiny brown man with a sparse white beard. His old, slender legs were twined in the lotus position, and a white silk scarf draped his lap, hiding his genitals. His brown eyes, peering out from a deeply lined face, regarded me with an unswervingly beatific expression.

"We must stay only a moment," Handsome Adam told me, indicating that I should sit at the edge of the rug opposite Old Adam. I nodded and sat down. Handsome Adam sat next to Old Adam and whispered in his old, crabbed ear. The old man smiled broadly at me. He nodded vigorously. His smile seemed to me practiced—the kind that would make his jaws ache if he kept it up.

"Adam is pleased that you have come to visit him," Handsome Adam said. "He will be happy to hear your questions."

I struggled to keep my expression solemn. Their pose was laughable. At best Old Adam was, in some basic way, theologically confused. At worst, he was transparently phony. In either case, his religious metaphors had been badly mixed—the patriarch of Genesis doing a rather bad imitation of Mahatma Gandhi. The Old Testament conflated with a diluted Eastern mysticism. Edenic nakedness in the lotus position.

"Tell him that I—"

"You may address him, Professor Theron. He understands all. I will in turn convey his answers. Words, for him, are a sign of mankind's Fall. Only silence is pure and sinless."

"I see." I stuck to a topic close to my heart, one that let me use the lecture material I'd wasted on Tuesday. "What especially interests me," I began, "are the sexual codes of utopian communes. The sects I've studied tend either to reject absolutely or embrace absolutely the sensual life. The Shakers, for example, practiced celibacy. The Perfectionists endorsed a kind of promiscuity. I take it that you favor something closer to the latter vision?" I had been speaking to Old Adam and studying his face. If there was comprehension in his eyes, I couldn't see it. His features maintained the same frozen, beatific expression.

Handsome Adam answered. "God did not give us our physical natures with the intention that we suppress them. But neither does God teach that we should waste our seed in promiscuity or profligacy. We believe that procreation is the final goal of the sexual act."

Old Adam sat there, nodding and smiling.

"How," I asked, "do you reconcile that notion with free love?"

"The men of our community practice *coitus reservatus*," Handsome Adam said.

"Does that mean what I think it means?"

Handsome Adam, I noticed, had trouble remembering to defer to Old Adam. The little man, mute and grinning, had virtually ceased to be the board off which we bounced our dialogue. "Our followers unite sexually as they choose, without inhibition, according to the strength of their desire. But the men discipline themselves never to achieve orgasm unless for the specific purpose of conception. In that way," Handsome Adam concluded, "we experience the intimacy and joy of sensual love without a sinful waste of our seed."

"I see." The idea made me shudder inwardly. It was an unpleasant variant of a notion that had persisted for centuries: precious bodily fluids must be conserved. And here, I thought, a chance for a shrewd insight that I could convey to Ciullo. If the Adamite men really practiced *coitus reservatus,* they were likely to commit suicide, not murder.

Handsome Adam got to his feet, signifying that our interview? audience? charade? had ended. I got up, nodding my thanks into Old Adam's frozen, brown-faced, yellow-toothed smile. I would have bet my life that he hadn't understood the first word of what we'd said.

I followed Handsome Adam across the room and down the stairs. "Is there anything else we can do for you?" he asked, pausing at the bottom of the stairs.

"I guess not. Thanks. You've been very helpful. On yes," I added, patting my rear pocket. "My faculty card?"

"Certainly. I must have laid it down. If you'll wait here, I'll have a look around."

It shouldn't have been a mistake to leave me there alone, but it was. I began to retrace my steps back up the stairs and toward the rug where Old Adam sat. What impulse moved me, I couldn't say. The imp of the perverse? That things weren't as they seemed didn't bother me— things rarely were. I just liked knowing about it. Ciullo might like knowing about it, too.

Old Adam must have seen me coming, because I found him just as his beatific visage settled into place; I didn't glimpse what expression preceded it. I had a feeling that earlier he had merely responded to the tone of my voice. Slowly, with a congenial smile, I approched him. "Getting back to sexual practices," I said, careful to keep a solemn tone, "if you never shoot your nut, why the hell are you grinning like an idiot child?"

Old Adam nodded, his smile intact, frozen. But his eyes tensed noticeably. Clearly he was unused to unescorted visitors.

"And tell me this," I went on. "When you take Eve back in a thicket, do you sniff her haunches and give it to her doggie-style?"

Adam either understood or picked up some flippancy in my voice. His eyes darted wildly, pathetically, like two tiny creatures trapped in his eyesockets. To his credit, he maintained his smile and nodded an affirmation.

"Old billy goat," I muttered. I had more questions, but I didn't have time to ask them. Old Adam hadn't cracked. The only thing I could tell for sure was that he knew how to smile.

I turned, took a couple of steps, and saw Handsome Adam watching me from the top of the stairs.

"Sorry . . ." I faltered. "I . . ."

"Your faculty card," he said, smiling ambiguously.

"Thanks . . . I . . ."

"I trust you found your visit instructive," Adam said, putting his hand on my shoulder. His eyes crinkled in amusement. Not only had he witnessed my interrogation of Old Adam, he seemed to have enjoyed it. I felt relieved, but hopelessly confused.

He took me outside, past the fat girl who still turned the pages of her *Mother Jones*.

"Good-bye," I said to her. I returned to Gerald, her image fresh in my brain. Another insight for Ciullo, I thought. Whether or not the Adamites sanctioned murder, they obviously didn't censure gluttony.

SEVEN

TWENTY MINUTES LATER, Gerald and I were back in the town of Waterville, sitting in a booth in the Snowden Cafe. I was having the special, Salisbury steak and two overcooked vegetables for $2.95.

Gerald devoured a plate of knockwurst and beans before he spoke. "What'd you find out?"

"Well, we're not dealing in precise measurements. There was an old man there who struck me as more comical than menacing. The young guy I couldn't figure. It's a little hard to place someone in the appropriate social category if he's only wearing a loincloth. He's no dummy. He must have known I was lying to him, but he didn't say anything. He just smirked."

Gerald ordered two thick wedges of custard pie. "So, where to now?" he grunted.

"What do you mean? We head back to Boston."

"Mr. Ciullo," he said, his mouth full of yellow custard, "said for you to talk to the guy who gave these people the filly. Beardsley."

I shook my head. "Uh-uh. Mr. Ciullo said for me to *listen* while Cleve Dickey talked to Beardsley, remember? Cleve's not here. Anyway, if I had mentioned Frank Beardsley back there, they wouldn't have let me in the door. Hell, anybody who would give the Adamites more than a funny look—much less a goddam ski resort and a twenty-five-thousand-dollar yearling—is not worth the time."

"Mr. Ciullo said for you to talk to Beardsley."

"You already said that," I sighed.

Gerald pushed away from the table and walked back toward the restrooms. He stopped by the pay phone. My mind felt a brief panic that gave way to resignation. He's calling Ciullo, I thought. Wants to know precisely how bad to hurt me.

In about five minutes Gerald returned, looking more sheepish than threatening. "I found him," he announced with a kind of shy pleasure.

"Found who?"

"Frank Beardsley," he said.

"How'd you manage that?"

"Looked him up in the phone book."

"Shrewd," I said. "Very shrewd indeed. But do you know the odds that he's the Frank Beardsley we want? Anyway, the disciples of Adam forgo the modern convenience of telephones."

"There's only one Frank Beardsley in the book," Gerald said stubbornly.

Gloomily I stuck my spoon into the pool of grease that had congealed on the surface of my spring squash. "Okay, you've got his telephone number."

Gerald hadn't exhausted his reservoir of revelation. "I called him," he said. "His secretary answered. We got an appointment with him in half an hour."

"Gerald, what the hell is an Adamite doing with a secretary?"

He glowered at me. "Ask him," he said, meanness gathering in his eyes. "That's what you're here for."

On the way out, Gerald handed the address he'd written down to the waitress. She was the same one who had given us directions earlier, and she was still smiling. I still didn't ask why.

"Quarter-mile down the road," she said. "Real-estate building. You looking for Frank?"

"Do you know him?" I asked.

"He only eats in here about five times a week."

"What's he doing with an office?" I asked, before I realized the question sounded imbecilic.

"Mister, if you sell real estate, you need an office. As for Frank, if you have an office, you can have a secretary. If you have a secretary, you got someone to chase around the desk. Understand?"

"Frank likes to chase girls?"

"He's a little slow," she said, "but he's got endurance." She handed me the tab: $7.25. I made Gerald pay for it.

We left the Mercedes on the curb and walked. I followed Gerald to a single-story building with Polaroid snapshots of houses and wooded plots of land in the front window. Inside, we found Frank's secretary in an outer office. She possessed very young, rural features hidden beneath lots of urban makeup. The fit of her jeans and blouse might have inspired a good chase.

"You guys just called?" she said.

"Yes."

The girl showed us into Beardsley's office. I wasn't expecting a loincloth and lotus position, but neither was I expecting what we got: a balding, middle-aged man wearing white shoes and a checked polyester jacket. A haze of cigar smoke hung in the air above his head.

"Hello, Mr. Theron?" he said. "Have a seat. Now what can I do you for? Property? Vacation home? I can get you in on a nice little time-sharing deal that—"

"No thanks," I said. "We've just come from the Adamite commune and—"

Beardsley looked at me as though I'd just confessed to an ax murder.

"And you can just slink the hell back there," he snapped. "Sonafa-bitch. And tell that scum-sucking bastard that Frank says—"

"If you'll just give me a second—"

Beardsley jumped out of his chair and stood up close to me. "I'll give you a second to drag your ass outta here. Or I'll kick it out." His head was six inches below me, but his belly made up for the difference in height. He jutted his chin up toward my face and flexed back his elbows, like a bantam rooster.

"If you'll take it easy a second—"

He stuck his right forefinger into my breastbone. "Take it easy your-self, you shit-eating flunky bastard."

I didn't see him get there, but Gerald suddenly appeared between me and the fat man. Gerald's shoulders blocked my view, but from the noises Beardsley was making, I could tell that he was being seriously throttled. Beardsley kept trying to say something, but he sounded as though he had a speech impediment. I stepped off to the side for a bet-ter view. Gerald had stuffed two fingers in the man's nostrils and clamped down on the outside, gripping his nose like a six-pack.

"*Uuunnnhhh. Aaahhhnnnnhh,*" Beardsley wailed, his arms flailing at his sides like two stubby hoses held too far from the nozzle. Gerald flexed his forearm to tighten his grip. Beardsley's arms went limp, as if the water had been cut off.

His secretary crept it. I looked at her and shrugged. She didn't know what to do either. She stood by me on the sidelines.

Gerald led Beardsley by the nose like a prize heifer, causing the man's head to jut forward bovine fashion. Gerald finally sat him in the chair and released him. Gerald shook his head back and forth to say *No.*

"Aw shit," Frank snuffled, rubbing his nose. He looked up at Gerald with the same horror that he would have regarded a Martian. "What the fuck—"

"Take it easy, Mr. Beardsley," I said.

"He ruined my fucking nose," he said. His nose was as red as a boil, and a little trickle of blood was seeping out of it.

"I'm sure there's no real harm done," I comforted him. "If you'll just listen a minute."

"He ruined my fucking nose," Frank whined again, though more quietly.

"What I'm trying to say is, we've just come from the Adamites, but we have absolutely no connection to them. As far as I'm concerned, they're buffoons."

Beardsley looked at me. "Why the hell didn't you say so in the first place?"

"You didn't give me a chance. Anyway, based on what we've heard, you were one of them. A convert. The rumor is that you donated the resort to them."

"A convert!" He made a loud spitting noise. "Do I look like I was born yesterday?"

With things calmer, Beardsley's secretary, who'd been standing next to me, said, "Frank? Is everything okay? Should I call the police?"

Beardsley regarded her with a pained expression. "Goddammit, Doris. You're about five goddam minutes too late. Go back out front."

"You might," I said to her, "bring us something to drink."

"Yeah, yeah," Beardsley sighed. "Bring us something. Go over to Wally's and buy some Scotch." He turned toward me suspiciously. "Who'd you say you were?"

"Thomas Theron."

"And him?" He nodded toward Gerald, flinching slightly, rubbing his nose by reflex.

"A friend." Gerald stood quietly at ease, in a classic pose of unobtrusive availability.

"Yeah, well," Beardsley started, "I don't know what you look like. Some prissy CPA, maybe. But as for your friend, I know a goddam piece of muscle when I see one. I haven't lived in the sticks all my life. Who do you work for?"

"That's not important. I need some information."

"Like what?"

"About the Adamites. You could start by telling me how they came into possession of your ski resort."

"Why should I tell you squat?"

It startled me how easily I slipped into the role. "Because my friend," I said calmly, looking at Gerald, "is a... ear nose and throat specialist."

"All right, shit. I don't mind telling you. Listen, I'm a businessman. He's a businessman. We made a business deal. He swindled me. Cleaned me out. And now I'm here shucking to make a buck. You think I like this nickel 'n' dime condominum crap?"

"Who's a businessman?" I asked. "Who are we talking about?"

"Adam."

I shook my head. "No way. I talked to Adam. Unless I missed something, he'd have trouble signing his own name."

"You talked to him?" Beardsley asked.

"Yes."

"Little guy wearing diapers? Didn't say nothing?"

"Yes."

Beardsley made a harsh sound that was somewhere between a laugh and a bark. "That's not Adam. That little creep couldn't steal quarters from a blind man. Adam found him five years ago in Boston, washing floors at the Star of Siam restaurant. Can't speak English. Adam put him on salary. Pays him just to sit there all day like a monkey."

"He's just show for the tourists?"

"There you go. Why do you think it's so easy to get in to see him?"

"So what Adam are we talking about?" I asked, though it wasn't hard to guess.

"Adam Feld. He's the young guy who does the talking." Beardsley looked at me as though something had just clarified in his brain. "You don't know their gimmick, do you?"

"You mean the return to Eden?"

"Nuh-uh. That was crap for the hippies. You know, Jesus says it's okay to run around naked with a hard-on. That used to be Adam's spiel, but there wasn't any money in it. Winters are too long around here. Anyway, most of the hippies started dropping off a couple of years back. From what I hear, Adam's just got a skeleton crew over there now." Beardsley had apparently amused himself, for he started laughing.

"I guess this means I don't know his gimmick," I said. "Why don't you tell me?"

"You want to see for yourself?"

I didn't, but I didn't want to say so in front of Gerald. "Possibly."

"You got some hard cash?" Beardsley asked.

I hesitated. I had a little over four hundred dollars, but I had no intention of giving it to Beardsley.

"Relax," he said. "Not for me. For Adam."

"What's he doing? Running a casino?"

Frank shook his head. He took a sheet of paper, wrote down some directions and a name, and handed it to me. "Now, when they ask you who your sponsor is, you give them this name. I got a friend, Sam Reardon, who's still active. They'll probably check on it, so I'll call him and let him know. Okay?"

Beardsley's secretary came in and placed three cans of Coca-Cola on his desk.

"Doris, what the hell is that?"

"Frank, you know Wally won't sell me anything without an ID."

"Jesus Christ," he sighed.

"That's all right," I told her as she left. "We're just leaving." I turned back to her boss. "One thing I don't understand. You didn't come to own a place like Waterville resort—or an expensive thorough-bred—by making naïve business deals."

"It's not that simple," he said. He put his hands in the air as though I were holding a gun on him. "Listen, I admit it. The guy fucked me up the ass, pure and simple. But I'm not the only one. People smarter than me, too."

I let that pass. "Why didn't you tell the police?"

"Tell them what? That here's this crook, getting a tax exemption just like he's the pope, and I'm all in heat to invest, to get him to let me do it too? Anyway, my name's still on some contracts over there. Legally, I'm still one of his backers. I just don't have any control, and I don't see any return. But if Adam goes down, I go down with him."

"It's still hard for me to imagine you signing any piece of paper that would—"

"I'm not too goddam proud of it," he interrupted. "Let's just say that I got very distracted. Let's just say he put my ass over a barrel. You'll see."

There was a chance, I thought, that Beardsley's story was merely self-serving. If he posed as victim, he would make a serious error in judgment more palatable to himself. He might accuse Adam of any-thing. "What about these news reports?" I asked. "Do you believe that Adam fixed that race, maybe even murdered the trainer?"

"I never said that. I hope to God he gets nailed to the wall for it, but I don't see it."

"Why not?"

"The shit robbed me blind, but the only thing he didn't want that much was the filly. Well, he wanted it at first. He didn't know shit from Shinola about horses, and he liked the idea of owning one. Thought naming it Jesus Saves was real clever. But when the filly started losing, he started bitching. All feed bills, no wins. Nothing he would kill over, though. Not his style. He's making too much money to worry about a few stable bills." Beardsley paused, his eyes brightening like those of a man who has remembered his only blessing. "If there's one thing that gives me satisfaction," he said, "it's that the filly turned out to be rotten meat. I wonder how many colts they had to stiff to let her win?"

He still didn't know, and I didn't tell him.

Before we left, he rehearsed the directions he had given me. "Why the hell do you look like you're going to a funeral?" he said. "I'm the one who got screwed. You're going there to have a good time."

=====EIGHT=====

WITH UNSPOKEN TENSION between us, Gerald and I walked back to the Mercedes. "Give me those directions," he said finally.

I looked at him guardedly. "Gerald, I've talked to Beardsley. I've talked to Adam—hell, to two Adams. To Eve. The way I see it, I've done everything Mr. Ciullo asked. More than he asked."

Predictably, Gerald shook his head.

I tested him further, though cautiously. "Listen," I reasoned, "it doesn't take a genius to figure out what Adam's up to. Beardsley ruled out gambling. So that leaves something roughly like an opium den, or something roughly like a brothel. The variations on vice are infinite, but the basic tune is simple. And there's no way Beardsley is a druggie, at least not primarily. He didn't hire Doris because of her superior secretarial skills. What it comes down to, then, is sex." Had Freud, I wondered, used similar logic to arrive at the pleasure principle? Eliminate a few possibilities, then conclude boldly, What it comes down to, Herr Doktors, is sex.

Gerald responded by reaching out his hand. "Give me those directions." Obviously we weren't communicating. This time I got in the front seat of the Mercedes. An egalitarian era demanded another strategy. We pulled back onto the Kancamagus.

After about a minute's silence, I asked him, "How long have you worked for Ciullo?"

"Eighteen years," he said. "Maybe nineteen."

His age was hard to guess; he must have been nearing fifty. "What did you do before that?"

"The navy for four years. Tried pro wrestling after that."

"Yeah?" I said, perking up. Until now, I'd never expected much benefit from the Sunday mornings I'd spent watching the World Wrestling Federation on Channel 25. I mentioned to Gerald a few big names from the old days—Antonino Rocca, "The Strangler" Ed Lewis, Bruno Sanmartino.

"You know about that?" he asked. He might not have been impressed, but he was genuinely surprised.

"Well," I replied, "I think it's safe to say that I'm the only Wesley professor who subscribes to *Pro Wrestler*." It wasn't a lie. In a darkly bemused moment, I had filled out a coupon, sent a sixteen-dollar check, and received a two-year subscription and a WWF T-shirt. Another of my quirks that Beth had found charming at first, and later embarrassing. During our courtship, she had even slept in the T-shirt. After marriage, however, I often spied her at the first of each month, waiting on the stoop for the postman, hoping to get the magazine before our neighbors saw it.

"What name did you use?" I asked Gerald.

" 'The Sailor' Gerry Valentin."

"Very catchy." I'd never heard of him. "Why'd you stop?"

"Had trouble with the promoters," he said. "Too many accidents. Had a pretty bad one once. Promoters don't like that."

"What happened?"

"I was wrestling Pretty Boy Billy Baker. 'Sixty-three, maybe '64. I got my timing messed up. Took a flier off the top turnbuckle, up about ten, twelve feet in the air. That's what the promoters wanted my specialty to be. 'The Sailor' meant the navy, but it meant sailing in the air, too. Anyway, my weight kept coming down on my knee instead of my foot."

I knew enough to guess that Gerald wasn't telling me he had hurt his knee. "I gather your knee landed on Billy Baker's throat?"

"Bridge of his nose," he said. "Pretty Boy was a real popular wrestler with the fans. A big draw. He couldn't work for maybe a year after that. When he came back, his face was messed up so bad, the promoters had to give him a mask and make him a bad guy. Called him the Executioner, I think. I was gone by then. The promoters didn't like that."

I waited, unsure whether he intended me to laugh. He didn't. "I see," I observed respectfully. "Gerald, what say we head back to Boston?"

"We make a right turn here," he said pointedly.

Thomas Theron, I thought, behavioral psychologist.

Beardsley had directed us back to White Birch Mountain, this time to a treacherous road that snaked up the mountain face opposite Waterville resort. We very nearly reached the summit before the road ended in a circular creekstone drive. Before us, a lodge, half the size of the resort, perched dramatically on a jutting cliff ledge. It was an A-frame with wings on either side. The illusion of woodsiness, I noticed, seemed to have been expensively created. Moss and ivy grew in symmetrical patterns along enormous, external oak rafters that appeared to be structurally without function. Slightly beneath the lodge and to the right, I glimpsed the corner of a swimming pool—large and kidney-shaped, from what I could see of it—that had been carved into the rock itself. A wispy cloud floated in the air a hundred yards out from the pool, above a gorge.

We turned into a small parking area that abutted the circular drive. "If we have to do this," I said morosely, "let's go." The Mercedes did not look out of place. We parked between a Ferrari GTSI and a Rolls Corniche convertible. I was feeling suddenly poor until I saw another Mercedes and a BMW. When I spotted a Lincoln Mark V and a Caddie, a portion of my self-esteem returned.

We crossed the drive and rang the bell on the left side of an elaborately inlaid oak door. A tiny iron ring at the center of the door swung back on its hinge, and an eye peered through the hole. A speakeasy? I thought hopefully.

"Good afternoon," a woman's voice said.

"Good afternoon," I said.

A pause. "I don't believe I know you gentlemen."

"We're guests," I said. I told her the name Beardsley had given us. "Sam Reardon is sponsoring us."

"Yes, of course. You don't mind waiting while I confirm that, do you, sir?"

"Not at all." Before that moment, it hadn't occurred to me that Beardsley might have revenged himself, revenged his nose, by not making the call. I didn't dwell on it. An even more unsettling thought was taking shape in my mind. If I had indeed come to a whorehouse— apparently an exclusive, profitable whorehouse—it was inconceivable that Vincent Ciullo didn't know about it. And if he knew about it, would he want me to be here? He'd hired an informant, not a participant.

Gerald stood behind me, calm, unconcerned. I toed the crushed stone uneasily. The door opened.

"Won't you come in?" An attractive woman, younger than her voice had suggested, greeted us. Dark eyes; a friendly, open face. A peach-colored, diaphanous blouse fit snugly across her breasts. Lower, the same fabric blossomed on her legs like jodhpurs or harem pants. I managed not to stare.

"Sam Reardon says hello," she said.

"Hello to Sam," I said.

"My name's Lynda—with a wye."

"I'm Thomas with a tee-aitch, and this is Gerald with a gee."

Lynda giggled—excessively, I thought—then ushered us inside to a small foyer with a reception desk. "You understand, of course," she said, "that a small contribution is expected from guests."

"Fine," I said agreeably. "Whatever's appropriate."

"Two hundred is usual," she said.

Affecting nonchalance, I handed her two hundred-dollar bills.

She looked at Gerald. "Apiece," she said.

I could swing it, barely. Swallowing a cough, I put my hand back in my pocket, hoping she didn't notice the effort required.

"Please make yourselves comfortable over there," she said, indicating a large, cherry-paneled room, where a sunken leather sofa faced a fireplace. "I'm afraid you're a little early," she apologized. "We have a very special party planned for this evening. If you'll excuse me for a few moments, I'll arrange to make your wait more pleasant."

Lynda left, and I sat on the sofa. Gerald remained standing, his posture conspicuously that of a bodyguard. I saw no one. Above us, on three sides, a balcony presided over the center space. More false beams ascended the walls of the A-frame, reaching an apex perhaps thirty feet from the floor. At regular intervals, on both levels, the walls held a series of doors. Bedroom doors, I guessed.

In the quiet rose a muffled voice. I followed the sound to a corner door that stood slightly ajar. I heard the voice again, more clearly. It removed whatever doubts lingered about the place we had come to. The utterance was feminine, urgent; the rhythm staccato.

"Oh jesus oh god oh jesus oh jesus. Oh yes. Aaahh."

Twice in a week, I thought. Twice in a week I'd heard someone calling Jesus' name. Bloomberg, lying poisoned on the toilet floor, naming the filly, had fooled me. But there was no mistaking the supplication I heard now. The unseen woman recited the most universal entreaty of all—truly, I thought, from the book of common prayer. Hers was an invocation to orgasm.

In a moment a masculine voice answered her, his litany obscene. "Oh fuck. There. Mmmmm. Oh shit yes. Oh god yes."

I sat eavesdropping, mesmerized by their bodiless sounds. Didn't philosophers speculate that, at some distant locus, all polarities fused? Even parallel lines are said eventually to touch. Polarities fused, too, I thought, in love's desperate oaths: Oh god oh shit. Oh please oh don't. Oh yes oh no.

A third voice startled me. Much nearer, calmer, even wryly amused. "Well, well," it said. "Professor Theron."

I turned and saw Handsome Adam. My mouth had barely begun to fumble for words when I saw him offer his hand. I shook it. "I thought I might be seeing you here," he said.

"You did?" Adam now wore white linen slacks and shirt. The shirt opened wide at the collar, revealing a slender gold chain. His brown hair was combed now, with stylish peaks swept back from a center part. With his clothes on, he was much easier to place. California outside, hardcore East Coast inside.

Lynda stood beside him, deferentially, and behind her a large man, tight-end-sized, whom I hadn't seen before. His arms bowed slightly away from the sides of his white suit, like a weightlifter's. I caught his eyes scanning Gerald in a quick appraisal. Competitors, I concluded. Same job.

"When I saw your Mercedes earlier," Adam said, coming around the sofa, "it was obvious that you'd driven to the wrong place. It happens occasionally. I debated whether to tell you outright. But in recent weeks, you understand, it's been wisest for me to err on the side of caution." He sat down next to me, patting my knee familiarly, as though he were about to sell me an imaginary tract of land in Florida. "You gave our, eh-hem, founder a bad scare."

"Sorry," I said.

Adam fluttered his hand in a dismissive gesture. "I admire a man with a sense of humor," he said.

I shrugged modestly.

A dying moan drifted from the corner room. "Lynda," Adam called, "close that, will you? Discreetly."

Adam turned back toward me and smiled. He glanced at Gerald. "Who's your friend?" he asked.

"Gerald Valentin," I said.

Adam gave me a knowing look. "I'm impressed," he said. "I suppose your family *is* well-to-do. I wouldn't have guessed that a professor would require that kind of protection."

"He keeps people from stealing my ideas," I said.

Adam laughed. Out of habit, I thought, and for the same reason he had patted my knee. He was selling. My image of him slowly sharpened into focus. He seemed to imagine himself a young executive. Full of

ambition, full of glib talk, full of himself. He was the second underworld figure I'd met in a week, and both of them had evolved far beyond Edward G. Robinson. Adam's speech seemed vaguely modeled on
something he'd heard on the BBC. "Masterpiece Theatre," maybe.

Adam was nodding behind us, toward the tight end in the white
suit. "Phil's nice to have around, too."

Phil looked younger, taller, more athletic, and better proportioned
than Gerald. But Gerald had him beat on intangibles, on sheer presence. Gerald looked competent. Phil looked, well, athletic and well-
proportioned. A barely perceptible bulge rose at the armpit of Phil's
jacket, the kind of detail I'd never noticed before this week.

"I'm wondering," I said to Adam, "about earlier today. Why do you
seem so certain that I wasn't simply interested in the Adamite sect?"

"If experience has taught me anything," he replied, "it's that people
who own fifty-five-thousand-dollar cars are interested in only one religion."

For ten minutes we sat thus, exchanging pleasantries. A happy gathering, I thought. A brothel master, a hooker, two hired guns, and
me—a john. Finally Adam stood up. "I hope we can continue this talk
later," he said. "In fact, if you have money you really want to put to
work, I have a few exciting ideas that you might consider. But no business now. Welcome. Enjoy yourself. The real festivities, I'm sure Lynda
told you, won't be getting under way for a couple of hours. A few
members and day hostesses are out by the pool. Why don't you have a
drink out there? Lynda will show you to the changing rooms."

"I don't have anything to change into," I said.

"A swimsuit's not necessary," Adam smiled. "In fact, the house rules
forbid it. It's our way of getting everyone in the spirit. The air is very
warm for this time of year. If it cools, Lynda will provide you with a
robe." Adam shook my hand again, his left arm resting proprietarily on
my shoulders. "By the way," he said, "how is Professor Kenan?"

"Professor Kenan?" I said. "Stephen Kenan? As far as I know, he's
fine—if you don't count senility."

Lynda leaned toward Adam, interrupting. "Excuse me," she said.
"Mr. Theron is here as a guest of Mr. Reardon's."

"I had assumed—" Adam began, studying me. The puzzlement in his eyes quickly cleared. "Forgive me. I shouldn't be jumping to conclusions."

I couldn't help but smile. "Stephen Kenan is a member here?"

"Our membership is confidential," Adam said. "I hope you'll disregard—"

"Of course," I said, barely suppressing my shock. "Hell, I'm impressed." Men of Kenan's age, if they thought about their penises at all, longed only for a perfunctory, painless piss. Or so I had believed.

Adam gave me to the care of Lynda, advising me with an urbane wink, "Save some energy for this evening. We don't practice *coitus reservatus* on this side of the mountain." I followed her, watching her legs revealed dimly through the diaphanous pants, contemplating where the week had taken me: from the strip clubs of the Combat Zone, to a religio-nudist resort, to here. There's a trend, I thought, a common thread running through it all. I had the growing conviction that the entire population of New England, swept along by a hormonal tide, looked for nothing more than an excuse to disrobe.

═══*NINE*═══

IS IT ABSOLUTELY NECESSARY," I asked Lynda, "that I undress?"

She had brought us to a wing of the lodge that held the apparatus of a health spa; a Jacuzzi, two hot tubs, a sunken whirlpool, an unused-looking Nautilus, and a door that led to a sauna. The air smelled of cedar and steam.

"Don't be modest," Lynda soothed. "You look in good shape. I promise, you'll be very popular with the girls."

"I haven't seen any girls."

"Patience," she said, smiling. "You're in for a pleasant surprise later. For now, our day hostesses are out by the pool." She opened the door of a private dressing room. "Your friend," she said, nodding toward Gerald, "is welcome to wait for you in the lobby or—"

"Mr. Valentin will require a dressing room," I said. "He'll be joining me poolside."

"Whatever you say." She led Gerald to a door at a far corner of the room—affording me executive privacy? I wondered. Gerald hesitated, then followed her. For the first time I saw on his face an expression that inspired pity rather than fear.

Lynda returned to me. "Now don't worry about a thing. A lot of first-timers are a little nervous. I'll be waiting for you at the deck bar with a drink," she assured me. "Do you have any special requirements that you want to tell me about?"

"I like Old Forester, if you have it."

"I mean girls," she smiled. "Fantasies."

"Oh."

"What makes you happiest?"

"I'm a little old-fashioned," I said, "so I prefer an old-fashioned girl." I paused. "Just so long as she's a few months shy of her thirteenth birthday."

Lynda regarded me neutrally. In her business, she couldn't afford to laugh at the wrong places.

"Just teasing," I said. "Sort of."

Lynda winked and left. Inside my dressing room I lit a cigarette and took a couple of deep drags, like a man about to be executed. I undressed slowly, hoping some escape might present itself. None did. Eventually a very pale, vulnerable-looking body confronted me in the full-length mirror. Why didn't I ever go to the beach? I asked myself. Get a tan? Lift weights? I turned slightly and looked over my shoulder. "Damn," I hissed. A tiny pimple rose near the center of my left buttock. I annoyed it briefly and succeeded only in making it redder. A small towel hung on the back of the door. I clutched it like a lifebuoy.

Clasping a towel to me, I crossed to Gerald's door.

I knocked. No answer.

"Gerald," I whispered. "Let's go."

Something rustled on the other side. Finally the door opened and Gerald appeared, haltingly, looking miserable.

"Christ," I said.

Gerald wore billowing boxer shorts with tiny images of frogs embossed on the fabric. He hadn't removed his black shoes and mid-calf socks. Worst of all, harnessed about his shoulder, down among the thick patches of body hair, he wore the holster.

"You forgot your hat," I said, turning him back toward the dressing room and stepping in with him.

"What?"

"Goddammit," I whispered, "don't go outside with that gun. This is no goddam fun for me either. Need I remind you who insisted we come here in the first place?" I glared at him. "Strip down."

"Please . . . I . . .," he stammered. He didn't look nearly so competent now.

"I gather you don't want to frolic by the pool?"

He shook his head pathetically.

"Tell you what," I said, pressing him for concessions. "You stay here, get dressed, keep out of sight. I'll go out by the pool and have one drink for appearance' sake. Then," I said, "we make our apologies and leave. Okay?"

He nodded.

I left him there and turned toward the pool door Lynda had shown me. Taking a deep breath, towel positioned for maximum coverage, I stepped outside and found myself on a large redwood deck. Lynda waved at me from a bar that sat beneath a blue canvas awning. I headed for her self-consciously, as though I were learning to walk anew. A breeze engulfed my body, insinuating itself into crevices usually private, exaggerating my feeling of nakedness.

"That wasn't so bad," she said, handing me a drink and patting the barstool next to her. I spread the towel in my lap. "Is Wild Turkey okay?" she asked.

"Fine. Thanks."

Lynda, similarly nude, rested her hand on my knee. "Relax," she soothed.

I absorbed the scene before me as quickly as possible. Under other circumstances the grandeur of a mountain notch might have punctured my cynicism. The bar and deck overlooked the pool, which, by means unfathomable to me, had been sunk into an enormous rock ledge. A thin gauze of fog clung to the surface of the heated water, broken only by the lithe forms of three women who swam and dived. Out from the precipice, through a dozen wisps of cloud that floated eye-level, another mountain peaked in the distance. The afternoon light, slowly fading, turned pinkish near the horizon.

Maybe a dozen people sat by the pool, separated into small groups. Nearest me, two men who could have passed for twins of Beardsley—or some miniature species of walrus—lay on recliners, angled toward the dying light. Naked, sprawled grotesquely, belly-up, motionless. Their positions vaguely resembled morgue photos of assassinated gangsters.

A peroxide blond knelt between the two men. She was offering herself to them, touching them intimately, whispering suggestions that I couldn't quite make out. She was not young, and her nakedness prevented her from hiding the imprint of the years. She compensated for her fading beauty, I saw, with aggressive salesmanship.

One of the men finally moved. Lethargically he reached down to free a hairy testicle that had wedged between his heavy thighs. He rolled his head toward the peroxide blond who ministered to him. "Get the fuck lost," he said, emphasizing the boredom in his voice.

With indifference born of experience, the woman rose and crossed the deck to the bar, passing me on the way. For a moment I caught her eyes, and what I saw in them belied her indifference. Her eyes glowed with hate and embarrassment. Part of the hate was for me, I knew, because I'd watched her.

"What's the matter, darling?" Lynda asked, her hand creeping up my leg.

"Nothing really," I said, morosely sipping the bourbon. "Nice view."

At one corner of the pool a group of five men—late forties to early sixties, I judged—sat around a glass table. Each, in turn, groped the woman who served them drinks.

Only one man remained. He sat at the opposite end of the pool, smoking a cigar, holding a tall glass with a piece of fruit in it, looking about casually. I knew immediately what had distracted Beardsley. A woman knelt between the man's spread knees. Her head, silhouetted against the softening pink sky, bobbed in a slow rhythm, sensual and efficient. So positioned, I concluded, Beardsley had scribbled his name on a contract.

I finished the bourbon. There was nothing left to see. I removed Lynda's hand from my leg.

"Relax, darling," she murmured. Her hand massaged the back of my neck. "Oh, that's tight," she said, "that's tight."

"Sorry, Lynda," I began. "I guess this just isn't what I had in mind. The lodge is beautiful, you're very beautiful, but I'm just not getting in the mood. I'm afraid I'd better leave."

"If you'll let me—" she started. Then she saw that I was serious. "I could have guessed," she said.

"You could?"

"From the moment you got here. You're not like our other clients."

Here it comes, I thought. The ageless flattery of an ageless profession. You're different. You're special. You're not at all like the dozen men who had me yesterday. "I'm not?" I said.

"You're spoiled."

"What?"

"I mean you don't like the idea of paying for it. A point of honor."

A point of economics, I corrected her mentally. Usually I couldn't afford it. But I said, "You're right. Inflated ego. Romantic self-image."

I half rose, then sat back down. I saw something that weakened my knees. My heart gave a thump. A young woman appeared suddenly by the pool. Long of leg, deep of thigh, she met and surpassed my image of Eve.

"Who's that?" I asked.

"Who? Oh, that's Rikki."

With a kay-kay-eye, I supposed.

"Lovely, isn't she?" Lynda said.

Lovely enough that, against my better judgment, I asked for another bourbon.

Lynda smiled. "You're in good company. Everybody falls in love with her. Men *and* women."

"I had something a tad less spiritual in mind."

With a graceful, self-possessed stride, Rikki walked the length of the pool—rousing the walrus-men to upright positions—then turned and mounted the steps to the deck. No longer Eve, I mused, but Venus Rising. Her appeal was not altogether one of innocence. Haloed by a mass of black curls, her green eyes, theatrically frank, seemed practiced in the art of temptation. She didn't need to resort to salesmanship, aggressive or otherwise. Hairs rose on the back of my neck. I, too, succumbed to the hormonal tide that swept about me.

"Feel like staying?" Lynda asked.

My eyes must have asked an obvious question.

"Sorry, Rikki's reserved. But we have other girls coming—"

"Reserved?"

"It's a special privilege we offer to some of our members. They call ahead and ask for a certain girl."

Rikki neared, and my eyes wandered lower. I cleared my throat. The black, tight ringlets of her pubic hair had been trimmed and shaved in an angular design. My eyes must have held a peculiar squinting expression, as though I were trying simultaneously to stare and not to stare. A lightning bolt, I finally realized. Why be coy? The design was there to be admired. She came closer. The lightning bolt seemed to strike the naked little man in her naked little boat. What would Freud have made of it? Eros and Thanatos?

"Nice effect," I whispered to Lynda. "I've seen hearts, but never lightning bolts. Require much maintenance?"

"I'm sure," Lynda replied, "that any number of gentlemen are willing to trim it for free."

"Can I get on a waiting list?" I asked.

Rikki approached the bar. When she was five yards away, I caught her eye and gave her my most engaging smile.

"Hello," I said.

She paused, green eyes briefly flaring. "Eat shit," she said. She kept walking and sat at the far end of the bar, but not before I enjoyed a view of the perfectly sculpted swells of her behind. She sat on the stool next to the woman who'd been rebuffed by the walrus-men.

Nice going, Thomas, I thought. You pay four hundred dollars to get into a bordello, and you can't strike up a conversation.

Lynda bristled. "I'll speak to her," she said, getting off the barstool. I pulled her back. "Don't. It's okay."

"Well, ignore her," she said, adding under her breath, "the little cunt." Lynda lowered her voice confidentially, intending to appease me. "It's no excuse, but Rikki's upset. She's not very happy about the gentleman she's entertaining tonight." Lynda paused, eyeing me, debating whether to go on. "I shouldn't tell you, but—" she stopped.

"Tell me what?"

"Well, that you know him."

"Know who?"

"Our member. Rikki's . . . patron."

"I don't know anyone h—" I caught myself before it slipped. "You don't mean Sam Reardon?"

She shook her head.

I thought for a moment. No, I thought. Too farfetched. But I said the name anyway. "Stephen Kenan?"

Lynda didn't move, but her eyes said yes.

"No wonder she's upset," I said, suddenly indignant. "What's he going to do, slobber on her?"

"Be nice," Lynda said.

She looked as though she regretted having told me. I regretted it too. The hormonal tide receded, leaving in its place the grim knowledge of what I was there for. I offered Lynda a not-too-graceful apology and left the bar. She seemed sorry to see me go, though not sorry enough to suggest a refund. When I passed Rikki at the bar, I shifted the towel from front to rear. For no reason. She didn't look up. She remained deep in conversation with the peroxide blond. If they were plotting elaborate schemes of mass castration, I didn't really blame them.

Kenan, I thought. It shouldn't have bothered me. If he were leading a secret life—hell, if he were able to lead a secret life—he deserved my respect. For twenty years Kenan had been the undisputed heavyweight of literary critics at Wesley, having single-handedly defined and established the field of Puritan studies. He had won virtually every literary prize known to man—two National Book awards, a Pulitzer, a host of lesser honors—but if you said hello to him, the best he could manage was a blank look of incomprehension. For most of his life he had been put out of touch with the world by genius, and now, I had supposed, by encroaching senility. I liked to think of him as the academic version of the Mystics at the track; certainly in recent years he had been no less pee- and saliva-stained than they. Now a professor emeritus, humored and pampered by his underlings in the department, his confused maunderings were received and explicated as if they were the utterances of an oracle.

I paused at Gerald's dressing room and started to knock. I heard a woman's voice on the other side of the door. "Fuzzy Wuzzy was a bear," she singsonged.

Opening the door, I found a petite young brunette, naked, curled like a snake on Gerald's trouser leg. He suffered her attentions silently. One of her hands had crept inside his open collar, and the other probed somewhere beneath his stomach. "Ooo!" she cried when she saw me. "Are we going to have a party?"

I said no. "I have to speak with Fuzzy Wuzzy here. Will you excuse us?"

She nibbled Gerald's reddening earlobe. "Is that okay with you, daddy?"

Gerald nodded stiffly. Uncurling herself, the girl squeezed past me. Her breasts, large for her small frame, buffeted against my stomach. "Mmmm," she murmured. "You're cute." She headed toward the pool exit, exaggerating the motion of her small butt with a hard heel-toe stride.

"How'd she get in here?" I asked.

"I left the door . . ." he faltered.

"Forget it," I said. "Ready to go?"

Gerald didn't speak. He just sat there, shifting uncomfortably.

"What's the matter?" I asked.

"Just give me a minute," he said, his voice oddly tremulous.

"What's the—" I started again. Then I knew. His hands rested awkwardly in his lap. The girl had aroused him. Gerald was concealing an erection.

I fought off an impulse to lean toward him and shout suddenly into his ear. Startle him. Wouldn't surprise cure an erection more or less the way it cured hiccups?

"Happens to the best of us," I observed benignly. "Just sit there a minute. I've got to get dressed anyway." I turned back. "Try thinking about the time you broke Billy Baker's face."

Kenan, I thought again. I knew what was bothering me. A repulsive image kept reappearing in my brain. The crabbed, grizzled organ of Age, pressed against the soft lips of Youth. Slowly the white teeth part to receive him.

My clothes weren't in the dressing room. Calm, I thought. Be calm. I checked the rooms on either side. One was empty, the other locked.

In a moment the lobby door opened and Adam came toward me. "There you are, Professor Theron," he said. "I'm afraid something's come up." Phil walked behind him, my clothes slung over his left arm. He carried a gun in his right hand.

"I called Sam Reardon. As a precaution," Adam was saying. "Asked him a few questions. He seemed unaware of some rather basic details about you. For example, what you look like."

"Goddam old Sam," I said.

Phil had pointed his gun casually in my direction. To be held at gunpoint is, of itself, emasculating. If one is also naked, the effect is much closer to castration. My scrotum shriveled, drawing my testicles up close to my abdomen; if my gonads were trying to hide, I didn't blame them.

"Could I have my clothes?" I asked.

"Where's your ugly friend?" Adam asked, ignoring me.

"He couldn't drag himself away from the pool," I said.

"We'll see about that in a moment. I'm going to ask you a couple of blunt questions, and I suggest that you don't bullshit me. It's hard to figure you as anything but a lousy schoolteacher, but I can't be too careful. These are perilous times."

"How perilous?"

"Nothing I can't handle."

He would have a chance to prove it. Behind the two of them, Gerald appeared from the dressing room, his approach matter-of-fact, all business, all speed without waste. He held his revolver in front of him. He looked competent again.

The prospect of violence induced in me a dream state. I felt the classic symptoms of shock: calm mind, shaking hands, dissociation from the event. The pageant played out before me in slow motion.

Phil sensed Gerald behind him an instant too late. Gerald reached up with his left hand, grabbed a handful of Phil's hair, and jerked his head savagely back onto the gun barrel. An excessive gesture, even theatrical, I thought calmly. The intimidating effect wasn't lost on Phil. He had collapsed to his knees, eyes wide, arms flung out submissively, dropping both my clothes and his gun to the floor. His head was bent backward at a painful angle across the barrel Gerald had thrust into his neck. Phil's trachea protruded against the muscled slab of his neck like a tiny forearm.

It had happened without a word. Without a sound, really.

For a moment Adam studied Phil's revolver where it lay on the floor, judging his chances to reach it. He reconsidered. Gerald didn't speak. Phil couldn't. They all deferred to me, the naked man.

My voice surprised me: a delivery clear, precise, and slow. The content wasn't much. "What we have here," I said to Adam, "is a simple, though apparently basic, misunderstanding." Appease him, I thought. Don't rub his nose in it. "I'm sorry it had to come to this. But, as you say, these are perilous times. I think we should be going."

"I hope you know what the fuck you're doing," Adam snarled, suddenly losing his BBC affect.

"I haven't the faintest idea," I said. "I'll just have to trust my baser instincts." I picked up my clothes and Phil's gun. As I bent over I thought, curiously, about the pimple on my ass.

Phil tried to adjust his position for relief. Gerald improved his grip. I heard a faint sound like popping knuckles.

I found a small storage room with an outside bolt. While Gerald ushered Phil and Adam into it, I dressed. My hands, still shaking, fas-

tened most of the buttons on my shirt; after a couple of tries, I gave up
on the shoelaces.

"You're gonna fucking regret this," Adam hissed when Gerald
bolted the door. "Count on it."

"I regret it already," I replied mildly. Appease him, I kept thinking.
"No harm done. Apologies to all."

Gerald sped down White Birch Mountain, using both lanes, taking
as much curve out of the road as he dared. Not until we left the Kancamagus for the security of the traffic on Route 93 did he ease his pace.

"Thanks," I said after a time.

He nodded silently. Then he glanced at me and said, "Apologies to
all?"

Above us, a black sky dissolved into a band of purple; lower, a thread
of whitish blue lined the horizon. Just before we reached the Massachusetts state line I asked Gerald to stop at the Country Barn liquor store.
I saved three dollars on a 1.75-liter bottle of Old Forester. It had been
an expensive day. My wallet held a ten and two ones.

We drove on. I nursed the bottle, cradling it in my right arm as I
slumped against the passenger door. Jesus Saves, I thought. Less than a
week had passed since I'd bet the filly, and already I had trouble remembering my life before that day at Suffolk. All I could see was an image
of myself now, caught in a rapid current that propelled me ever closer
to the swirling mouth of an enormous drain.

The more bourbon I drank, the more things seemed to clarify in my
mind. My time at Suffolk Downs had taught me that race-fixing was a
primitive, unpredictable method to make money. I couldn't imagine a
man like Vincent Ciullo resorting to it. But if Ciullo were setting up a
competitor, the fix made more sense. Ciullo and Adam Feld, as far as I
could tell, sold roughly the same merchandise to roughly the same customers.

What would I tell Ciullo? Whatever I'd learned in New Hampshire,
it wasn't anything, I'd bet, he didn't know already. And whatever I'd
done, it clearly wasn't anything he'd asked me to do. What bothered
me most was that I'd left the sidelines and entered the field of play. I

could blame it on Gerald, of course. I could blame it on Cleve. But what if Ciullo weren't satisfied with that?

By the time we passed through Concord and got on Route 2, the bourbon had deepened its grip on me. The phase—illusion?—of heightened clarity passed, leaving me confused, but oddly buffered from my predicament. I had a plan.

We reached the crest of a hill on Route 2, and the skyline of Boston lit the black sky like a beacon.

"What time does Ciullo want to see me on Monday?" I asked Gerald.

"Seven o'clock."

I gave him Beth's address and said, "I have to run an errand." If Ciullo considered the $31,000 a retainer, then I would be prepared to give him the money when I saw him. Simplicity itself. Buy my way out. I could then resume my life of genteel professorial poverty and quiet self-destruction. No more aging mafiosi, no more rising vice kings, no more large men bearing arms. After all, I told myself, the point of self-destructiveness is to inflict one's own wounds at one's own pace.

The bourbon succeeded in removing every logical obstacle to this strategy. The plan seemed increasingly foolproof. I drifted toward gentle acceptance.

After four months of silence and separation, I found myself knocking on Beth's door for the second time in a week.

The door opened about a minute after I stopped ringing the bell. Beth appeared, the second remarkably beautiful woman I'd seen that day. Both too young for me; neither friendly.

"Do you know what time it is?"

"Within an hour or two." I started to tell her that I missed her, but her frown stopped me.

"You're drunk," she said.

"You might say that."

She looked past me to the street, where the Mercedes was double-parked. "Did you drive here in that?"

"No. Gerald drove me."

"Who is Gerald?"

"He's a little hard to describe. He's kind of a chauffeur."

Her head shook in exasperation. "My God," she said. "Listen, Thomas. I hope you don't want to sleep on the couch again, because Breck and I have—"

"Is he here?"

"Yes, he's here. Why shouldn't he be here?"

"I don't need the goddam couch," I said. "I'm going to sleep in my office tonight."

"I'm almost afraid to ask," Beth said, "but why?"

"Well, there's a fellow who runs a very expensive whorehouse in New Hampshire who probably would like to have me shot."

"Thomas," she sighed.

"Did you get that check I sent?"

"I got it."

"Beth, I hate to ask this, but could you not cash it?"

Her eyes shone with hostility. "I didn't ask you to send the damn check in the first place."

"I know, I know. So you tore it up?" I asked hopefully.

"No. Breck convinced me that the money was mine, so I should keep it."

I debated momentarily whether to summon Gerald to drag Breck into the street and beat hell out of him.

Silence. Finally she said, "Thomas, you're unbelievable. You know that? I'd really forgotten—" She stopped. "You get driven here in a goddam Mercedes Benz and—" She stopped again. "Listen, anything so I don't have to put up with this shit. I don't think Breck has deposited the check yet. I'll have him tear it up."

"Thanks, Beth."

More silence.

"Is that all, Thomas?"

I heard myself mumble something about the IRS taking ten percent. I belched. Then I heard myself, slurring against my will, ask Beth for a three-thousand-dollar loan.

Without a word, she took a step back. Very slowly, not slamming, the door closed.

PART II
SHE

═══ *TEN* ═══

FOR MOST OF SUNDAY I hid in my office, possessed of an armadillo-urge to curl up inside myself, withdraw from the world. The American Civilization Department occupies Talbot House, a refurbished Cape Cod on the outskirts of the Wesley campus—on weekends a peaceful refuge. My office, formerly an attic room, took up a quarter of the top floor, affording lots of floorspace without a corresponding amount of headspace. Two dormer windows offered a good view of the entrance and the street, just in case an automobile priced out of the academic range should park there.

Long after my hangover had stabilized, my neck still ached from sleeping in the desk chair. The phone rang several times in the morning; I didn't answer it. At noon I slipped out for Chinese food at the Ta Chien. On the way back, I detoured a half-mile to Everett Street and cautiously entered my apartment—to collect a change of clothes, some aspirin, a toothbrush, a pillow, and the Philco, if I could manage it. I didn't seriously expect Adam Feld to be waiting there for me. The apartment would have been hard for him to find. I'd lived there four months without bothering to notify anyone officially of a change of address. I hadn't even unpacked.

I was wrong, partly. Adam wasn't there, but someone had been, someone who wanted me to know about it. A dozen cartons of books had been overturned and strewn about the floor. The Three Boxes were similarly scrambled. I quickly stuffed a few things into an empty box, glanced back into the room, and left.

The past week had almost inured my mind to panic. Wildly inappropriate thoughts popped into my head. One good thing, I thought, starting the Volkswagen. About forty yellow-and-black pamphlets comprised part of the clutter on my apartment floor. For weeks I'd been wondering in which box I had stored my Cliff's Notes.

Awake early the next morning in my office, my body suffering more than ever the effects of sleeping upright, I went for a breakfast of eggs and fried salami. When I returned, I found Talbot House rousing itself for the coming week of pedagogy. I tried to slip up the stairs unnoticed.

"Hiding from your students again?" Jeanne, the department secretary, had spied me. "What kind of getup is that?"

I was wearing a raincoat, a Kangol cap, and sunglasses. "You don't like it?" I said, going to her desk.

"You look like a pervert. Why are you holding your neck like that?"

"Got a crick in it," I said. "Haven't been sleeping well."

"Poor baby." Jeanne was in her mid-thirties, recently divorced. Her eyes, far livelier than those of the academics she worked for, gave energy to her plain features. She had taken a fancy to me, mostly because she liked to talk dirty, and I was the only member of the department willing or able to oblige her. Last week she had posted the sign on my classroom door, informing my students that I was sick.

"Feeling better?" she asked.

"Not much," I said, taking off my sunglasses.

"God, you look like shit," she said.

"Thanks."

"Want some coffee?"

"Sure, thanks."

"I've been trying to reach you," she said. "Braithewaite wants to see you." Gayle Braithewaite was the department chairman.

"About what?"

"Who knows? It'll be interesting to see if he remembers. He's in there now. I'll have the coffee for you when you get out."

I liked Braithewaite. If Stephen Kenan were comparable to the Mystics at Suffolk Downs, Braithewaite, a medievalist, was more like the Stoopers, the old men who searched among the trash for discarded tickets. With myopic, nearly insane deliberation, Braithewaite poked about in the arcane texts of Old English, Old Norse, Old Germanic, hoping to find . . . well, it wasn't clear to me precisely what he hoped to find. An hitherto unnoticed word variant? A translator's error? A discarded bookmark? But when he found it, whatever it was, he was no less ecstatic than the Stoopers, jubilantly sending the discovery off for publication in some unread newsletter. I liked, too, that Braithewaite never talked shop; he held in his heart the ludicrous suspicion that scholars were lurking everywhere, waiting to jump his claim.

I knocked on his office door and stepped in.

He looked up at me quizzically. "Oh, hello Thomas," he said.

"You wanted to see me?" I watched his mind struggle to surface from some unfathomable depth of thought.

"You're not looking too well, Thomas," he said presently. The reason for my visit had obviously slipped his mind.

"I've been a little under the weather," I said.

"Well," he said, delaying, "how's the biography of Lowell coming along? You don't want that fellow from Yale to scoop you."

"No complaints," I said. "A little slow." More than a little. I'd been knocking off a good two pages a month.

His eyes finally cleared. "Oh yes, yes," he said. "I've been getting these phone calls."

From Adam Feld? I thought nervously. Ciullo checking up on me?

"The parents of that young man called again," Braithewaite said. "Potter? Roger Potter?"

"Yes," I replied with relief, "he's a student of mine."

"Well, his parents are of the mind that young Roger is not getting the kind of education to which twelve thousand dollars a year in tuition entitles him. Any problem?"

There was no need to squirm; not the slightest hint of censure entered his voice. "The problem, Gayle, is that Potter is not getting the 'A' to which he thinks he's entitled. He could give a damn about anything else. You know the type."

"Yes I do, Thomas. I certainly do. His parents said something about you missing lectures, or delivering the wrong lectures, or giving quizzes instead of lectures. Anything to that?"

"The quizzes motivate them to do the reading," I said.

"I see. His parents mentioned that while these tests are in progress, it's your habit to read . . . I think they called it a *Racing Form.*"

"That's possible. I don't see that it matters."

"What's a *Racing Form,* Thomas? Anything I should look into?"

"Nothing that would interest you. It's kind of a research tool. For my hobby."

"I see, I see. Fine, Thomas, fine." Braithewaite was perfectly satisfied. The only thing he really objected to was fielding calls from irate parents. "Tell you what," he continued. "Why not cut back a bit on these quizzes and give the students the benefit of your hard-earned wisdom a little more often. I've heard you lecture a few times. Wish I had your aptitude for oral delivery. Very witty indeed. I think your students would enjoy that. Anyway, I think it's best to keep everyone happy just now. The tenure committee meets in less than a month, and though I don't foresee any difficulty, we shouldn't roil the waters just now." He regarded me benignly. "But I do understand. It's hard getting students these days to work to the best of their abilities."

"No problem, Gayle," I said. "More lectures it is."

He looked at me vaguely, his eyes already drifting, his mind sinking back to whatever obscure depth it usually occupied. "By the way," he said dreamily, "how's the biography of Lowell coming along?"

"No complaints," I said. "A little slow."

Outside, Jeanne handed me a cup of coffee. "Everything go okay?"

"Without a hitch," I said. "He's the perfect administrator."

"From your point of view," she said. "More work for me."

"Jeanne, there's something I'd like to ask you. Confidentially."

She raised her eyebrows comically. "Anything."

"Didn't you work for Stephen Kenan before he retired?"

"Absolutely," she said. "I was in the major leagues."

"Anything, well, unsavory about him? Anything that goes beyond the ordinary gossip?"

Jeanne smiled. "Are you looking to blackmail him?"

"Why would I want to do that?"

"Even in his dotage, our beloved Professor Stevie still sits on the tenure committee. It wouldn't hurt your chances if you could yank his cord."

"Come on, I'm serious. What do you know?"

"Well, whenever he got preoccupied with his latest opus, Kenan never took the time to go upstairs to the bathroom. He peed in his wastebasket."

"That's old news," I smiled, "though it continues to amuse."

"I never thought it was so funny," she said. "Guess who had to clean it up?"

"I guess there's no point in beating around the bush," I said. "What I really want to know is whether he led some sort of double life."

"Who doesn't?" she said, smiling provocatively. "Want to hear about mine?"

"I don't think my heart could take the shock."

Jeanne eyed me thoughtfully. "I guess I could drag up a few juicy Kenan stories. On one condition."

"What's that?"

"That I tell you over dinner tonight. I'll get a couple of steaks, a couple of bottles of wine. No telling what smut will surface."

I don't think she really expected me to accept. "You're on," I said. "I can't make it till ten-thirty."

"Yeah?"

"Yeah." Highly unethical, I thought. Would no doubt cause future headaches. But my neck couldn't take another night in the chair. "What should I bring? Another bottle of wine?"

"Since you ask, you could stop by the pharmacy."

"What for?"

Her eyes twinkled brightly. "Ortho-Gel?"

"Seriously?"

"Nothing lasts forever."

"I was thinking of bringing those little knockout pills, slipping them into your wine. You wake up, never know what happened."

"Don't you dare," she warned me laughingly. "I want to watch."

The suggestiveness of her tone eased the ache in my neck. Not eased, really. The ache merely relocated to a point on my body somewhat lower.

Off and on for most of the day, my office phone kept ringing and I kept jumping at the sound of it. Finally, in the afternoon, it got to me. On the next ring, I gingerly picked up the receiver, covered the mouthpiece with the palm of my hand, and listened silently.

"Hello? Thomas? Thomas?"

"Hi, Elizabeth," I answered.

"I've been trying to reach you. You okay?" Her voice had softened remarkably.

"So far. Sorry about the other night," I said.

"If you really need the money, I can—"

"No. It was a crazy idea."

"I don't know what kind of fix you're in, but—"

"I don't want you to know," I said.

"Things have been hard for me too," she said. "I'm sorry about this mess."

"Me too."

"I mean about us," she said.

"Me too."

We talked on quietly, almost whispering, as though we were in the sickroom of a patient whose prognosis was uncertain. When we hung up, another ache joined the others, this one in the region of the heart.

*   *   *

Without benefit of bourbon, the plan to give Ciullo money seemed more foolish than foolproof. Maybe things wouldn't come to that; if I had unwisely intruded into his affairs, he would surely understand that my intentions had been good.

Even so, I took precautions. I planned to carry a cashier's check when I arrived at the Pink Lady that night. The Wesley credit union bestowed on me an emergency loan at 15.25 percent; the payroll office extended a salary advance, minus a "processing fee." The bank charged five dollars for the cashier's check. I completed my financial errands feeling as though I'd swallowed a fishhook.

At six-thirty I took a drink to steady my nerves from a flask I kept in my office, then drove twenty minutes to the Combat Zone. I found the back alley where Gerald had led me precisely one week ago. Ciullo wasn't in his office. Alex was, wearing a black velvet sports jacket. He greeted me warmly; I could have sworn that he was genuinely happy to see me.

"So how was your trip?" he asked.

"I think I should wait and tell your uncle," I said.

My expression must have been forbidding, for Alex didn't press me. "Mr. Ciullo will be here within the hour," he said. "Would you care to wait here?"

"I think I'll have a drink out front."

"Sure. I'll send word to our manager. Drinks on the house."

"Thanks."

Wedging myself between two drunken businessmen, I sat at the bar and watched the strippers. A thin girl in her late teens was just finishing a spastic dance to a song by the Dead Kennedys. Hair spiked and gelled, movements jerky and rebelliously unsensuous, she rebelled, too, against the plush burlesque costume of the past. The red and black lace of Frederick's of Hollywood lay on the stage all round her.

After her, Saffron, a child of the sixties. Straight brown hair well down her back; tie-dyed sarong for a costume. Eyes closed, she swayed to some inner rhythm, dreamy and drugged. A self-expresser, I guessed, and a sensitivitrix. In the background, Donovan sang "I'm Just Wild About Saffron."

I sat thus for nearly a half hour, while the cultural trends of recent decades paraded before me. A bass guitar began to thump so loudly that it resonated in my stomach. An old Eddie Floyd song that I liked:

It's like THUNDER, LIGHTNING,
The way you love me is frightening . . .

The drunk next to me leaned over and confided, "Wait'll you get a load a this one. I been waiting here two hours." He squinted knowingly.

Suddenly a girl appeared between a parted red curtain. Taking quick, rhythmic steps, she sprinted the length of the stage, stopped abruptly at the edge of the bar, and tossed her black hair over her head like a stallion throwing its rider. The men at the bar erupted.

When she flung her head back, I recognized her immediately. And I knew what design lay hidden beneath the silver-lamé triangle that covered her mons veneris. A lightningbolt. And I knew her name, too. Her first name. Rikki.

Rikki, whirled, shimmied, spun, and dipped, at times holding her black curls high in a pose of sexual abandonment, at other times cupping and squeezing her breasts until a fleshy Y appeared at the open collar of her silver-lamé jacket. Her spike heels caused the muscles on her legs to clinch spectacularly. Her rhythms came from the intuition of a heartbeat or the memory of sexual union.

Someone tapped me on the shoulder. "Mr. Ciullo's just arrived," Alex said.

"Oh." I looked back toward the stage. "Just let me finish this drink."

"I see you've found her," Alex said.

"Found who?"

"Rikki Storm."

"And so has everybody else," I started. I turned and looked at him. I felt it coming. I somehow knew what he was going to say. It conformed to the dream logic that had taken over my life.

"Of course, Rikki Storm is just a stage name," Alex said. "It was a bitch finding her. She'd put Rachel Bloom on her W-2, so that gave me a hunch. The hard part was getting access to the name that matched her social security number. But there it was. Rachel Bloomberg. Apparently," he added, "she's coping rather well with her father's death."

"Apparently," I said.

I lingered over my drink while my brain struggled to assess the significance of her identity. Ciullo would surely want to know, I thought, that she'd been moonlighting in Waterville; I just as surely didn't want to tell him. The jukebox now played a slow Boz Skaggs tune, and Rikki's movements became slithering and full of sexual promise. A brief but intense melodrama played in my mind. I imagined myself with Rikki, talking intimately in a dark bar, until finally I let her know the secret that I possess. Did you tell anyone, Thomas? she would ask anxiously. No, I reply gravely. I hint at what peril I have withheld the knowledge. Later, Rikki would be grateful. Precisely how grateful, and in what manner her gratitude would be expressed, comprised the climactic and most graphic act of the melodrama.

"Did you tell your uncle about her?"

"Oh sure. It's a pretty useful piece of information. Jake was pretty secretive about her. Ashamed of her, I think. Thanks for the tip."

I stalled Alex awhile longer, until Rikki shed a final triangle of silk, and I once again glimpsed the voltaic façade of her pudendum.

The absurdity of Vincent Ciullo's library-office struck me again—the only printed material within ten blocks, I supposed, without full-color photography on the covers. Alex had led me into his office, then exited without a word. Gerald, who had positioned himself with vague menace by the door, didn't return my nod of greeting. Ciullo himself looked vigorous and more professorial than ever, wearing a maroon cardigan sweater, starched white shirt, and gray silk bow tie. He rose from behind his mahogany desk and greeted me with his customary display of fastidious courtesy. "Professor Theron," he began, "I'm very pleased to see you again," inviting me to take a seat. No initial interrogation, I noticed, as though I'd achieved the status of colleague, even friend. Ciullo's eyes conveyed the complete openness that is habitual with persons secure in their authority.

Whatever humiliation I was to experience, I wanted to get it over with immediately. "I guess Gerald's already told you what happened," I said.

"No, no," he said. "Gerald is invaluable to me, but I didn't employ him for his verbal skills. That's why I employed you." Ciullo raised his hand as though I were about to interrupt him. "But let's postpone all that for a minute," he said. "I have something here I think might interest you." He opened a briefcase, removed a medium-sized volume, and pushed it toward me across his desk. Ciullo wanted to talk books. A cruel preliminary, I thought.

Not just any book. I recognized the jacket immediately.

"Captivating reading," he continued. "I spent the entire weekend with it. Very impressive."

"Fortunately," I replied equably, "the hiring committee at Wesley thought so too." Solid block letters ran the length of the binding: VOY-EURISM IN THE AMERICAN NOVEL. At the bottom, perpendicular to the title, the author's last name appeared in tiny letters: Theron. My complete works.

"Your argument fascinates me," Ciullo said, gathering himself. "Here's how I would paraphrase it"—he paused and looked up—"now correct me if I stray. The romantic vision of the American novelist originates in a limitless expansion of ego. In fact, *self* becomes identified with, even interchangeable with, the *world*. Hence, to observe the outside world becomes a technique of self-examination. Put another way, voyeurism becomes a kind of introspection. A very neat, a very pretty argument. Is that a fair summary?"

"That's about the size of it," I agreed. "I don't know how pretty it is. One critic called it a remarkable piece of sophistry. No substance, all sleight of hand." I shifted uncomfortably in my chair. Ciullo's digression was fraying my nerves. I politely requested a drink. "A bourbon?" I said. "A double?"

Ciullo sent Gerald for the drink. "But wouldn't you agree," he persisted, still hoping to provoke a lively exchange of ideas, "that an unfortunate side effect of this habit of voyeurism—a danger implicit in your book—is that the observer is reduced perpetually to a state of pas-

sivity? An enormous amount of mental activity without corresponding
action in the world. A harmful way to lead one's life, I think."

I shrugged. "But safe."

"Yes," Ciullo murmured. "Safe." He uttered the word as though it
filled his mouth with an unpleasant taste. Ciullo sat quietly for a moment, regarding me with a kind, pitying expression, as if I were a small
child with polio. And somewhere in the recesses of his gaze, I watched
his hope fade that he might cure me. He returned my book to his
briefcase with obvious remorse. "You disappoint me, Professor
Theron."

"Listen," I appeased him, "I appreciate your enthusiasm for literature. But for myself, I think it's a serious mistake to confuse books
with life. Frankly, it's an old-fashioned mistake."

"Then I choose to remain old-fashioned," he replied, shaking his
head with a queer sadness. "If literature has no meaning for our lives,
why should we bother with it?"

Who's bothering? I thought, but kept the opinion to myself.

"Very well," Ciullo said. "We have other business to conduct." His
eyes demonstrated again their unsettling capacity to turn hard and
opaque, devoid of any discernibly human quality. His stare made me
wish that I hadn't been so eager to change the subject. "So tell me," he
said, "of your trip to New Hampshire."

I'd rehearsed carefully, coaching myself to keep a reasonable tone, an
assured manner. "Mr. Ciullo," I began formally, "the request you made
last week was simple enough. The execution of it, as things turned out,
was rather complicated." I explained that the stewards hadn't asked
Cleve, after all, to interview the filly's owners. After Bloomberg's death,
I told him, the investigation had been turned over entirely to the police.

"I see," he observed neutrally.

I searched his eyes for a clue to his thoughts. There wasn't pleasure
there, but there wasn't anger either. There wasn't much of anything. I
plunged ahead. "Of course, I've heard a lot of rumors about the investigation. Some people have guessed, or think they have guessed, how
Jesus Saves was held back in all those races. They believe the filly was

trained to stop whenever a jockey used the whip. As for the case against
the Adamites, the police have little more than circumstantial evidence,
really nothing more than what's been aired in the news reports. But
they remain confident of an indictment. I gather that they're hoping
for a conviction for the sake of political expediency as much as from
hard facts. Some prosecutor is trying to make a reputation for himself.
Cults don't play well in New Hampshire."

A prolonged silence followed, during which Ciullo gazed vaguely in
my direction through a cloud of pipe smoke. I'd prepared for every
conceivable question, for every conceivable accusation, for every conceivable suggestion that I'd failed in the task he had assigned me. The
problem was, Ciullo didn't ask any questions, didn't accuse, didn't suggest. I recognized this technique; it was one I'd often used myself in
the classroom. Uncomfortable Silence. If I were willing to sit in front
of a class long enough without speaking, the silence would eventually
drive the students to the edge of panic; finally, in their distress they
would babble forth whatever minuscule knowledge and whatever wild
opinions they possessed about a subject.

Ciullo manipulated the silence expertly. I babbled forth.

"So when Gerald showed up," I started in, feeling foolish and too
eager, "I guess I didn't explain the situation properly. We went to
New Hampshire anyway. We probably shouldn't have. To put it
mildly, we ruffled some feathers there."

No response, but I thought I detected a glimmer of interest in his
eyes. He finally said, "Tell me about it."

I did not embellish or delete. First I recounted the session with Old
Adam and Handsome Adam, then the confrontation with Beardsley,
then the visit to the brothel, and then, well, our escape. To edit the
story would have been dangerous, I decided; I felt certain that Ciullo
knew everything I knew about Adam Feld and a good deal more. I
didn't mention Stephen Kenan—what was the point? But I told him
about Rikki/Rachel's part-time employment. So much for my melodrama of gratitude. "The Adamites," I heard myself saying, "are an elaborate—too elaborate, it seemed to me—front for prostitution. Adam is
clever enough, but he's also something of an egomaniac. I think he

gets a thrill from playing everyone for a sucker. I can't imagine why he bothers with the biblical ruse or the tax-exempt business—except for the sheer risk of it. My guess is that Adam Feld enjoys playing a joke on the entire state. Thumbing his nose at the locals, swindling his own customers. The whole operation seems foolhardy, but it's worked. Up to now, at least."

Ciullo emptied, then reloaded his pipe, an activity that engaged his full attention. I sat there, leaning toward him, at a complete loss for something to say. Ciullo finally rested back in his chair and surprised me by saying, "I find all of that very interesting, Professor Theron. Truly." His eyes softened and he smiled—not one of his courteous smiles, but one that appeared genuinely affable.

"You do?" I emitted a nervous laugh that sounded in my own ears uncomfortably close to a giggle. "To tell you the truth," I managed, "I had the impression that you knew all of this already."

"Oh that. Oh I do. Of course I do. I wouldn't be much of a business man if I didn't. Actually, the news about Mr. Bloomberg's daughter has come to me only recently. The poor man went to great lengths to keep his family affairs private. It must have been stressful for him." Ciullo drifted into some silent reminiscence, then fluttered his hand. "But that's not what I find extraordinary," he said, looking straight at me. "You've been misrepresenting yourself, Professor Theron."

"I swear. Everything I've told you—"

"I think I've misjudged you, Thomas," he interrupted. "You surprise me. This unlikely adventure in New Hampshire shows initiative. It impresses me. I think you relished the opportunity to test yourself." Ciullo was again looking at me as if I were a crippled child, yet this time his gaze was full of hope. He apparently believed that I'd taken my first halting, brave step, bespeaking adolescent courage. "I doubt that you would ever admit it, but I suspect that you're not so satisfied with your life of passivity as you imagine. What was it Conrad recommended in *Lord Jim?* 'In the destructive element immerse.' "

"*Lord Jim,*" I observed with rare insight, "is a novel." The real meaning of our dialogue was beginning to dawn on me. Ciullo hadn't the slightest interest in the facts of the story I'd just told him; he sought only the chance to play amateur analyst. My role, it seemed, was captive, unwitting analysand. "Mr. Ciullo," I protested, "I don't want to test myself. I don't want to prove myself. I went to New Hampshire only because I couldn't talk Gerald out of it. Whatever I did there was motivated by fear. Purely self-interest."

"Really?" he challenged. "I think, Thomas, that you're far easier to read than you imagine. Consider all of the days you've wasted at a third-rate track in East Boston, all of the nights you've wasted right here in the Combat Zone—yes, I've heard about that, too. What does this behavior suggest to you? Simply this: a man obsessed with cultivating desperate lives and desperate environments. And for what purpose? To what end? To correct a monotony in his own life, to fill a gaping void at his very center. Even the book that you've written," he said, nodding toward his briefcase, "as much as I admire it, suggests this. Who else but a man perplexed by his own inactivity would set out to compose a treatise on voyeurism in the American novel? No, I tell you honestly, Thomas, your deepest wish is to enter the world. To act. You are a man who whips himself not for what he has done, but for what he has not done."

I felt a sudden empathy for small laboratory animals who are the victims of esoteric research. What was worse? I wondered helplessly. The presumptuousness of Ciullo's insights, or merely my own guilty recognition that he was more or less right? I bristled anyway, just as another man might bristle upon hearing his honor impugned.

Ciullo wasn't finished. "Consider what has put you in this situation to begin with. A kind of self-destructiveness that compelled you to bet on a horse that you believed had no chance of winning. Consider—"

"Are you going to bill me for this?" I asked evenly.

"Even your sarcasm," Ciullo declared, not missing a beat. "Your ego lashes out, revenges itself on a world in which you do not participate."

Suddenly my mind clutched a thread of hope that I'd been too preoccupied to notice. "If we could put aside my psychic history for a minute," I started, "is it fair to say that you're not . . . displeased with this Waterville business? I was pretty worried that I'd messed things up."

"Thomas, I'm not sure what impression you have of me, but I'm not an unreasonable man. These things happen. Gerald was only trying to do his job. You aren't my sole avenue of information. I appreciate your efforts on my behalf."

"So that's it?" I asked hopefully.

"That's it. I would hope that we can maintain some sort of social acquaintance in the future. I've enjoyed our talks. It's not often that I have the chance."

He didn't mention the $31,000, so who was I to bring it up? Inexplicably, I found myself liking him. Well, not inexplicable. I liked him as any victim likes his oppressor: I liked him for not hurting me.

Relief, fear, and curiosity were so conflicted within me that I'd forgotten an unsettling fact. I reminded Ciullo that Feld had pulled a gun on me, and most probably had later ransacked my apartment. "Even if Feld is a lightweight," I flattered him, "I can't help but be a little concerned."

"Adam Feld," he said, "is more dangerous than you imagine. He's a lightweight, as you say, but he doesn't know it. That's a volatile combination. Your impressions of him were very much to the point. An insufferable egotist. Delusions of omnipotence. He doesn't think anyone or anything can harm him. That's why he persists in misusing his own clients and flaunting that religious charade"— Ciullo said "sha-ROD"—"I'll give him his due, however. He's resourceful. He's survived much longer than I would've thought possible."

Something in Ciullo's voice told me that Feld's luck had run out.

"If I were you," he advised me, "I'd be circumspect for a day or two. Stay away from your apartment, your office if possible." Then Vincent Ciullo offered me a chilling reassurance. "After a day or so, you shouldn't worry about Mr. Feld. You might keep an eye on the newspapers."

On that note our bizarre meeting concluded. The check remained safely tucked in my pocket, and except for my nerves, I wasn't any worse for wear. On balance, undeniably, a success.

At his office door Ciullo grasped my elbow familiarly. "I have a chapbook of poems," he said, flushing slightly, "that I should be very pleased for you to look at. They're not very polished, but—"

"Happy to," I said diplomatically.

"I'm very interested in your work, too. Any projects under way?"

"Well, sort of. A biography of Edmund Lowell."

"Really? Very ambitious. How's it proceeding?"

"No complaints," I said. "A little slow."

══*ELEVEN*══

GIDDY WITH RELIEF, I stepped into the Pink Lady, hoping that my drinks were still on the house. My movements were tremulous and shaky, like those of a man who has narrowly escaped being run over by a truck. But I felt like celebrating. I felt rich again. I felt like watching Rikki Storm take her clothes off. No matter what Ciullo said, a life of voyeurism and passivity was a fine life indeed. I was humming off-key an old Ray Charles standard, "It's no kind of life . . . da-da, ba-boom! . . . but it's my life."

I checked my watch. Hard to believe, but I'd been with Ciullo less than an hour. That gave me a full hour and a half before dinner with Jeanne. The bartender remembered me. I gulped down a free bourbon, ordered another, and thought, Jesus Saves. The anxieties of the past week evaporated and the ninth race at Suffolk replayed vividly in my mind. The filly surging powerfully forward, nostrils flaring, wide belly heaving. A genius. Rourke frantically trying to stiff her. An idiot.

"Alex!" I called.

Ciullo's nephew was leaning across the bar, talking to a stubby man who appeared to be the club manager.

When Alex came over to me, I said, "You weren't telling him to cut off the free drinks, were you?"

"Oh no," he said quickly, then grinned sheepishly.

"Good. Then join me. Put it on my tab."

"I don't really have the—"

"Come on," I urged, "a couple of drinks. We have to talk."

Alex took the stool next to me. He didn't have his uncle's gift for being polite and scaring someone witless at the same time. Alex was just polite.

"I guess everything went okay," he said. "You look like you're in good spirits."

"Good spirits? Hell, I'm hysterical." In truth, the voluptuousness of relief was gradually fading. Curiosity was beginning to set in. "Alex," I said, "would you mind telling me what the hell all of this is about?"

He was shaking his head. "I'm not supposed to, uh . . . do you really want to know?"

"Shit, Alex"—I said "shit" because I still regarded him as a student, someone with whom I could take liberties—"none of this was my goddam idea to begin with. If I had my way, I wouldn't want to know any of it. But it's too late. I seem to know just enough to get me hurt. Things are looking up right now, but who knows? I've been hearing footsteps all week, and I'd just like to know why." I tried to stare at him the way his uncle had just stared at me. "Let me put it this way. If anybody ever writes the story of my life, they're sure to want to know who murdered me."

"No one's going to murder you," he said uncomfortably, looking around. He moved uneasily on the barstool, as though he'd found out too late he was drinking with a lunatic.

"That's good to know. Tell me more." I took no pleasure in badgering him, but I had no choice. I forced another drink on him.

"I shouldn't say anything," he repeated.

"I'll make this easy. I'll do all the talking. You don't have to say a word. I've pieced most of it together, anyway. I'll just speculate about this and that, and you listen."

When he shook his head, I ignored him. I began listing my suspicions, giving each one the aura of fact. Adam Feld was trying to break out of the minor leagues, I said. Trying to establish himself in a business dominated by your uncle. About a year ago, Feld swindles Beardsley out of the ski resort, gets the filly to boot. Only Feld is a dunce when it comes to thoroughbreds. Your uncle sees that a rising competitor is ripe for picking. It's simple enough to have his own man, Bloomberg, put in charge of Jesus Saves. Jake holds the filly back, frames Feld. The police come in and take Feld to jail free of charge. "Except," I concluded, "Feld found out that Bloomberg was diddling him."

Alex hadn't mastered a poker face. His eyes seemed to confirm my speculations, but he still wouldn't speak. I forced another drink on him. I switched tactics.

"It sounds like a goddam harebrained scheme to me," I said indignantly.

No response.

"Your uncle must be getting old. Losing it." Pause. "Reading too much poetry. Out of touch with the real world."

Alex finally came to Ciullo's defense. "It worked, didn't it?" he said, emptying his drink with a gaudy swallow. "You read the papers. Feld's got police crawling out of his ears." Alex couldn't hold his liquor either; he was having trouble with his clichés.

"Tell that to Jacob Bloomberg," I said.

"Feld will pay for that," Alex said. A hint of nastiness surfaced in his voice, as though the alcohol had revived some recessive trait for violence. "This thing with Jesus Saves was just a precaution, you know. Uncle Vinnie never thought he'd have to use it. You saw how Feld is . . ."

"He's the type who usually hangs himself," I said.

"Yeah, a nuisance. A zero. Until . . ."

"Until what?" Now Alex just required a nudge here and there to keep his momentum going.

"He started expanding. A couple of months back he got the crazy idea to start soliciting girls in Boston. Right under Uncle Vinnie's nose. Offering easy money."

"How come?"

"He'd been using these New Hampshire girls. Hippy girls."

"So he decided to hire skilled labor in Boston?"

"Yeah. A serious mistake."

As if on cue, Rikki Storm appeared through the dressing room door, modestly outfitted in a lavender shirtwaist and belt. With her was someone else I'd seen in Waterville, the fading beauty with the peroxide hair. Rikki sat at the bar. A couple of patrons, I noticed, were already eyeing her, debating whether to fork over for the nine-dollar drink and the pleasure of her company. The aging blond sat with her for a moment, then headed for the stage. She wore a silver sequined costume, a large pink boa around her neck, throwbacks to the burlesque era.

Alex was looking at Rikki too. "Sitting over there," he announced drunkenly, "is the reason Feld found out what Bloomberg was up to."

I'd finally got my answers, but I didn't like them. And I didn't like the way Alex was staring at Rikki. "You're saying that Rikki informed on her father? And then Feld murdered him?"

"Yeah. Why not? Look at her. She's not too broken up about it."

"For starters, it doesn't make any goddam sense. Why didn't Feld simply hire another trainer? Fire Jake, not murder him. Otherwise things get worse, not better. Look what happened." That I should suddenly take Feld's side didn't bother me; I was taking Rikki's side. But I refused to contemplate my motives for wanting to protect her.

"Nothing Feld does makes sense. He's out of control."

"The rash act of a rash man? He finds out he's being used and can't take the blow to his ego?"

Alex finished another drink. "Right."

"What about the Butazolidin they found in Jake's whiskey bottle?"

"I don't know. Maybe Feld was trying to confuse the police. Cover his tracks. What does it matter?"

"Then it ceases to be a rash act."

"You don't understand," he said. "In this business you got to be decisive. That's what Uncle Vinnie keeps telling me. Be decisive. Act. If you waste too much time thinking about things, you won't get anything done. So we don't have time to answer every crummy little question."

Alex was clearly waging his own private battles, but I didn't feel sympathy for him. Instead, through some curious displacement, I knew an urge to take him to task for the sins of his uncle.

"That's bullshit," I said.

"What?"

I should have stopped there, but I didn't. "Your uncle may not be as goddam smart as you think he is. He's got this whole shitty business about Feld and Bloomberg figured wrong. There are a lot more ways of looking at it."

"You know something you're not telling?" he said.

"I might," I lied.

"What way do you look at it?"

"Well, if you could forget the politics of vice, you might think about hearth and home. Maybe it all comes down to, say, a domestic tragedy. It's worth looking into."

"There's no time for that," he said. "Anyway, it's too late."

"Your uncle's going to shoot first and ask questions later?"

Alex put his empty tumbler down and pushed away from the bar. "That's not a smart thing to say," he said, rising unsteadily, "even to me."

I finished my drink alone. Onstage, the peroxide blond was bumping and grinding and shimmying to the sounds of the Billy Rose Orchestra. Her eyes still carried the same hate and embarrassment that I'd glimpsed in Feld's brothel. Everything about her was a throwback to the fifties, from the stylized movements of her routine to the awkward pun of her stage name, Ursula Undress. She shed her sequins and boas the time-honored way, striving for large, dramatic effects.

A drunken businessman near me stage-whispered, "What are we in? A goddam time warp?"

The rest of the men remained equally unimpressed. They had been jaded, I supposed, by their repeated exposure to genitalia. Ursula's evening-glove routine inspired only derision. It hurt me to watch. But she pressed on, clinging somehow to the illusion that she was in show business. When the time came, at song's end, it obviously mortified her to display her vagina.

I circled the bar; an old man made it to the stool beside Rikki an instant before I did. He just couldn't wait, I thought, to hand over his social security check. I stood poised behind them, self-consciously, not really knowing why I was there. To blurt out some warning? Instead, I eavesdropped.

"You know I've missed you," the old man was saying in a grave voice. "I depend on you."

I leaned closer, remembering Rikki's response when I'd merely said hello. What obscenity would this declaration of affection provoke?

Her voice full of weariness, Rikki sighed, "Oh God. Can't you just leave me alone?"

Not as bad as I'd expected.

In a moment the old man sensed my presence behind them, my intrusion into his moment in the sun. He turned and looked up at me. "Do you mind?" Stephen Kenan said.

"No, no," I managed, slinking away.

===*TWELVE*===

Once a large anxiety is removed, I was learning, a host of lesser anxieties rush in to fill the void, like air sucked into a vacuum. Standing in the bright fluorescent light of the CVS Pharmacy in Cambridge, I thought: Damn. No wonder Jeanne had wanted me to buy Ortho-Gel. A tube no larger than a giant-sized toothpaste cost $7.45— three dollars more than the wine I'd just bought. I took a minute to scan the shelves, hoping to find signs of a price war. No generic brands. Not even a product claiming, "Compare. We kill sperm for a lot less." Having a $31,000 check tucked in my pocket had transformed me, paradoxically, into a bargain hunter.

I was relieved to find the drugstore deserted. A short, bearded man in a white coat worked behind the pharmacist's counter. Up front, a heavyset young woman with short black hair presided at a cash register. I hesitated. I didn't particularly like that I was purchasing a contraceptive while cradling a bottle of dinner wine in my left arm. Of what crime might a Cambridge wit accuse me? Unseemly optimism? Pride? I finally turned and approached the man in the white coat, trying my best to appear sober and businesslike. I laid the Ortho-Gel on the counter with an air of elevated purpose, as though I'd put there a *U.S. News & World Report*.

The man looked up and frowned. "Would you mind putting that filthy thing out?"

"Pardon?"

"Cigarette," he said curtly.

"Whoops," I replied agreeably. "Sorry." As discreetly as possible, I dropped the butt and gave it a turn with my toe.

"Not on the fl—" he started. "Christ." He glared down at the counter. "You'll have to buy that up front."

"Right." I headed toward the front register, thinking, Ah Cambridge. I lived in a community of militant nonsmokers, militant non-sexists, militant non-meat-eaters, militant no-nukers. I found peculiar comfort in the knowledge that I could, on short notice, offend the entire population by sitting over the remains of a rare T-bone steak, smoking Camels, telling dirty jokes, occasionally interjecting belligerent asides about the Russian threat. My pleasure in this was only slightly tainted by the deeper knowledge that I, with my own militant cynicism, was every bit as predictable as they.

I presented my purchase to the stocky woman—this time, for the sake of my expression, imagining the spermicide to be an obscure seventeenth-century literary journal.

"That it?" she said abruptly, without comment.

I nodded and counted out eight singles. "There must be a cheaper way to do this," I observed cheerfully, self-consciously.

She took the money and eyed me nastily. "It would be cheaper," she muttered, "to cut off your nuts." She looked very much like she wanted to volunteer for the job.

So chastened, I humbly avoided her eyes and busied myself by studying a sign posted behind her head on the window. The outer border of the sign held an elaborate pattern of intertwined oak leaves. Lower, large red letters proclaimed: CVS MONTHLY SPECIAL. The center space was hand-printed with a black felt marker: 100 MG. BUTAZOLIDIN CAPSULES, $16.00 PER 250.

I read it twice more before the word BUTAZOLIDIN clicked in my brain.

Pointing at the sign, I asked, "Is that the same drug horse trainers give to thoroughbreds?"

She received the query suspiciously, pausing as though to examine it for aberrant political ideology. She finally said, "Ask the pharmacist."

In a moment I stood at the rear counter again. I repeated my question to the pink-lunged man in the white jacket.

"Yes," he sighed, regarding me with a look of finite patience.

"Do trainers come here to buy Bute?" I persisted.

"No."

"Listen," I said evenly. "Maybe I'm not asking this the right way. But if trainers don't buy it, who does?"

His eyes registered a brief internal debate; he deferred to his role as friendly neighborhood pharmacist. "Mostly senior citizens," he said. "Bute affects people the same way it affects horses. Anti-inflammatory. Loosens the joints. Eases pain. Gives freedom of movement."

"Are we talking about arthritis?"

He nodded. "A very common treatment."

"A prescription drug?"

"Yes."

"What would happen with an overdose?"

By this time a few customers had drifted into the store; two of them were standing in line behind me. "Listen," he said, "I've never heard of that happening. Excuse me, but I've got customers."

"I know," I said, holding up the CVS bag that held the Ortho-Gel. "That's what I am."

"All right, all right," he sighed. "Bute overdose. Let me check." He turned the pages of a book the size of a telephone directory. "Well, the same would happen with Bute that would happen with most nonlethal drugs. Nausea, vomiting, gastric pain."

"Thanks. That helps." I turned back. "Oh, by the way, how tough is it to acquire Quaaludes these days?"

The resignation on his face disappeared. His eyes darkened, as

though his mind were piecing together the clues to a puzzle of unima-
ginable depravity: a bottle of wine, a spermicide, horses, arthritis medi-
cation, Quaaludes. And all from a man with whiskey on his breath.

"Don't worry," I smiled ambiguously, "I never kill more than I can
eat."

Jeanne Godwin lived in a small one-bedroom apartment in a four-
story brick building on Chauncy Street. One good thing about Cambridge militancy, I thought, pressing the buzzer to number 12. The citizens were virulently anti-landlord. Most apartment buildings were
rent-controlled, which meant that a tenant only paid about double
what an apartment was worth.

At the door Jeanne reached up and kissed me, half on the cheek, half
on the mouth. At holiday parties for the department we had indulged
in fleeting, social kisses. This time the touch carried an unfamiliar
cargo of meaning. She led me inside, where I found lots of old, comfortable furniture on hardwood floors, the stain dark and rich with age.
Here and there a sparse placement of rugs of an Indian design. A wall
of books, another wall with Japanese watercolors. Everything neat and
in its place, as though she'd just cleaned. A small oak dining table was
set with two white candles and a bouquet of daffodils.

"Never thought I'd see the day," she said, smiling. She wore a white
kaftan that contrasted handsomely with her dark complexion. Her
thick black hair, freshly brushed, swept back boldly from her face in a
way I hadn't seen it before. It suited her.

"You mean you and me?" I asked.

"Of course you and me," she replied. "We've been flirting all this
time. There's a kind of security in that. Mutually acknowledged limits.
But now—here—it seems . . . it just seems kind of funny. I mean, look
at me." She gestured at the informality of her kaftan, then at the novelty of her hairstyle.

"So now we have to put up or shut up?" I asked, but I was thinking,
she must have been joking about the Ortho-Gel.

"I don't know. Something like that. What was it Wordsworth said?
The burden of too much liberty?"

"Don't start quoting old poets," I said. "You'll confuse me. It's not as bad as all that. Relax. We'll have a nice dinner. We can even pretend we're back at the office." I handed her the bottle of wine while discreetly stowing the CVS bag in the side pocket of my jacket.

"Ah," she said, giving the wine label an appraising glance, "New York State. You shouldn't have."

"Read the fine print at the bottom," I responded, "thirteen-and-a-half-percent alcohol. That's at least a point better than the higher-priced spread."

"A real connoisseur."

Thus we retreated from the ambiguous expectations of our dinner date. We opted for the relative safety of a familiar joking back-and-forth across the sofa, shying away from an unknown, serious in-and-out under the sheets. Which was fine, really, I told myself unconvincingly. I could probably sleep on the couch. I needed to be—how had Ciullo put it?—circumspect for a day or two.

We drank, exchanged more witticisms, until we drifted to the dual topics obligatory for Cambridgians of our age and social station: work and divorce. Jeanne's marriage to an architect had ended two years ago, "on amicable terms," she said. "A great phrase, isn't it? 'Amicable terms.' We sat around for five years, amicable as all hell, boring each other to death. I don't know how we worked up the nerve to call it quits. But what was the point? No children, not a whole lot of money. We just sort of petered out. But there's no such thing as a clean break. We still see each other. Comfortable habits are hard to break."

"I don't know," I said, taking the lead in our dance of commiseration. "Elizabeth's very good at clean breaks. Before this week, we hadn't even talked. She's already involved with some guy named Breck."

"She's a very pretty girl." Jeanne paused. "Breck?"

"Says it all, doesn't it? I can understand it. At her age she still feels that she's living in a world of pure possibility. A world with lots of good things still to happen. When you think like that, it's not all that hard to leave things behind, make mistakes, start over." I gulped the last wine from my glass, finishing the New York State Chablis. "Of course, for me, lately, it's been more a question of what bad thing's going to happen next."

"You worried about tenure?"

"I wasn't thinking about that. But now that you mention it, frankly, my dear"—I executed a little drunken flourish—"I don't give a shit."

"Damn," Jeanne corrected. "Don't give a damn."

"Whatever. Anyway, should I be worried? Have you heard any depressing rumors?"

"No. There's a little friendly wagering going on within the department. I placed a sentimental bet on you."

"A small one, I hope. But thanks anyway."

"Well, if you'd finished that Lowell biog when everyone expected you to, there'd be no question. Of course, in your favor, the students still hold a grudging respect for you," she winked. "Maybe you ought to have Beth write an effusive letter."

"Cute," I said. "It looks like the interview may be more important than it usually is."

"Maybe. Braithewaite's so spaced out, who knows what's going on in his head."

"Or in Stephen Kenan's," I said.

Jeanne opened another bottle of wine, a Côtes du Rhône, and started the steaks on a little hibachi she'd set up on the fire escape outside her kitchen window. Before long she brought to the table two large plates, each holding a gorgeous medallion of tenderloin, a bundle of asparagus, and a heap of garlicky sauteed mushrooms. The wine, I noticed, was having its effect on Jeanne, too. Whatever tension there'd been between us disappeared. No longer self-conscious about the kaftan, she moved easily back and forth from her small kitchen. When faced with a choice of missing me or brushing against me, she brushed.

Midway through my steak, I sat back. "So tell me about Kenan," I said comfortably.

"You're serious about that, aren't you?"

"Not as serious as when I first asked you. But yes, I'm interested. So, does our celebrated professor have a secret life?"

"His whole life is a secret. He's the only person I've ever been around who is certifiably a genius." She smiled at me. "No offense."

It was odd, I thought, that the phrase *certifiably a genius* came as naturally to mind as *certifiably insane.* I recalled that distant locus where polarities fused. Oh please oh don't.

"As far as I'm concerned," Jeanne was saying, "that makes his whole life a secret. I don't think any part of what goes on in his mind is comprehensible to me."

She was right. Kenan was a genius, the intellectual equivalent of the great explorers of old. He had created the entire field of Puritan studies out of nothing; before Kenan worked his mind upon the sermons, journals, and artifacts of our forebears, the collective expression of America's first century had not offered respectable ground upon which to pitch one's literary tent. And having created a subject, he then became its leading exponent. He remained the definitive interpreter of Puritan history, sociology, literature, philosophy, theology. Even if you disagreed with him, you had to concede that he was an industry unto himself; he had created literally hundreds of jobs for lesser scholars.

"And that business about pissing in his wastebasket. Of course it's a big joke around college, part of the Kenan legend. But I used to get so angry at him! My God. He had me so cowed I only mentioned it to him one time."

"Yeah? What'd he say?"

"One morning he seemed to be in an uncharacteristically good mood—when I look back on it, I'd bet he'd been drinking. So I went in and said, Professor Kenan, I like working for you, etcetera, I know you have a lot on your mind, but why in God's name do you urinate in your wastebasket? You say the word, I told him, and I'll run out right now and get one of those little porcelain jobs with a lid on it. Keep it right here in your office. Well, he got a little agitated. I don't think he was mad at me; it was like I wasn't there. He said, 'I'm making a beast of myself.' Then he kept saying it over and over, in this mechanical voice, rocking back and forth in his chair. 'I'm making a beast of myself.' That was that. I finally went back to my desk. I didn't know what to make of it."

I did, or thought I did. "Do you remember that Dr. Johnson story?"

"The Dr. Johnson who died two hundred years ago?"

I nodded. "He was always getting blind, stinking drunk, so his patron—Mrs. Thrale—finally asked him, 'Why do you make such a beast of yourself?' 'I make a beast of myself,' Johnson told her, 'to get rid of the pain of being a man.' " One of my favorite quotations.

"Do you think Kenan was referring to that?"

I shrugged.

"Well," Jeanne said, unappeased, "I wish he'd done something to get rid of the pain of cleaning up his piss. There's still a big stain on the carpet. Looks like the continent of Africa."

We laughed through the rest of dinner, then moved to the sofa. Jeanne put a Dura-Flame log in the fireplace and brought out a bottle of port. "You'll like this," she said, suppressing a hiccup. "Eighteen-percent alcohol." She sat very close to me on the sofa, tucking her legs beneath her, knees touching my left thigh. She circled an arm behind me and rested her fingers on my hair.

"Do you think Kenan's getting senile?" I asked.

"Can't we talk about something else?" she complained. "I was just thinking how nice it is that we're not in the office, after all."

"I know. Me too. Just a couple of questions more. This Kenan thing has been preying on my mind."

"God knows why," she said, momentarily, sobering. She asked abruptly, "You don't know how old he is, do you?"

"Well, he retired three years ago, so I guess that makes him about sixty-eight."

"Uh-uh." She shook her head. "He *looks* sixty-eight—hell, he looks a lot older than that—but he retired voluntarily. Old Steve Kenan is fifty-four years old. Look it up in *Who's Who*."

"Jesus. What put the age in his face?"

"Booze, for starters. The same thing, Thomas dear, that's going to make you look old before your time. But, technically speaking, you could say that Kenan's been alive longer than most men his age."

"What the hell are you talking about?"

"Not alive, really. Awake. Have you ever heard of those people who don't need sleep? Or can't sleep? I don't know what the doctors call it, but it's like a radical version of insomnia. I heard he can only sleep two, maybe three hours a night. Before I'd heard that, I asked him one morning if he had slept well. Just being friendly. He got this look of incredible pain on his face. It scared me. Almost a look, well, of sexual longing. I felt sorry for him."

"No wonder he's so prolific," I observed. "Sounds a little grotesque." Kenan's condition put me in mind of something I had heard recently, something similarly repulsive. It came to me: *coitus reservatus*. Sleep, no less than orgasm, offered release and slaked the fires of consciousness.

"One more question," I said.

"Aw," Jeanne pouted, leaning toward me, noticeably unsteady.

"I'll ask it all at once. Quicker that way." I gathered myself. "Is Kenan chaste, is he gay, impotent, a satyromaniac, a masturbator, or," I asked, completing the catalogue, "does he seek the company of prostitutes?"

Jeanne rolled her eyes. "You do want to blackmail him," she teased me. "Thank God, but I don't know anything about any of that."

"Nothing?"

"No." Her eyes were vacant, as if she were remembering. She giggled to herself. "Well . . ."

"What?"

"I never told anyone this before." She looked at me. "Don't get all excited. It's not much."

"What?" I repeated.

"Well, sometimes I'd come into his office in the morning and there would be this smell."

"That's hardly surprising," I said, deflated. "Kenan wasn't a stickler for personal hygiene."

"I know, I know. But this was something else. Sometimes I could just swear that his office smelled . . . well, smelled like, you know, sex." She hiccuped.

"Smelled like sex?" I said, grinning.

"Don't pretend to be naïve, Thomas. You know exactly what I mean."

"Don't be too sure," I laughed. "I told you that Elizabeth was very good at clean breaks. It's been a long time."

Jeanne wasn't laughing. She leaned toward me and put her mouth close to my ear. "You want me to freshen your memory?" she whispered.

In a moment we lay coiled on the sofa, the Dura-Flame log flickering a reddish light over us. Suddenly Jeanne pulled away and sat upright. "Damn," she said, slightly flushed. "I forgot. You know I told you to stop by the pharmacy? I was teasing, sort of . . . I really am out—"

"Not to worry," I reassured her.

"Thomas!" she cried in mock embarrassment, when I told her what was hidden in the right-hand pocket of my jacket.

In her bedroom we shed our words and submerged ourselves in motion and inarticulate sounds. We pursued the moment as if we both had learned that here resided the one unqualified pleasure that life had to offer. At first we embraced the athleticism that is common to first-time lovers; then gradually we drifted into the calmer waters of affection and tenderness. I found myself wondering, Why did I seek the love of strangers? For novelty's sake? If anything, Jeanne and I were too familiar with the urgency, with the places that yielded to the touch, with the finite number of embraces. Ours was a knowledge mutually conveyed through the minutest of signals, a subtle sexual shorthand. But if it wasn't novelty we sought, what was it?

Whatever it was, Jeanne found it before I did. Raised on extended arms, I watched her move beneath me.

Her time came, then passed. Mine still eluded me. Sweat collected at the tip of my nose and dripped down onto Jeanne's face. Eventually fatigue set in, and with it, self-consciousness. I found myself caught in the ridiculous paradox of the inebriate who seeks orgasm: by thinking intensely, I sought to rid my mind of thoughts; through an effort of concentration, I sought to relax.

Sensing that my moment was fading, Jeanne made me the object of all of her amorous science. She raised her knees closer to her chest and snaked her left hand behind the juncture of our torsos. She tickled, then tugged at my testicles. With her right hand she tweaked my nipples, then raked her fingernails delicately over the taut skin of my lower abdomen. She ground her hips wantonly. She moaned with a depraved and ostentatious enthusiasm.

Her labors weren't in vain. She brought me to the brink; I wavered there precariously. Our reward near, Jeanne redoubled her efforts, orchestrating every tweak, every tug, every teasing rake of her nails, every obscene utterance, as though she had commenced the final movement of a tactile symphony. She bowed forward and up to lick my chest. She clutched her whole body.

I came. I knew the unqualified joy of those seven, eight, nine? seconds of muscular spasm joined to utter forgetfulness. That little oasis of time when I didn't ward off some unseen doom by making a joke.

We collapsed, sweating, intertwined, breathless. We lay silent.

"God," Jeanne finally breathed, "we should have done that a long time ago."

"Done what?" I asked, still catching my breath. "Oh, that." The jokes were already back. The brevity of the moment always unnerved me. Everything flooded back with startling rapidity—my memories, my worries, my whole doubtful life.

Jeanne, too, must have experienced a similar metamorphosis, for she was laughing softly.

"What?" I whispered.

"That's the smell," she murmured, yawning.

"Kenan?"

"Hmmm." She turned onto her side, rooting languidly down among the covers, fading fast. I molded myself to her like a spoon.

"Jeanne," I whispered, "does Kenan by any chance have arthritis?"

So close to sleep, she didn't find the question peculiar. "Mm-mm," she yawned, "don't think so."

Good, I thought. Keep things simple.

Jeanne roused herself momentarily. "Had a bad hip . . . some mornings he walked with a limp . . . wha'?"

I didn't like the grotesque speculations that kept surfacing in my mind.

"Jeanne?" I whispered.

She was asleep.

Good, I thought again. Better that way. I couldn't ask her if he took anything for his hip. I couldn't ask her if he took anything to help him battle those sleepless nights.

She couldn't answer: Butazolidin. Quaaludes.

═══THIRTEEN═══

AT SEVEN-THIRTY the following morning, after coffee with Jeanne—both of us hung over, sheepish, idiotically polite—I drove toward Talbot Hall. I'd already parked before I remembered what Ciullo had said: stay away from the office. So I drove on, through Central Square, and had another cup of coffee and an Egg McMuffin at McDonald's. My head buzzed mildly, but I was full of good intentions to follow Braithewate's advice that morning in class. No more quizzes. What were his words? Give them the benefit of my hard-earned wisdom. Above all, I told myself, don't disturb the placid collegiate waters a month prior to my tenure decision. If tenure was granted, I could splash about all I liked. Better still, I could drift and sleep.

Lecture prepared, mind focused, at five past nine I appeared before the class. Their eyes wavered, half-opened and bloodshot, men unshaven, women tousled, all evidence of some Dionysian revels I hadn't time to contemplate. Of course, Roger Potter sat no more than four feet in front of me, well rested, composed, his expression expectant.

I plunged in, secretly thanking whatever god had blessed me with the dubious theatrical ability to make the oldest saws of American literature appear original and interesting. I led with a ribald segue from

Hawthorne to Melville (Hawthorne dropped portentous veils from ministers' faces; Melville dropped the cloths from islanders' loins, blah blah). I quickly rehearsed Melville's early South Seas novels, making sure to paint suggestive portraits of the guilt-free natives he found there. I explored the reservoir of sexual myth behind whale hunting ("Moby-Dick, at the most fundamental level, means just that. The pursuit of the whale is also a pursuit of epic sexual potency," blah blah blah). I traced the vulgar etymology of the title itself, an exercise that I defied any student to sleep through.

Halfway through the hour I was well into contemporary views of *Moby-Dick,* sprinkling in glamorous references to constructionism, deconstructionism, Foucault, Derrida. Not name-dropping for its own sake; I wanted my charges, at pre-game cocktail parties, to hold their own with their vacuous Ivy League counterparts.

"It is possible," I said, finally positioning myself for a conclusion, "that Melville, in the end, retreated from the more frightening implications of his vision. In 1857, after *The Confidence Man,* he stopped writing fiction altogether. He refused to pursue his art, we are free to conclude, because he feared where it might lead him. He feared what he might see."

Potter's hand shot up. Ordinarily I would have ignored him. But it was wisest for now to keep his parents off the phone to Braithewaite.

I smiled pleasantly. "What's on your mind, Potter?"

"Professor Theron, what is it precisely that Melville was afraid he might see?"

At the rear of the room, a low, masculine voice stage-whispered, "Your mother."

Subdued laughter. I cleared my voice authoritatively. "That's a fair enough question, Mr. Potter. Would you care to speculate on that?" The most fundamental abuse of power in the classroom: answer a question with a question.

The quality that set Potter apart from his classmates was his absolute indifference to appearing foolish. "Well," he began, "maybe Melville didn't want to think about—"

Potter stopped midsentence. A huge, unsightly man opened the door and entered the classroom. Potter's mouth fell open, as though some evil spirit had conjured the very thing Melville hadn't wanted to see. Perhaps Melville's whale itself, beached, somehow ambulatory had flopped into the room.

Gerald, looking larger and uglier than I remembered, leaned across the small half-lectern on my desk and said, "Outside."

I managed a smile, hoping to persuade the class that the monster they saw was expected, even awaited. I followed Gerald out of the room.

Once I'd closed the door behind us, I whispered tensely, "What is it?"

"You have to come with me," he said.

"Listen, goddammit. Do you plan on dragging me to the Pink Lady every time Ciullo reads a new book and wants to discuss it?"

Gerald regarded me implacably. His eyes blinked slowly, unperturbed. Then he said, "We ain't got time for you to whine." Placing his large palm on my arm, he closed his fingers above my elbow, where a muscle had been in my youth. He squeezed.

"Jesus, all right. Just wait a second. Let me cancel class."

He shook his head. "They're in college. They'll figure it out."

Gerald led me out of the building and across the main quadrangle to the visitors' parking lot behind Emerson Library. I saw Alex leaning against the Mercedes. He opened the rear door for me with an apologetic tilt of his head. Sober, I noticed, and his usual, ineffectual self. "Sorry," he said. "I know this is a bad time, Professor Theron. But something's come up."

"What is it with you, Alex?" I said angrily. "The same shit every time. 'Beg pardon, professor. Veddy veddy sorry, professor.' I feel like I'm in a nightmare of courtesy. When is this going to end?"

"Sorry," Alex apologized, then, realizing what he'd said, flushed and apologized again. Gerald had maneuvered through the heavy traffic in the Square and turned down Kennedy Street toward the Charles River Bridge. "I thought you'd want to know about this," he said, handing me a late-morning edition of the *Globe*.

It didn't take long to find what he was talking about. At the bottom left corner of page one, set off in a bordered square reserved for late-breaking stories, the headline appeared: NEW HAMPSHIRE SUSPECT FOUND DEAD. The account was brief, two columns, each no longer than four inches:

> Adam Feld, a member of the controversial Adamite sect, was found dead early this morning, the apparent victim of an overdose of barbiturates. Feld, 33, originally of Queens, New York, had been questioned this past week in connection with a Suffolk race-fixing scheme and the homicide of a New Jersey trainer. Police sources say that the investigation of Feld also revealed the existence of a prostitution ring. While suicide has not been ruled out, sources say the death is being labeled accidental.
>
> These latest allegations, if proven, will terminate the Adamites' two-year effort to maintain legal status as a religious entity. The sect, already the target of various local religious organizations, has been involved in a long-term legal battle that most observers consider futile.
>
> Referring to Feld's death, one officer who chose to remain unidentified said, "It just means we clean up the mess a little sooner. The [deletion] was about to hit the fan, anyway. Those Adamite girls weren't on their knees, not praying anyway. They were on their [deletion], and the meter was running."

A full report, the story promised, would follow in the evening *Globe.*

My stomach felt queasy, my shoulders suddenly cold. It was the type of story that usually provoked only my detached curiosity. But my nearness to the events—my virtual participation in them—triggered a less abstract response. My esophagus bulged; for a moment I thought I would gag. I held the newspaper spread beneath me until the nausea subsided. Then I slumped back, quietly thankful that I hadn't deposited little gobbets of Egg McMuffin on the plush upholstery of Ciullo's Mercedes.

"You okay?" Alex asked.

"Yeah," I finally managed, "sure." Then I calmly observed, "I guess your uncle wasn't kidding when he told me not to worry about Adam Feld."

Alex was shaking his head. "You don't understand."

"Alex," I sighed, "for a week now I haven't understood a whole hel-luva lot—" I stopped and looked at him; then I looked down at the newspaper in my lap. "Are you saying that your uncle had nothing to do with this?"

That's what he was saying. "It's looking more and more," Alex said, "as if you were right last night."

"Right? Right about what?"

"Remember? You said the whole Bloomberg thing might turn out to be a domestic tragedy. You said there were other ways of looking at it."

"Listen, Alex. In case you haven't noticed, I talk out of my ass a lot. It's kind of an occupational hazard. You didn't tell Mr. Ciullo what I said?"

"There's nothing for you to worry about," he said.

Despite this assurance, I leaned back and glanced uneasily out of the side window. Wherever we were heading, it wasn't the Pink Lady.

"Beacon Hill," Alex told me. "Mr. Ciullo's home."

And apparently the oldest, most exclusive section of Beacon Hill. We turned up a steep, narrow street and I studied the town houses. Bleak façades, I thought, understated as only the very wealthy can understate them. The Hill had once been the domain of the Sears, the Lodges, the great Brahmin families who inhabited a privileged world of exquisite codes and obscure values. Now true Brahmins were all but extinct. Beacon Hill had long since become the habitat of wealthy Bostonians who merely lusted after the Brahmin legend. No different, really, than wealthy Virginians who lust after the mythic glories of the Old South. Or wealthy Texans who lust after a frontier ethos. The Virginian in his white linen, the Texan in his cowboy hat, the Bostonian in his bow tie. Only the money behind the illusion really existed. Serious money.

The Mercedes turned into a garage built into the lowest level of a four-story, gray stone town house. I followed Alex to a small door that led inside.

The interior surprised me, so full of contradictions that I couldn't guess what image, if any, Ciullo lusted after. A heavy odor of food hung in the air—not a fresh odor, but antique, as though the entire dwelling had been seasoned from repeated use, like a skillet. The toys of small children lay strewn about the floor. Some of the furnishings bespoke humble origins; others, high aspirations. What appeared to be an original Cezanne hung on the wall above an ungainly sofa upholstered in a hideous, embroidered fabric of pale green. A beautiful antique dining table reflected the light of a garish cut-glass chandelier. Half of what I saw might have been purchased through agents at private auction, the other half wholesale. Not really bizarre, I decided, just full of contradictions. The environment of someone who juggled several identities, or had climbed too rapidly some aesthetic ladder.

Gerald stayed behind with the Mercedes. Alex led me up the stairway. On the first landing a shadowy figure startled me; then I realized that a large—menacingly large—crucifix decorated the wall. We continued up until we stopped at a door on the third floor. Alex knocked once and opened the door for me, then remained behind.

Vincent Ciullo sat at an enormous desk that held pile after pile of books, haphazardly arranged. At the center of the desk a small lamp focused light on a clutter of paper and an ancient typewriter. More books were stacked on the floor beside his chair—an old, comfortable barber's chair, I noticed. Ciullo plinked a few more keys of his typewriter before he looked up. He wore a blue robe, slippers, and on his head, a green visor. He swiveled the chair toward me and sighed. "It seems that events have conspired to keep us from our work," he said, glancing back at the pages spread out on his desk.

I didn't reply. I vowed to keep silent as long as possible, at least until I discovered what was what.

"Has Alex shown you the news reports?"

I nodded.

"And what was your response to it?"

"A brief nausea," I said truthfully.

"Yes, well, I appreciate your delicate sensibility," he observed, "but I was asking for your intellectual response. Do you think Adam Feld capable of suicide? Or an accidental overdose?"

"I didn't know him well enough to say."

"From what Alex tells me, you weren't so cautious in giving your opinions last evening," he said, studying me. "Would you tell me on what basis you theorized that Bloomberg's death might be—your words, I think—a domestic tragedy?"

"Mostly on the basis of bourbon and a vivid imagination," I said. I was kicking myself and thinking, Here's my punishment for badgering young Alex, apprentice mobster.

Ciullo stood up angrily. For the first time, I heard him swear. "If you weren't so preoccupied with protecting your own puny ass, Professor Theron, then perhaps you could comprehend what's going on here." He looked toward the door. "Now, I can call Gerald up here to assist me. I was hoping that we had gone beyond that."

"We have," I said humbly. I tried to set my body in some obvious pose of cooperation.

Ciullo composed himself, but remained standing. "Now," he said, "do you think Feld capable of suicide? Simply your opinion."

"If I read him correctly," I began, "I'd say no. I don't have much to base it on, but I'd say he was too ambitious, had too high a regard for his own future. And for much the same reason, he's not the sort who would experiment in any serious way with drugs. Men like Feld have an exaggerated opinion of the value of their own minds. If anything, he went to the opposite extreme. A health nut."

"Good," Ciullo said. "Good. We agree." He sat down again and took out his pipe. "Let me put this in perspective for you," he said. "Feld's death, whether by his own hand or someone else's, pleases a lot of people. Especially the police. They are inclined to accept without question the present account of his demise, however implausible it seems to you or me. The police are not immune to selfish motives; they crave the convenience of simple solutions. To their way of thinking, Feld's death conveniently solves the Bloomberg homicide. It speeds up the decline of the Adamites. And it accomplishes all of that without the unpredictability of a trial. The citizens of New Hampshire wouldn't have enjoyed, week after week, watching Feld on the court-house steps, smiling confidently into TV cameras. All in all, much more than the police could have hoped for. They won't question their luck. The newspapers will bear me out."

Ciullo raised his palm as though I were about to contradict this ac-count of the bureaucratic mind. "Oh, I'm not saying there won't be some lingering media interest. Prostitution posing as religion is a form of hypocrisy that the media will find hard to resist—far more compell-ing, really, than mundane revelations of vice alone. So you can expect to read a few news stories, to watch a few television reports. There may even be the usual unfounded rumors about me. But sooner or later the entire matter will die its own natural death and sink from view. Some other scandal, fresher, more titillating, will take its place."

I cleared my throat. "I'm willing to believe all of that, Mr. Ciullo, but I'm not sure that I get the point of it."

"The point is simply this. I don't have the same luxury the police have. I can't be satisfied with the first convenient explanation, however shoddy, that presents itself. It may turn out that Feld's death was acci-dental, after all. But I have to know that beyond doubt." He eyed me impatiently.

"So that's why you need to know," I said, "what was on my mind when I spoke to Alex."

"Yes," he sighed.

The mention of Gerald had resolved whatever fine point of ethics I might have debated. "I hope you haven't got your expectations up," I began. "This isn't much. In fact, it's pretty outlandish."

Ciullo wasn't buying that. "If you really believed that," he observed, "you wouldn't have made an effort to conceal it."

"It's just that I didn't want to throw out the name of a man who is most likely an innocent bystander."

He wasn't buying that, either. "What you call tugs of conscience," he said, "I would call a desire to absolve yourself from responsibility."

Silently asking forgiveness of the God of Pedagogy, I informed on

Professor Kenan. Kenan was a member of Feld's club, I said. Kenan had some sort of hankering after Rachel Bloomberg. Kenan conceivably had access to the drugs found in Bloomberg's whiskey bottle. And Kenan was, I said, more than a little strange. "Of course, that in itself doesn't mean much," I concluded. "What would really be odd is if a man like Kenan were completely normal."

"Ah," Ciullo said, "the eccentricity of genius." He smiled faintly, shaking his head. "Stephen Kenan. One of the few men whose work I admire without reservation. Really, a giant. I agree with you, Thomas, the notion that he's somehow involved is outlandish." He added, "But we'll see."

Incapable of passing up an opportunity to discuss books, Ciullo for the next ten minutes demonstrated a detailed knowledge of Kenan's monumental works. I joined in, too eagerly if anything, thinking that my confession hadn't been so bad after all. I relaxed.

"That's not a name I expected to hear," Ciullo said finally.

"I feel a little queer about it myself," I said. "Hell, the man's on my tenure committee."

"Really? I had the impression that you already had tenure."

I shook my head. "Five years as an assistant prof, then a tenure decision. In a couple of weeks, as a matter of fact."

"A formality, I imagine."

"Not really. Department sources tell me I'm even money."

"Well," Ciullo offered, "if I can help in any way, don't hesitate to ask. I'm not without influence—"

"No, no thanks," I said quickly. What did he mean by 'influence'? "Braithewaite is committee chairman, and he's pretty hard-nosed about these things. I don't think anything short of donating a new library wing would sway him. Anyway, my chances are decent right now."

"Yes, of course," Ciullo said. "I wish you the best of luck."

Still in his robe, he escorted me downstairs. "I'd like to ask a favor," he said, his voice casual.

"Sure," I said. "I can take those poems right now."

"No," he said. "That's not the favor."

"Yes?"

"If you learn anything about this Kenan business, I'd certainly like to know."

What was he up to? "I doubt I'll hear anything," I said.

"Of course, I wouldn't expect you," he went on, ignoring me, "to pursue this gratis. I think we could arrange, if anything turned up, an appropriate remuneration. I have the impression," he added pointedly, "that you've been asking a few questions anyway."

So that was it. Ciullo was dangling a hook, thinking he might draw me back into his world. I wasn't biting. "Well, I doubt—"

"Like it or not," he persisted, "you've become something of an expert on these events. You seem to have a knack for uncovering things."

"Just a bad case," I said, "of being in the wrong place at the wrong time."

He still ignored me. "I'll need whatever information you can turn up within the week. I have other people looking into this from other angles. But Mr. Kenan seems right down your alley. I want to get this matter resolved."

I started again, "I doubt that—"

"Alex pointed out Bloomberg's daughter to me," Ciullo said, setting the hook, sure of himself and even surer of me. "She's a remarkably beautiful girl. It would be unfortunate if something should happen to her."

=====*FOURTEEN*=====

CLEVE DICKEY PUSHED a *Boston Herald* across our table at the Paddock Bar. "So here's why you been bugging shit outta me to go to Waterville," he announced. "This guy Feld was running a goddam whorehouse. Why didn't you just say you wanted a little action?"

I balanced three candy-striped swizzle sticks on the pile of losing tickets stacked in front of me. Things were back to normal. Two races. Down two hundred dollars. "Too embarrassed, I guess."

"Bullshit you were. A lot of things that ought to embarrass you," Cleve said, smiling, "don't."

Just then an unshaven man with feverish eyes stuck his head between us, shouting, "Cleve! Just nailed the trifecta! Nailed it fucking cold. Didn't even watch the race. Fucking knew I had it. Knew it."

"Nice going, Freddy," Cleve replied blandly. "Good for you."

Freddy sprinted past us, shouting like a town crier, succumbing to the deep compulsion that drove bettors to proclaim their success indiscriminately.

"Knew it, my ass," Cleve hissed, watching him.

Cleve was right, I thought. The certainty always came later. Bettors were like overmatched boxers throwing wild punches. When a punch finally landed, the task became simpler: to convince oneself of one's aim and premeditation.

I'd played the third and fourth races, and the only thing of which I had to convince myself was that I could afford to lose one hundred dollars every time I went to the window. Concentrate, I urged myself. My mind wandered; erotic bolts of lightning flashed in my brain.

"You keep playing those stupid combinations," Cleve frowned, "you're gonna give yourself high blood pressure." A purist, Cleve scorned, action bets: the trifectas, perfectas, daily doubles, twin-tri's which made the most money for the track, while putting most bettors in the poorhouse. Real horseplayers didn't hedge; they bet only to win.

"Cleve," I began casually, "did you know that every drugstore in town sells Bute on prescription?"

"Sure."

"Yes?" I prompted.

"Old folks buy it. Limbers 'em up. My first wife's mother took it for her arthritis." He smiled. " 'Cept in her case, it had a bad side effect."

I could tell from his grin that he was setting me up, but I played straight man anyway. "What's that?"

"It limbered up her jaw muscles. Haw. Haw."

I laughed politely. "I wish you'd told me."

"Tell you? I thought everybody knew that. Anyway, you're the asshole who teaches college." He eyed me suspiciously. "You got something on your mind, boy?"

"Just curious."

In the fifth, I wheeled a perfecta, playing a longshot plodder named Huggamee in combination with three decent colts, and lost another seventy dollars. Cleve watched disdainfully as I shuffled the tickets into the burgeoning pile.

"Didn't you say it was Petey who knew that Bloomberg had a daughter stripping in the Zone?"

"Yeah, Petey," he said absently. Then he leaned forward and studied me with an air of triumph. "So that's what you're sniffing around for.

You trying to track down that girl? I wouldn't mind another look at her myself."

"Something like that." If that explanation satisfied Cleve, I wasn't going to contradict him. Finally, a small benefit from a dubious reputation.

"How's Petey know about her?" I asked, remembering that Ciullo hadn't known until this past week.

"Shit, Petey just hears things. You would too, if you just sat around the jockeys' room in a wheelchair."

"Petey's crippled?"

"Naw, he just likes riding around in a chair," Cleve jibed. "Petey used to be a pretty fair jock. Been about fifteen years now. A shitty claimer broke down under him. The horse rear of him stepped on his spine. Fifteen hundred pounds wearing steel shoes."

"Do you mind taking me down to the jockeys' room? I'd like to ask him some questions."

"About that little stripper?"

I nodded.

"Tell me," Cleve said, "What's it like to be led around by that tube of meat between your legs?"

It was early afternoon now. That morning, after an absence of three days, I'd awakened in my own bed, amid the overturned cartons and scattered books in my apartment. Adam Feld had been trying to frighten me; he had only succeeded, I thought, in helping me unpack. I cleared a path to the bathroom, then to the kitchen, and then retraced my steps to the bed and the TV. I found it impossible to stare at the Three Boxes. The manuscript pages lay scrambled on the floor, a gargantuan, incomprehensible collage of novel, biography, and criticism. I briefly considered tossing the entire random mess into a single box and submitting it to an avant-garde literary press. Hell, they just might publish it. Small presses valued inscrutability above all else.

On TV, Phil Donahue interrogated a homosexual couple who had been married in California. For the sake of a balanced show, Donahue solicited the sympathy and understanding of the matrons in his audience. Once he had achieved this, he turned back toward his guests and resumed his attack. "You plan to adopt children"—brow knit challengingly—"am I right?"

The morning passed. I didn't bother to scrutinize my motives for what I was about to do. It would have been futile anyway. My capacity for self-delusion, like most people's, far exceeded my capacity for self-knowledge. What I thought didn't matter. It only mattered what I did. And what I did was reach for the phone and begin my pursuit of Stephen Kenan. Thomas Theron, I thought, bounty hunter. Soft-boiled detective.

Three calls to colleagues at Wesley yielded the following: Since his retirement, Kenan had held a series of lucrative visiting professorships. Classic academic sinecures, I knew; short hours, high pay. Most small colleges couldn't afford fulltime, big-name talent, so they settled for the transient prestige of a man like Kenan. Then, long after Kenan had moved on, the college would display him prominently in the brochures that they forwarded to prospective students.

This spring, Kenan's services had been acquired by Channing College, a small suburban campus six miles west of Boston. One detail of note: last fall, I learned, Kenan had taught at Pine Manor, a junior college *cum* finishing school in Chestnut Hill. The school Rachel Bloomberg had dropped out of three months ago.

Next I called the Pink Lady and spoke with Alex. "Tell the club manager that I'll be in to ask a few questions," I said. "Tell him it's okay to cooperate with me." I couldn't imagine myself slipping the bartender a couple of sawbucks. I wasn't sure how much a sawbuck was, anyway.

"Sure, Professor Theron," Alex replied cheerfully. My request didn't seem to surprise him. "Anything else?"

"Not for now."

"I thought you might want to know," he offered, "Rikki Storm missed her shift last night."

"Thanks. Is she supposed to work tonight?"

"Nope, tomorrow."

"Thanks."

The most difficult call still lay ahead of me. Kenan's secretary at Channing College refused to give me an appointment. There was a dogged protectiveness in her voice that didn't succumb to my flattery or, after that, my bullying. Then I remembered the magic words.

"Oh, Professor Theron," she softened, "why didn't you say you were at Wesley? Surely Professor Kenan will want to see a former colleague." The mention of Wesley College elicited the respect of any person who had ever secreted away the tiniest intellectual insecurity.

She assigned me a slot for four o'clock that afternoon. "I guess that will be okay," she said, reconsidering. "I don't know—" I hung up before she had the chance to retreat further.

By noon, not yet out of bed, I already felt as though I'd put in a full day. I dressed in a herringbone jacket and red tie, ate a bowl of raisin bran, went out to my Beetle, and drove to Suffolk Downs.

Cleve was now leading me out of the grandstand, through a mob of bettors that pressed in close against us. Faces nurturing hope; faces creased with despair; still other faces arrested at that instant when hope or despair is transformed into its opposite. All of the wild schemes, I knew, all of the recriminations, the curses and the brave laughter, could be reduced to two sentences: before a race, "Maybe . . ." After a race, "If only . . ."

Outside, we crossed the wide asphalt spectator grounds that spanned the length of the homestretch, walked past the saddling area adjacent to the winner's circle, and headed toward the jockeys' room. Blue cloudless sky, a mild salt breeze from Boston Harbor, less than two miles away. Despite the fine weather, few among the six thousand patrons watched the races live. Most stayed inside, lurking by the bars, staring transfixed at the closed-circuit TVs. Flesh-and-blood horses were incomprehensible to most bettors; reduced to electrons cast upon a screen, the images seemed familiar, accessible, and therefore, so the delusion unfolded, predictable.

"So what's going to happen to Jesus Saves?" I asked Cleve as we walked.

"Feld's lawyers are looking to unload her. Trying to recover some of the money Feld owed them. They'll sell his cemetery lot out from under him if they can."

"Isn't she damaged goods? She took a lot of abuse."

"Maybe. But then again, maybe somebody will get a helluva race-horse cheap. Bud Spina's negotiating for her. He's willing to take the risk." Bud Spina trained a small stable of horses at Suffolk, but always made it to the top of the money list. "He might be able to salvage her. If he can get the papers, he's thinking of running her in a starter allow-ance next week. See what's he's got."

"You think he can un-train her?"

"He's gonna try. You remember that colt I was telling you about, chased seagulls? Once he got blinkered, he turned out all right. Well, this other time I was hot-walker for a two-year-old named Pell-Mell. Lots of promise. Fifteen hands, sound as a dollar, good speed. But he did the craziest thing I've ever seen. He'd come up on a clod of dirt on the track—didn't have to be a big one, just a clod of dirt that didn't get raked over—and that son of a bitch would jump *over* it. Swear to God. Fucking riot. This big beautiful horse, hauling ass down the stretch, and he would be jumping over these little bitty mudpies. It took all of us put together a couple of months to figure what the shit he was doing. At first we figured he was having some kind of goddam seizure. Some smartass reporter from the *Form* started calling him Petty-Mall."

"How'd you cure him of that?"

Cleve shook his head. "Didn't. Couldn't. Sold him for a song. That's my point. Maybe Bud Spina can do something with Jesus Saves. Maybe he can't."

We found Petey in his wheelchair, a broom in his lap, parked in a quiet corner of the jockeys' locker room. "That's why Petey knows everything," Cleve whispered to me, loud enough that Petey could hear. "He don't do shit but sit there and exercise his ears."

Fifteen years in a wheelchair had wasted Petey's lower body; there didn't seem to be anything at all within his pantlegs. His shoulders had compensated for the injury. With a quick, powerful swipe, he jabbed the broom handle at Cleve's belly. "I'll exercise this up your sorry ass,

Cleveland." Petey looked over at me. His aggressive black eyes presided over a small hooked nose. "When's this shithead gonna get him a rug that fits?"

While the two men exchanged insults—the hot surface pools of a subterranean affection—I got my first look at the jockeys' room. The air smelled of leather, liniment, and, like most locker rooms, testosterone. Rows of green benches alternated with gray metal lockers on one side of the room; scales, massage tables, whirlpools on the other. Most of the conversations I heard were in Spanish. I saw maybe six riders, and three times that number of hangers-on. In silks, or with towels knotted about their small waists, the men flashed confident smiles and moved about the room with cocky, self-possessed strides, full of hip. Each of them lean, a thin sheath of skin drawn taut over sleek muscles. They needed strength to make a tired animal finish fast; they needed sensitive hands to identify a thoroughbred's rhythm, then blend with it or change it. Mostly I sensed the presence of big egos. Kevin Rourke, I supposed, had been an aberration. These jockeys expected deference from strangers. No different, really, from the locker rooms of test pilots or surgeons.

Cleve pulled me toward him. "This friend of mine," he said to Petey, "wants to ask you some questions about Jake Bloomberg's daughter." He winked. "Says he's just curious. I think he's got a dirty mind." Cleve patted me on the back, then left us alone, resuming his station at the Paddock Bar for the sixth race.

"Hello, Petey," I began, taking a seat on the bench next to him. "My name's—"

"I know who you are," he said. "I've seen you around. Theron, right? You teach college in Cambridge."

"Yep." Petey, I thought, was establishing his credentials as an informed source. He probably relished his role as keeper and dispenser of oral history. Wouldn't hurt to stroke him, I decided. "Cleve tells me," I said, "you're the man to see for reliable information. He says there's not much that you don't know."

"Depends."

"Depends on what?" Was now the time to scrounge around in my wallet for a couple of sawbucks?

"Depends on whether you're gonna stand there and blow smoke up my ass. Tell me what a smart guy I am. See, a lot a people see this wheelchair, they start acting funny on me. They think because I got bad legs that somehow I'm feebleminded too. You're not gonna start that shit, are you?"

I didn't make things worse by apologizing. "Okay, let's start over. Cleve told me you were a dumb son of a bitch. Said if I gave you a mirror, you couldn't find your own asshole."

"Teacher, huh?" Petey said, his dark eyes gleaming. "Cleve says you couldn't teach a puppydog to piss on paper." He smiled. "So what you want to know?"

"I'm just wondering how you knew that Jacob Bloomberg's daughter dropped out of school and took a job in the Combat Zone. I've heard that Jake was very secretive about his family affairs."

"Didn't hear it from Jake, that's for sure," he laughed. "Jake would think twice before he'd tell you the time of day. He sure wouldn't spread it around that his daughter was a whore. It was eating him up. Made him crazy. But it's mostly just a secret around here. I heard about it from some friends of mine at the Meadowlands. Jake was from near there, in Jersey. You can't really keep that kind a thing from people you work around for long. I even knew Jake a little, back when I was riding. He was still a small-timer back then. Beats the shit outta me why he ever started training. Never had a gift for it. Horses made him nervous. Jake was always a hustler first, trainer second. I figure that's why he got mixed up in all this shit with Feld in the first place." Petey shook his head. "I can't believe what he did to the filly. Fucking ruined her."

"I heard."

"Goddam gruesome shit, if you ask me. It's trainers like Bloomberg who put me in this two-wheeler. Shooting their stock full of dope to keep 'em running. Give 'em nerve operations so they don't feel nothing in their knees. Don't rest 'em. Horses get sore, get gimpy, bad legs, but the Bute'll keep 'em running. Got to pay their keep. Look what happened to me. A goddam two-bit gelding that didn't have no business running snaps his leg. Clean in two. And there I am, laying in muck, with about four thousand pounds of horseflesh still wanting to pass."

"I take it you're not upset that Jake's dead?"

"Don't bother me one bit. Didn't bother his daughter either."

"Do you know her?"

"Uh-uh. I just saw her the day she stopped by for some of Jake's things. Cleve saw her too. If she gave a goddam that he was dead, she sure as hell didn't show it."

"You have any idea why?" I asked.

"I got lots of ideas, but I don't know what they amount to. There were always stories making the rounds about Jake. That happens when you try to hold on to your secrets. He probably beat hell out of the girl. I know he beat hell out of his wife, 'cause I saw the results a couple a times. Pretty girl that worked in the barns, 'bout half his age. When she left him, he figured she was a slut anyway. So he was going to make damn sure his girl wouldn't turn into a slut too." Petey looked at me. "You know how trainers believe in bloodlines."

"So you think he might have pushed his daughter into it?"

"All I know is that he was mean. I don't know why she stayed with him as long as she did. But if she wanted to piss him off, she knew just how to do it."

"Show business?"

"Yeah. Especially the 'show' part."

"Thanks, Petey," I said, standing up. "That helps."

"Let me ask you something," he said.

"Sure."

"What Cleve said. You're not looking for Jake's daughter just to get in her pants?"

"No," I said. Not consciously, anyway, I thought.

"You don't think Feld killed Jake, do you?"

"I don't know. No, I guess not."

"You think maybe his daughter had something to do with it?"

"I hope not."

"If you find out it's not like they're saying in the papers, you'll let me know?"

I hesitated.

"I'd just like to thank whoever did it," he said.

=====*FIFTEEN*=====

IT TOOK ME forty-five minutes to get from Suffolk Downs to Channing College. Route 3 to the Mass Pike West, then eight miles to the exit for Route 16. While I drove, I chain-smoked and thought: Maybe Cleve had me pegged, after all. Maybe all I had was a dirty mind. Then again, I had a sufficient number of rationalizations to cleanse it. If some dark lobe of my brain contrived to seduce Rachel Bloomberg, that was news to me. I flipped a butt out the window and drove on, thinking, What's the harm in asking a few questions?

Channing was a small, pleasant college in Newton. A central pond for winter skating, a narrow, winding car path, plenty of footpaths through well-kept grounds. The buildings were judicious revivals of the nineteenth century, ivy-covered red brick. Taken together, the campus was an exemplar of planning and taste so exquisite that the result remained merely picturesque.

After a student directed me to the Humanities Department, I entered Kenan's outer office at precisely four o'clock. His secretary was wearing a brown tweed suit over a white Victorian blouse. Tortoise-shell glasses hung from her neck on a black string. Wesley College or no Wesley College, she didn't seem pleased to see me.

159

"I wished you'd called ahead," she said. "I'm afraid Professor Kenan won't be able to make the appointment."

"I did call ahead," I said, leaning over her desk. "Miz . . .?"

"Mrs. Vaughan," she said uncomfortably. "He's not in."

I'd broken enough appointments myself to guess that she was covering for him. And her embarrassed eyes told me that she didn't particularly enjoy it. I looked past her face to the door of the inner office. Our celebrated professor was in there, I'd bet. Doing what? Hanging his pecker over his wastebasket, mid-pee? Forcing his antique organ on some underaged hooker?

"You don't mind," I said, walking past her to Kenan's door, "if I wait in here?"

Bolting out of her chair, close on my heels, she whispered plaintively, "You can't go in there," just as I entered the door.

Stephen Kenan sat alone in his office, behind a large oak desk, his head in his hands. He didn't look up. The air in the room was gamy, I noticed, but not from sex or urine. A strong odor of whiskey, a fog of stale cigarette smoke, and—undeniably—the lingering, acrid odor of flatulence.

Mrs. Vaughan tugged at my elbow. "You have to leave," she whispered.

"In a minute."

"I'll have to call campus security."

I rolled my eyes. "Call them. Tell them I'm mad as hell and I'm not going to take any more broken appointments."

Kenan sat with his eyes closed, his gray head wobbling on a pedestal made by his hands, oblivious to the warnings exchanged in front of him.

"Mrs. Vaughan," I soothed her, "I know it can't be easy working for Mr. Kenan. I'm aware of his eccentricities. This will just take a minute."

Her face was full of nobody-knows-the-troubles-I've-seen. "He's in no condition to talk," she replied, barely concealing her contempt.

"I know Stephen," I said familiarly. "Everything's fine."

"Well . . . I mean, it was such an honor to have him at Channing.

The last thing in the world I expected . . ." she faltered, turning toward the door. She looked back at Kenan with disgust. "I'm not a nurse," she said, closing the door behind her.

Kenan still hadn't raised his head. I cleared my throat loudly. "Professor Kenan?"

His head wobbled.

"My name's Thomas Theron. I'm Am. Civ. at Wesley. Up for tenure this month. Professor Kenan?"

Slowly, shakily, Kenan's head levitated off his hands, revealing an enormous, forbidding countenance, chiseled out by time and by some deep agony I could not name. A forehead high and broad and slightly bulbous, a configuration that for centuries has signified genius. Deep ruts creased the length of his jowls and disappeared into the loose flesh of his neck. An intricate inlay of wrinkles fanned out from the corners of huge blue-gray eyes that struggled to focus.

Nonplussed by my presence, the old man—old, even ancient, no matter what Jeanne had said—fumbled in his jacket pocket, found a cigarette, then hung it on his lower lip. He fumbled in his pockets again until I reached over with a light. One long, deep drag ushered forth a harsh, painful-sounding cough. He bent redfaced over his desk, veins pulsing at his temples, tendons tortured out from his neck. His sputtering propelled the cigarette out of his mouth, into his lap, then onto the floor.

What a piece of work is man! I thought, wondering if such a future lay in store for me.

Circling his desk, I retrieved the cigarette. The carpet held a dozen burned spots, and butts with long gray ashes intact. Here and there, gobs of an unidentifiable brown matter spattered the floor. I balanced his cigarette on the teeming ashtray on his desk.

The cough finally let go of him, and he breathed heavily, like an exhausted wrestler. Then he said hoarsely, "What time is it?"

"A little past four," I said.

His mind seemed to work upon this answer as though it contained the Riddle of the Ages.

"Pee-em," I assisted.

Kenan reached for a pot on his desk and poured a tiny amount of amber liquid into a dirty cup. "Teatime," he said. Then he filled the cup from a nearly empty bottle of Scotch that he took from a desk drawer. He took a hard swallow.

The alcohol roused him, braced him, and deepened his voice. "Who," he began with exaggerated precision, "the fuck . . . are you?" A wonderfully theatrical voice, I thought, a voice that endowed a curse—or a banality—with depth and substance.

I told him again who I was. "That name may not ring a—"

"Theron," he said. He belched. "You wrote that book on Peeping Toms and the novel."

"One and the same," I said.

He fixed himself another cup of tea and used the last of the Scotch. He got another cigarette, ignoring the one I'd retrieved from the floor. "Professor"—the word uttered as though it contained a profound insult— "if no one's already told you, then let me be the first. Your book is a piece of shit. Pure . . . unalloyed . . . fucking . . . shit." His eyes glazed, and at the same time he seemed to lift a leg slightly off the seat of his chair. I heard him pass gas.

How noble in form! I thought. How godlike in bearing!

"I guess you won't be giving me an . . . enthusiastic recommendation for tenure," I said.

The Scotch had revived him. His eyes moved distractedly about his office, then rested on me. "Don't be parochial," he said. "Actually, I'm inclined to support your candidacy."

"I'm not following you."

"Of course you're not. Do you know how I'm compensated for evaluating a tenure candidate?"

I shook my head.

"Seven hundred and fifty dollars. Regardless of a candidate's credentials. Most applications are submitted with two published books, sometimes three." He tilted his head back to swallow the remainder of his drink. "You, Theron, have not been so eager as they to impose your tiny mind upon the world. I'm grateful for that. It disposes me to look favorably on your application."

"Thanks," I said and took a deep breath. "Now, what I've really come about—"

"You want to know what to expect from the interview," he interrupted impatiently. "Everyone does."

"No," I said, shaking my head.

"Never mind. I don't mind telling you." As with most men who had lived their lives on some distant planet of thought, Kenan didn't listen, didn't converse. He made speeches. The responses of a second party were merely pauses in a monologue. "Knowing the questions beforehand makes things pleasanter for everybody. For myself, I'll make it very easy indeed. I won't fucking show up. You can't ask for more than that."

"What I really want to know—" I began again, shaking my head furiously.

"Still not satisfied? Let me see. I can give you an idea what old Braithewaite will ask you. He asks the same questions every time. Don't suppose you will be the only ignorant bastard there. Braithewaite likes to start off with some gibberish about the great adventure that is education, the lifelong mutual learning process, the scholar and his disciples, etcetera. Then he will ask, 'What have you learned from your students?' "

"I'm here about you and Rachel Bloomberg," I said.

"Now, you and I know perfectly well that we haven't learned one goddam thing from any snot-nosed student who ever lived. But Braithewaite expects some sentimental answer to his sentimental question. Think of one."

"Rikki Storm," I said.

"Since you're an Americanist, he'll probably recall his days at Oxford, where the librarians keep American literature on a shelf labeled 'Easy Reading.' Then he'll twitter and ask you why you've spent your life studying children's books." Kenan paused to rummage in his bottom drawers, scattering papers, emptying the contents onto his desk. Finally he found a fresh liter of Scotch.

I stared at the junk on his desk and blinked. A stapler, a bundle of letters, three amber vials, a pewter flask, and a small silver pistol. He had tossed the articles onto his desk with apparent randomness, but the pistol—squarish, no larger than the palm of my hand—was positioned where I couldn't help but see it.

"Do you like William Faulkner?" he asked me, breaking the seal on the whiskey bottle.

I hesitated, eyeing the small, menacing weapon between us. "I like some of his novels better than others," I said noncommittally.

Another fierce cough got hold of him. Kenan hacked his throat clear and spat a globule of brown phlegm onto the floor. If nothing else, I'd identified the glop that afflicted the carpet at his feet. He stuck another cigarette in his lips. He picked up the pistol.

"Faulkner has a character named Addie," he said, gesturing casually with the gun, not pointing it at me, but not pointing it away from me either. "She has a rather interesting insight. The reason for living, she says, is to get ready to stay dead a long time." He studied me. "Are you ready to stay dead a long time, Professor Theron?"

The hairs on the back of my neck were bristling. I shook my head slowly.

"Well," Kenan said, "I am. There is nothing in this world so over-valued as consciousness."

He pointed the pistol toward his mouth. His finger moved on the trigger. A click. Silence.

Kenan set the pistol on his desk. "The spirit is willing," he said with a faint smile, "but the flesh is weak."

"The flesh," I suggested shakily, "is smart." Making a show of checking my watch, I said, "I think I've taken up too much of your time."

Kenan tilted back his head, set the whiskey bottle to his lips, and bubbled it. "You're right," he said, shivering. "The flesh preserves it-self. So the spirit resorts to subterfuge. Circumlocution. We commit countless symbolic suicides daily, hourly. Our mishaps, our willful fail-ures, the pain we inflict upon others, all spawned by a failure of nerve to inflict pain upon ourselves." He smiled at me. "What strategies for suicide have you devised?"

I didn't answer.

"Cigarettes? Alcohol?"

I shrugged.

"An amateur," he scoffed. "A novice."

"Would a more sophisticated strategy," I asked, still staring at the pistol on his desk, "include murder?"

Kenan pushed the bottle of whiskey toward me. "I'm sure it happens all the time," he said. "Join me for a drink, professor. I think you're trying to tell me something."

"I'm trying to ask you something," I replied, accepting the bottle, "about Rachel Bloomberg."

He sat quietly for a moment. "So you know my little Jewess?" he said sardonically. "She's very easy to get to know."

"I've seen her."

"You've been stricken?"

"She's very beautiful."

"There's a thorn on her rose," he said. "You may find your brain impaled on the barb of her lightningbolt."

"Is that what happened to you?"

He smiled patiently. "Professor Theron, if you have notions of blackmail, you'll have to wait in line."

"Was Adam Feld trying to blackmail you?"

His face turned surly. "If you peep into others' lives," he said, "you may not like what you find. Your prey might turn on you. Might bite you on the ass."

"I'm only trying to help," I said quickly. "A certain man thinks you might be involved in two murders. He's got a lot of power, and some peculiar ideas to go with it. He won't hesitate to hurt you. Whether you're involved or not, I think it would be better for you to tell me."

"You want to save me?" he asked incredulously. He began to laugh, and the laugh produced another body-wrenching cough. Recovering, he whispered breathlessly, "You haven't been listening. I don't want to be saved." A wry, contemptuous smile curled his lips. "Bring your powerful friends with you next time."

I sighed and turned toward the door.

"Do you know what this interview has cost you?" Kenan said. "Think hard."

I turned back. "Tenure."

He nodded. "At the very least."

═══SIXTEEN═══

THE NEXT MORNING I called Elizabeth. After a brief, awkward exchange of greetings, I startled her with an invitation to dinner that night.

She might have made a face at the other end of the line, but all she said was, "Can't."

"How about tomorrow night? I'll even force down some quiche and salad," I offered. "On me."

"If you're trying to confuse me, Thomas, you're succeeding," she sighed. "Shouldn't we think a minute before we jump right back into—"

"This is strictly business," I replied. "Well, almost strictly. I want a professional consultation. I'll pay the going rate." I probably shouldn't have offered to pay. Beth worked at Booker Hills Institute, a posh mental-health clinic in affluent Milton. Booker Hills did a booming business in mental difficulties symptomatic of little more than excess wealth: alcohol rehab, stress, depression, I've-got-it-all-but-I-still-feel-like-shit. Occasionally an exotic sexual deviation. The fees went off the scale. The rates had to be high, Beth argued, so that the wealthy clientele would *value* the therapy they received. Hmmm.

"You're not faking a mental breakdown for my benefit?" Beth said. "Playing for sympathy?"

"No, Beth. I just want to pose a few abstract problems and get your reaction."

"What kind of abstract problems?"

"You might brush up on suicidal murderers. Depression and violence. Maybe obsessions."

"Anything else?" she said dryly.

"Maybe May-December romances, if you get a chance."

"I don't believe . . . Do you remember how many fights we had about my job? All mumbo-jumbo, you said. Patrician witch doctors, you said. And what was it you called my clients? Macabre nabobs? Remember?"

And I was right, I thought. "Elizabeth, we don't have to rehash our opposing world-views. I'm just working on this problem and I want to cover all the bases, that's all."

After a few seconds of silence she said, "Strictly business? You pay my usual fee?"

"Right. And dinner to boot."

I could tell that she still didn't believe me. "Thomas, do you remember the first time we slept together?"

"I remember the first time fine," I said. "It's the last time I have trouble with."

"That was supposed to be business, too. You said you wanted to talk to me about my essay on Cotton Mather."

"Okay, Beth," I said, beginning to regret that I hadn't just gone to the library and checked out a few psychology texts. "Maybe I *am* having second thoughts about us. But I'm asking you to dinner because I need a professional opinion. As for our first time in the sack, don't try to paint me as the young prof with the lickerish eye. As I recall, you'd been planning to seduce me for weeks. At least that's what you said while you were unfastening my belt buckle."

We battled a while longer, each of us knowing too well the other's softest spots. We probed efficiently, like physicians, familiar with the tender regions where the slightest touch would elicit pain. But battle fatigue eventually set in. We fell into reminiscence. And before we said good-bye, we even managed a laugh or two. She agreed to dinner, warning me, "It will cost you."

At a little past eight that evening, I was sitting across a booth from Frank DeVito, the manager of the Pink Lady. Alex had talked to him. He had been expecting me. He was forthcoming. But what was coming forth wasn't much.

"Rikki Storm?" Frank was saying. "What's to tell? She does good work. Hustles more than her share of drinks. Gorgeous girl, got her muff shaved down to look like—whatchamacallit?—Zorro?"

"I think she was trying for a lightning bolt," I interrupted. "Rikki *Storm.*"

"Shit," Frank said, closing his right eye against the smoke from his cigar, "I never thought of that. You musta seen her."

"Yes." The side booth where we sat served as Frank's makeshift office. The neck of a low-wattage fluorescent lamp bent close over a stack of receipts. Handmade signs were taped to the mirrored wall next to us. DANCERS AND BAR PEOPLE CHECK SCHEDULES CAREFULLY. Frank wore a well-tailored jacket that hid most of his belly. His Vandyke would have served as a beard on a face of normal size. Frighteningly hirsute; a single black eyebrow spanned his protruding forehead. His facial hair, I was thinking, must have nourished itself at the expense of his brain.

Frank excused himself and chewed out one of the dancers—for my benefit, it seemed. Alex must have insinuated that I was a VIP. He came back and sat down with an air of satisfaction. "Keep 'em on their toes," he said. "Ain't none of us here for our health. In this business, a dancer's got to get down and spread it open, lickety-split. You know, an unobstructed view. Show a little pink. Ain't like the old days, vaudeville. Guys now got to see it all." He surveyed the handful of customers at the bar. "That's the only thing'll keep these fuckers heads outta their beer. They don't give two shits about dancing."

"Rikki Storm?" I prompted, checking my watch.

"She works the second shift, three nights a week. Didn't show night before last. Hasn't shown tonight."

"Is that it?" I asked.

"Whaddaya mean?"

"Do you know anything about her? Does she have any special problem . . ."

"Mister, that's all these girls have got is problems. They got problems with drugs, they got problems with men, they got problems with each other. And," he said with ludicrous solemnity, "they fuck up, they got problems with me."

I must have looked annoyed, because Frank said, "Tell you what. If you want to know about Rikki, ask Norma. I hear she lives with Rikki." There was a crazy gleam in Frank's eyes as he spoke.

"Are you saying that they share an apartment," I said, "or do they *live* together?" I had the feeling he was going to tell me something I hadn't planned on.

"Well, I ain't never seen 'em humping each other, if that's what you mean. But yeah, I'd say they *live* together. Norma's worked here for years, and I know sure as hell she's queer for women."

Perhaps I had harbored some plot to seduce Rachel. Otherwise, why did Frank's revelation depress me?

"But who cares?" he said generously. "Dykes make the best strippers anyhow. Good actresses. And they hustle the hell outta the drinks, which is where we make our money. If a real charmer comes in, a straight girl will sometimes dawdle over her drinks. They can't help theirselves. But Norma's real cold-blooded about it. I don't care if Frank Sinatra was buying her drinks, she'd keep sucking 'em down. Run his tab outta sight. And leave him cold the first time he don't reach for his wallet."

"Norma's a dancer?"

"Yeah, a career girl. Been working here longer than I have. She used to be the best, a real looker. Now she's got to work hard for it. She don't like that."

"That's not the most appealing name I've heard for a stripper."

"What?" Frank said. "Oh yeah. She goes by Ursula Undress. All the young girls tell her she ought to change it on account of it's too old-timey. Myself, I think it's a good one. Somebody told me there was an actress that had that same name."

"Almost," I said. "Is Norma a peroxide blond?" I asked. "Beginning to show her age?"

Frank looked at me. "You know 'em all, don't you?"

"You think I could talk to her?"

"You kidding me?" Frank laughed. "Mister, these girls'll talk to a leper if he's buying."

I moved to the bar. In a matter of seconds I felt a body hugging me from behind, insistently molding itself to me. Arms circling my shoulders; a fog of perfume enveloping me.

"Frank said you wanted some company."

I turned and saw Ursula's face. Up close, the effect was startling. A thick mask of makeup, caricatural, more appropriately viewed from a distance. Tiny clumps of mascara hung at the tips of her false lashes. Hair frayed from repeated bleaching. Black roots. Less than a foot separated our noses, and I still didn't know what she looked like.

"You know Rikki Storm," I said.

"Ooo," she replied throatily, sweetened breath washing over me, "you've got good taste. But Rikki's not here tonight. Why don't I just fill in? My name's Ursula," she whispered, her hand encircling, caressing the bottom of my tie. "What's yours?"

The bartender leaned toward us across the bar. "You want to buy Ursula a drink?" he asked me, placing a cocktail napkin in front of her. Everyone helped hustle the drinks. The dancers tipped the bartenders from their commission.

After I paid for the drink, I said, "I think I may be able to help Rikki."

"Ooo, that's nice," Ursula said. "You want to help me too? Why don't we just carry our drinks over to one of the back booths and we'll help each other?" Her hand was working me over beneath the bar. Expert technique; from above the bar, a plainclothes cop couldn't see her upper arm moving.

Ursula had already finished one skimpy drink—nonalcoholic, of course—and the bartender brought her a second, extracting another ten dollars from my change on the bar.

"Let me put this another way. I don't want to help Rikki Storm. I want to help Rachel Bloomberg."

Ursula pulled her hand from my lap. Her mask of sexual availability vanished. "Who are you?"

"I'm just who I said I was. Thomas Theron. I live in Cambridge. And I happen to be caught up in the same events I think Rachel is caught up in. If you're suspicious, I don't blame you." I offered her the same assurance I'd offered Kenan. "I promise, I'm only trying to help."

Similar result. "Why don't you try minding your own fucking business?" she hissed. "Rachel doesn't need help."

"She may not. I hope she doesn't. But there are some people around who think she might have something to do with her father's death. With Adam Feld's death. I'm willing to believe she doesn't. I just want to know."

"What other people?"

"Just other people. And they're not nice. I'm nice."

Ursula laughed. There was no humor in it, only bitterness. "You're nice? You asshole. Do you know how many times I talk to nice guys from Cambridge? What are you, a lawyer maybe? You don't dress good enough to be a doctor. Maybe a hip Cambridge architect?"

"Professor," I said.

"Figures. Professors are the worst. No money, lots of bullshit. Always want to talk their way into something free."

Free? I thought. She'd put away three drinks now at nine dollars apiece. And all I was getting was a hard time.

"Every damn one of them acts nice," she was saying. "Like they pride themselves on how nice they are. You wanna know what's behind it?"

At these prices, I thought, no.

"Hate," she told me anyway. "They hate women. They want to use you. Get their rocks off. Simple as that. Give me a truck driver from Brighton any day. At least they don't kid you about what they want. They buy you a drink, then say, 'Give me a little head, Red.' None of these fucking mind games. The only difference with you professional types is that you bullshit more. Maybe you don't even know yourself what you want. But what it all comes down to, what everybody's saying is, 'Come on, let me fuck you.' Ditchdigger or doctor, truck driver or professor. You know what I see? A mouth to bullshit you with, two fists to hit you with, a cock to fuck you with, and a wallet to get your attention. That's every man who ever lived. That's what love is."

She wasn't making things easier. I wondered what personal history provoked such venom. "You've got reason to be suspicious. I won't argue with your view of men. Hell, you're probably right—"

"Shit," she snarled. "That's the way all you white-collars start out. Yeah, you say, you know how men are. But you're not like that. You're in touch with your goddam emotions. You want to get to know me as a person. Then a few drinks later all the nasty shit comes out." She paused to gulp about five dollars worth of her drink. "Truck drivers just want an old-fashioned hump. You Cambridge types want the heavy stuff. Tie me up. Hurt me a little. Asshole sex. Or maybe get tied up themselves." She glared at me. "Is that what you like? You want me to tie you up? Pee on you?"

I was paying for this? "All right," I sighed. "Just listen. Then I'll leave you alone. If you hate my guts, fine. If you care about Rachel, hear me out. I know that you and Rachel have been moonlighting for Adam Feld. I also hear that Rachel had good reason to hate her father. Had a bad home life, mother left early, whatever. About Feld, I don't know. But I do know that some people out there think she's got something to do with all this. And since you live with her—I don't know, love her maybe—could be you're somehow in it too."

"I take it back," Ursula said angrily. "You're not like all the guys from Cambridge. You're fucking crazy."

"Then tell me how I'm wrong."

"Read the papers. Feld killed Rachel's father, then OD'd. And fucking good riddance. I can't think of two men who needed killing more than they did."

"Some people don't believe it happened that way."

"So? Who cares? Who are these people you keep talking about?"

"People who'll hurt Rachel unless they get some answers."

She fell silent for a moment. The mask of makeup emptied of expression, as though the face behind it had withdrawn.

"Do you know Stephen Kenan?" I persisted.

"Buy me another drink."

I dug into my pocket again and brought out a twenty. "Stephen Kenan?" I prompted.

"Never heard of him."

"Well, Rachel's heard of him." I took from my wallet a small photo of Kenan that I'd cut from the dust jacket of his book on Puritan theology. I showed it to her.

"The professor?" she laughed, her interest momentarily piqued. "We call him Daddy-boy."

Daddy-boy? I thought.

"Somebody ought to lock him up."

"Why's that?"

"That's what you do with crazy people."

"Tell me about him."

She handed back the picture. "I'm not telling you shit. Why should I?"

"Because I've bought you sixty dollars worth of ginger ale?"

"Kiss my ass."

"Tell me about Rachel, then."

Ursula's expression transformed once more, again theatrical, ruttish, full of lewd insinuations. She snuck her hand back into my lap. "That's what this is all about," she cooed, "isn't it?" She rubbed my penis through my trouser leg. "Rachel's the most beautiful thing you've ever seen, isn't she? Everybody wants her for something. Feld wanted her to make money. Daddy-boy wants her to keep him from killing himself." She was massaging me harder now, approaching the boundary of pain. She moved her face close to mine, the eyes behind the prurient mask alive with disgust. "And Jake," she whispered. "Old Jake just liked to rape her."

"Her . . . ?" I managed.

"What do you want?" she urged. "You want to fuck her too?"

I shook my head.

Ursula maneuvered a testicle between her thumb and forefinger. Before I could move, she squeezed, familiar with the particular pressure that elicits pain. "You can't," she hissed, kneading me. "Stay away from her. She's mine."

She released me and left. My eyes began to water.

=====SEVENTEEN=====

NO, THOMAS, I TOLD MYSELF, lying in bed till early afternoon. Pull your little turtle head back into your turtle shell.

I'd wanted to know the harm in asking a few questions. Now I knew. An alcoholic, suicidal, and very probably psychotic scholar had pulled a gun on me—sort of—and then scuttled my fading hopes for tenure. A wildly confused feminist had lectured me on misogyny, tried to sterilize me, and made me pay for the privilege. And for whom had I suffered these humiliations? A young lesbian who'd uttered only two words to me. "Eat shit." No, Thomas, I repeated. The world is no place for you.

Eventually I rolled out of bed and got down on my hands and knees amid the snarl of manuscript pages on the living room floor, sorting and restoring them to the Three Boxes. By three o'clock I'd finished the task. I lifted to my desk the box containing the aborted novel, *Helpless Laughter.* Two hours later I'd skimmed all 244 pages. Not bad, really. Salvageable. The only serious flaw was not with the book, but with myself. I'd never given myself to it completely, never been desperate enough to risk a total commitment. Well, what was stopping me now? Soon to be unemployed, no prospects, and a little over $25,000 to see me through. A fresh cigarette at my lip, I turned a fresh sheet of paper into the typewriter carriage, nurturing a fresh hope in my uncertain heart.

Two hours passed and the sheet of paper stared back at me, pristine. The ashtray teemed with ash and filters. My hope remained, modified. It would take time, I assured myself resolutely, to retrieve the elusive rhythm of fiction.

Dressing as spiffily as my wardrobe would permit, I walked to Grendel's Den to meet Beth for dinner. What other past failures, I wondered, might I begin to salvage that day?

"So what are these abstract problems you were telling me about?" Beth asked, sitting over a plate of baba ghanouj.

"I don't know," I replied diffidently. "I'm sort of losing interest."

She eyed me impatiently. "I knew it."

"What?"

"I knew that you were just trying to get me out. Remember? You lost interest in that Cotton Mather essay too. I bet you've lost interest in paying my consultation fee, too."

We were sitting at a small table in the no-smoking section of Grendel's Den. Elizabeth was looking spectacular in a black, clingy knit dress, a single strand of pearls around her slender, model's neck. A touch of makeup—which she rarely used—yielded dramatic results. Had she dressed for me? I sat there trying to recall the secret places beneath her clothes, once familiar. I was getting ideas.

"Calm down," I sighed. "I'm not backing out." I didn't tell Beth everything, but I mentioned enough details so that she would take me seriously.

"*The* Vincent Ciullo?" Beth asked, eyes wide. "The gangster they always mention in the papers when something bad happens?"

"You know me," I said, scooping a large dollop of hummos onto a wedge of raw onion. "Never a dull moment."

"What's he like?"

"Not what you'd expect. He's an Ezra Pound freak."

"The Ezra Pound?" she teased. "The poet you made us read in that survey course? The one nobody could understand?"

I nodded. "Ciullo has some funny ideas."

"Such as?"

"I don't know. I guess he gets it from some perverted reading of Pound. Something a philosopher might call 'amoral vitalism.' "

"Translation, please?"

"Any passion is better than no passion at all. Which means roughly that it's okay to pillage, loot, and murder—just so long as you don't sit around the den all day watching TV."

"No offense, Thomas, but if that's the case, what does he see in you? Didn't he notice the *TV Guide* you carry in your back pocket?"

"Clever," I said. "Actually, he thinks I'm seething with repressed passion. Thinks that I secretly want to escape my cozy library corner. Thinks I'm not suited for life with my nose in a book."

"He's got a point," Beth smiled. "You're gonna ruin your eyes."

I'd stuck a cigarette in my mouth, unlit. "Do your patients enjoy this laughing-psychologist routine?"

"Sorry."

I'd shocked her by ordering tofu lasagna; I didn't shock her by actually eating it. "I don't know why the hell he picks on me to practice his half-assed analysis," I said. "It's not like I do anything to invite it."

"Do you want a truthful response to that?" Beth asked, studying me soberly.

"Only if the meter's running."

She ignored me. "I don't know if you realize this, Thomas, but you sail through life with a very superior expression on your face. It's as though you have this sign stamped on your forehead that says 'All the Answers.' But all people ever get from you is smug cynicism. If you go around ridiculing everything, you're in effect claiming that you know the right way to do things. The way that's not ridiculous." She tried to fix me with an honest gaze. "Except," she said, "you never *do* anything. You just sit there and make jokes. That's what frustrates people. I know it sure as hell frustrated me."

"Haven't you heard? Behind the mask of every clown, there's the soul of a tragedian."

"See, you're incapable of saying anything serious." Her voice dropped with resignation. "Maybe it's congenital. Maybe you've got a gene for glibness."

"I'm a nurturist. It's all environment."

"See? Come on," she prompted, "say something serious."

"Hell, I don't know." I thought for a second. "Gross national product?"

She was right. I couldn't. She started laughing.

"I love you?" I tried.

Beth laughed harder.

"Okay, you tell me something," I interrupted. "Seriously. Did you get dressed up for me?"

Her smile vanished. "Forget whatever it is you're thinking, Thomas. I'm meeting Breck later."

We finished and moved to the bar downstairs. I took care of the dinner check. Reluctantly. I didn't like paying good money for food that didn't have meat in it. The restaurant upstairs was Beth's favorite in Cambridge, the bar beneath it was mine. The owners of Grendel's had won a liquor license after a long court battle with the church adjacent to the restaurant. The Supreme Court had finally declared unconstitutional a Cambridge law that prohibited the sale of liquor within a five-hundred-foot radius of a church. A high-powered Harvard law professor had won the case with ridiculous ease. Every time I got drunk there, I considered myself merely promoting a healthy separation of church and state; I would stumble home secure in the knowledge that the Constitution was safe.

Beth, oblivious to the predatory stares she received when we entered the bar, sipped a brandy Alexander through a cocktail straw. Without naming names, I described Kenan to her, his apparent obsession with a young stripper, his seeming preoccupation with suicide, his alcoholism, his tragic shortcomings in personal hygiene. "He's got what amounts to a death wish," I said.

"You understand," she said, "without interviews, without talking to this person, what I say won't mean much."

I nodded. "I'm just spinning this out of thin air, anyway."

"Well, generally the goal of suicide isn't to do away with oneself, per se. It's more of an attempt to rid oneself of unacceptable pain. The man you're describing is obviously in a great deal of pain."

"Do you think the pain could lead him to commit murder?"

She raised her hands diffidently. "That's outside my clinical experience. Of course, it happens. Just pick up the *New York Post*. Husband kills his wife, then himself. Except the man you're telling me about hasn't committed suicide. He just talks about it."

"Talks like he's in love with the idea."

"It's absurd to draw conclusions from that," she said.

"I understand."

What I didn't understand was why a man across the room kept staring at us. I'd noticed him upstairs in the restaurant, too. Don't be paranoid, I told myself. He's looking at Beth. Men in bars always looked at Beth.

"Well?" she said.

"Let me see," I began distractedly. "What about insomnia?" Insomnia, I figured, would be right up Beth's alley. All those clients of hers lying awake at night, worrying about fluctuating interest rates. "I've heard that dream deprivation can cause psychosis, hallucinations when someone's awake."

She shook her head. "Not really. Not if a person is healthy. That's largely a myth." She paused, studying me. "Is something bothering you?"

The man kept staring. A handsome man, wearing an expensive trench coat, blond hair styled impeccably; he looked like a newscaster. Blue eyes clear, unswerving, and apparently riveted on me. He reminded me of Adam Feld. Did Adam have a partner I didn't know about?

"Speaking of hallucinations," I said, "have a look behind you. Discreetly. Am I imagining things, or is the man sitting in the corner staring at us?"

Beth turned toward him, then turned back to me. "Which man?"

"The blond Geraldo Rivera," I said.

"Not nice," she said. "That's Breck. I told you I was meeting him later."

I'd seen hostility in those eyes, after all. Right emotion, I thought, wrong reason. "He's been watching you like a hawk," I said, smiling, relishing his jealousy. I moved my chair closer to Beth and leaned toward her, cutting off his view. "He looks a little pissed off."

"Do you want to talk about your mystery man or not?" she said impatiently.

"What's Breck do for a living?"

"Why don't I invite him over and you ask him?"

"No way. Not while I'm paying for your time. So what's he do?" I was betting salesman. That's why he reminded me of Feld. Something crass, maybe. Something philistine. Something in the world of getting and spending.

"If you had ever come with me to the symphony, you'd know. He's first violin in the BSO," she said. "Satisfied?"

"La-ti-da," I said.

She ignored me.

"I bet he's got tiny, sensitive hands, huh?"

"As a matter of fact," she said pointedly, "he's got very large hands. Does this mean you're through with our psychology lesson?"

A moment's hesitation. "All right," I said, resigning myself. I told Beth the few unsavory facts I had gleaned from Rachel Bloomberg's past: outrageously abused by her father, a victim of Jake's grotesque beliefs in breeding; a mother who had early on escaped similar assaults; and finally, I said, blessed—more probably cursed—with a face and physique so stunning that it provoked obsessions in strangers.

"Including you?"

I said it again, testily. "Jesus. I'm just trying to help her."

"Okay. Just asking."

"Lately, she's been sharing her bed with an aging stripper named"—I cleared my throat—"Ursula Undress. Norma, when she's off duty. Norma's view of life makes mine seem hopelessly romantic."

"That," Beth said, "I'd pay to see. A colleague of mine, a feminist, does some community service in her off-hours. She works with prostitutes, some dancers. A lot of working girls, she says, are drawn to other women. Technically they're not homosexual. They just seek affection from other women because they never get emotional satisfaction from men."

"I know. Ursula didn't phrase it so delicately. She didn't give me much of a chance to feel sorry for her."

"Ah, poor baby," Beth said dryly. "She didn't see right off that you're pure of heart? She wouldn't let you make it all better?"

"Don't throw stones," I said. "What the hell would this colleague of yours have done? Let her talk for fifty minutes, then send a bill to Blue Cross for a hundred twenty-five bucks? Great."

"Okay," she relented. "Let's not get started. What is it that's really eating you?"

"I don't know. Rachel, I guess."

"Yes?"

"I keep assuming that she's not involved, at least not primarily. Maybe that's too sentimental."

She tried to hide a look of astonishment. "Patricide?"

"Why not? From what I'm learning about her father, who could blame her? Statistically, family violence is a better bet than old professors heading for the bughouse."

"Well, more women *are* committing murder," Beth offered. "One of the most unpleasant side effects of liberation."

I gulped my drink. "I get the feeling that I'm missing an obvious fact. But I'm tired of thinking about it. I'm tired of talking about it." I looked across the room. Breck still scrutinized our every move, like a dog waiting to be fed. "I'd hate for all this depressing talk to ruin your evening."

"I'm afraid what I've told you doesn't amount to much," she said. "Sorry."

I shrugged, excused myself, and went to the john. What it amounted to, I thought, was horse manure. With a disgruntled sigh, I stood in front of the urinal, propping my hand on the bathroom wall. A short poem confronted me at eye level. Pretentious Cambridge graffiti. Title, "Jane Goodall Among the Apes":

> Opposéd thumbs, opposéd toes,
> What dreams this trait suggests!
> My hands forced high above my head
> While heavy feet molest.

Well, Ursula Undress had a point about Cambridge types. They hated women, only they kidded themselves about it. Tried to turn their hate into art. The thing was, in a better mood, I would have found the poem amusing. Pretentious, yes, but not too bad.

Someone tapped me on the shoulder. "I'd like a word with you."

Turning my head slowly, careful not to spoil my trousers, I saw Breck. I had to look up to him. He was big for a violinist.

"Why don't we go outside?" I suggested, thinking, where Beth can see us.

"In private, if you don't mind."

"Who are you?" I just wanted to hear him say it.

"I'm Breck."

I smiled. "Is that Breck oily, dry, or normal?"

"I wish I had a nickel . . ." he sighed. "Elizabeth told me you had a mouth."

"So you just followed me in here," I said, zipping up, "to get a peek at what else I've got. Beth tell you about that too?"

"She told me," Breck said evenly, bringing himself full height, "that you always talked about it a lot more than you did it."

I rolled my eyes. "But not you, huh? You're the good farmer. Got to plow your land every day."

"I don't want any shit off you, Theron. I'm just telling you to quit screwing around in Elizabeth's life. Give it a rest. If you want to crawl in a corner and rot, fine. Just do it in private. Don't bring her into it."

"Ah, Breck," I sighed. "Nothing climbs up my ass like a roughneck violinist." I felt a little embarrassed, a little childish, exchanging insults with a rival in the men's room. But I was enjoying it, too. A pleasant switch from the time I'd spent with Ciullo, Feld, Gerald, et al. They'd inhibited me, left me tongue-tied. I needed oral exercise.

"You see, Breck—" I began.

I never saw the punch. Blackness, then a blurred light. A brief but intense dream transpired. Wild faces peering into mine. Loud, angry voices. Awake in the emergency room of Cambridge City Hospital. What felt like knitting needles tried to pierce my skull from the inside out. Beth leaning over me.

"How you feeling?" she said gently.

"Aw shit," I muttered groggily.

"You jerk."

I tried to sit up. The pain kept me down. "Ah . . . goddammit. Me a jerk? Ouch. He took a swing at me for no reason."

"You're both jerks. He said you provoked him."

"I'll provoke his ass in jail. I hope he broke his goddam sensitive hands."

"He's fine," she said. "He barely grazed you. You banged your nose on the edge of the sink. I think you lost your balance, trying to duck."

"How bad?"

"Doctor said it's broken in two places. No concussion."

I silently transported my mind to every appendage, taking stock, seeking out other regions of pain. My right knee throbbed. When I looked back at Beth, she smiled. "What did you say to him, anyway?"

"Say to him! I told him I hated Wagner. Then the blue-eyed bastard cold-cocked me."

"Calm down," she said softly. Beth's knit dress was rumpled and splotched. With my blood, I guessed.

"You got a mirror?"

She rummaged in her purse, brought out a compact, and handed it to me. Gruesome. Two enormous plugs of cotton had been stuffed into my nostrils. A wide band of gauze was taped across my nose. Black skin was visible at the edges of the gauze, black from the blood deposits beneath the skin. By tomorrow, I knew, color would spread across my cheeks, beneath my eyes. Hideous bruises of yellow and green.

"Where's my car?"

"Wherever you parked it. I got you here in mine. It wasn't easy. You were unconscious for a few seconds. Scared Breck to death. He thought he'd killed you."

"Good."

"I can give you a ride home," she offered gently.

"I wouldn't want this to spoil your fun," I said glumly.

"It won't. Breck and I had a tiff."

"Is that what you have with a violinist? A tiff?"

"If you really want to know, it was more serious than that."

A half an hour to fill out insurance and release forms, another twenty minutes to wait while a wheelchair was brought around for me. "You got to ride outta here," the nurse said, casting an unsympathetic eye on my bloodied clothes. "Policy."

Beth waited outside in her car, an old Ford Granada. I apologized for the blood on the seatcovers. We drove to my apartment silently, a gentle confusion in the air. Inside, I poured myself a bourbon.

"Put water in mine," Beth said.

We sat quietly, drinking.

"How's the nose?"

"A lot better, now that I've shut up."

She carried her drink around the apartment, diplomatically withholding comment. "What's that in the typewriter?" she asked. "Resurrecting Lowell?"

"No. I sort of started fiddling with the old novel this afternoon."

"I'm glad." She looked at me. "As long as you're not using it to escape."

"That's not the sort of question you can answer—until it's too late."

She came and sat next to me, her eyes serious. "I've missed you," she said. "A lot. Despite—"

"Despite what's-his-name."

"Yes. It's lonely. Thing is, I felt sort of lonely when we were together too."

"It's a basic condition," I said.

"Have you been seeing anyone?"

"No."

"Happy?"

"As a lark," I said solemnly. "Now if only I could breathe through my nose."

Beth set her tumbler on the packing carton I used as a coffee table. "Well . . ." she said.

"Well?"

"You going to be okay?"

"I don't think my nose is going to let me sleep," I said, testing it gingerly with my fingertips. "We should have stopped to get that prescription filled."

She looked at me for a long time, her eyes studious, as though she were adding columns in an invisible ledger. "Maybe I can fix that," she said softly, putting an arm on my shoulder and planting a small kiss on my cheek. She rose and walked toward the bedroom. I followed her.

Inside, I watched as she pulled her black dress over her head—the moment, all lovers know, to stare frankly. I reacquainted myself with the secret places I'd been striving to remember all evening. A flesh-colored little nothing of a bra; a minuscule strip of white bikini panties, Saks Fifth Avenue. Gloriously bare-legged. All firmness and youth.

The sight of her made my heart hurt. Made my nose hurt too.

Then she was nude. "Let's get you out of those clothes," she said. I eased myself onto the bed.

I paused. "You're not doing this to get back at Breck?"

"Don't ruin it, Thomas," she whispered. "I'm here. You're not fighting Breck for territory. This is what I want."

She unfastened my belt. I raised my hips while she slid my trousers off, acquiescing in my role of injured warrior. My shirt came off, more awkwardly, then my socks. She sat beside me on the bed, hands massaging my chest.

She smiled at me, tenderly, playfully. "You look like a hockey goalie," she said.

"Beauty and the beast. You like that?"

"Will it hurt for me to kiss you?" she asked.

"Depends on where you kiss," I said.

"Mmmm," she murmured, leaving a path of wet kisses down my neck, down my chest, down my stomach. Down.

"Mmmm," I replied.

Later I pulled her toward me. "I want to try it," I said.

"You think you're up to it?"

"What is it weightlifters say? No pain, no gain?" I eased myself— ow!—onto her with underwater movements.

"Careful," she said. "There."

"Yes."

"Hallo."

Each exertion, I soon discovered, each surge of blood through veins, triggered a fresh torment to my nose. Every time I gave myself to the pleasure, a thump of pain brought me back. The golden ring that awaited me seemed cruelly positioned at the end of a gauntlet. I didn't complain. Please, God, I prayed silently, let me enjoy this.

"You sure this isn't hurting?" she whispered gently. "You're not very hard."

"Maybe I lost too much blood," I smiled painfully. "Feels great." My nose not a nose, but a raw pulsing nerve. Please, God, I prayed.

"Let me get on top," she whispered. "That will help."

It helped. At first. The pain returned like a brutal tax on luxury. I briefly considered feigning an orgasm, simply to stop the sharp pounding of blood through my nose. It would have been easy enough. Cries of pain and cries of sexual pleasure are not easily distinguished.

"Beth?"

She paused. "Yes?"

"We'd better give it a rest. I—"

"Hurting bad?"

I nodded.

She gently took herself off me and snuggled up.

"What I like best, anyway, is holding you."

"I know," she said.

"Give me a raincheck?"

"Mmm," she nodded. "Think you can get to sleep?"

"Sure."

Long after she had fallen asleep, I watched her. The mingled pleasure and pain of life. Not poignantly mingled, I thought. Just mingled.

In the middle of the night the phone rang. Still half awake from keeping my nose company, I picked up the receiver after the third ring. I glanced at the clock. A quarter past three.

"Yes?" I whispered.

"Thomas Theron."

"Yes."

"You said you wanted to help," the voice said. "So help."

I was fully awake. "Ursula? I mean, Norma?"

"No. Rachel."

"You need help?"

"More like Norma told you. We can help each other."

"How's that?"

"You wanna know who killed Adam and . . . uh . . . my old man?"

"Tell me."

"You know the Redmont Hotel? On a side street, between Washington and Tremont? About two blocks from the Pink Lady."

"Yes." I passed the Redmont every time I went to the Zone.

"Meet me there."

"Now?"

"Uh-uh. Four o'clock tomorrow, suite 914. That good for you?"

"Yes."

"Don't be late," she said. "Don't be early, either."

"Okay. That it?"

"Yeah . . . wait, no. Get me a cup of coffee on your way over," she said and hung up.

Replacing the receiver, I jostled Beth. She rolled over and draped her leg over my stomach. I stayed awake the rest of the night.

=EIGHTEEN=

For the first time in nearly two weeks, a classroom hour passed without incident. Gerald's appearance the previous hour, now followed by the startling effect of my grossly discolored nose, unnerved my students, rousing them to fresh—if uneasy—participation. It happened, too, that our topic sustained the mood. I lectured on *The Mysterious Stranger,* the satanic offering of Twain's decline, a dark shudder of old age.

After class I walked to Talbot House, my blood tingling with caffeine and nicotine, my mind riveted on a single question. What name would Rachel utter? Kenan? Ursula? A confession of her own guilt? Perhaps a name I had never heard? I mounted the steps to Talbot House, my expression rapt, like a man who expects to hear a final secret of life divulged.

"My God," Jeanne said, her eyes wide, "what happened to you?"

"A melodrama," I began, preparing to recount the details. Curiously, no questions followed.

"Thomas," she said, "there's something I need to tell you."

I paused. The nervousness in her tone worried me. "Bad?"

"Sort of," she said. "It's—"

189

"If it's bad, I don't want to hear it," I interrupted.

"It's something you have to know—"

"If it's tenure down the tubes, I already—"

"Would you give me a minute? This is not easy for me to say."

"Sorry, I'm a little keyed up."

"Okay," she said, collecting herself. "You know that I've been seeing David again. I mentioned it the other night. We've been dating, re-member?"

I nodded, wondering if our night together had seemed to her a standing invitation to swap marital woes.

"Well, David has been seeing someone else, and this girl has been seeing someone else. You know Cambridge social life. Like a soap opera, right?"

"Jeanne," I said, "what's the bad part? I'm not following you."

"Well, shit," she said, "there's no pleasant way to say this. The girl David's been seeing thinks she has herpes. So David thinks he might have been exposed. So I . . ."

The sentence dangled ominously. I thought of Old Testament gen-ealogies: Shem begat Terah, Terah begat Abraham . . . "So I might have it," I said.

"Maybe. I'm still hoping it's a false alarm."

Nice going, Thomas, I thought. Give Beth herpes. Part of the di-vorce settlement. Split everything right down the middle.

"I just found out last night," Jeanne said. "You angry?"

"Doesn't anyone get VD anymore?" I began, but the misery in her eyes stopped me short. "Hell," I consoled her, "these things happen. Let's not worry about it until you're sure." But I was thinking, Herpes are like diamonds. They're forever.

"There's something else," she said.

God, I panicked, don't tell me the Ortho-Gel was defective. "Okay." I mustered my courage. "What?"

"Braithewaite wants to see you. It's funny, but this is the first time I've ever seen him pissed. What'd you do?"

"Hell if I know," I sighed. "All right, set up an appointment. To-morrow would be okay."

Jeanne shook her head. "He's in there now. He said he wanted to see you as soon as you came in."

"Tell him you haven't seen me," I said. "He won't know the difference."

Just then, Braithewaite's office door opened and he peered out. "Is that you, Thomas?" he said. "Could I have a word with you?"

"How about tomorrow, Gayle? I'm a little pressed for time," I lied.

"Why don't you step in here for a moment, Thomas," he repeated.

He must have been worked up. Usually he could take no for an answer.

Jeanne and I exchanged a private glance. I entered the chairman's office just as one of his young, otherworldly protégés was leaving. Inside, Braithewaite eased his frail body behind his desk, rested his mild eyes on me, and shook his head sadly. Whether out of delicacy or a profound obliviousness, he didn't comment on the gangrenous-looking excrescence at the center of my face.

"I've been getting some disturbing phone calls," he announced quietly.

Starting at the top of the list, I suggested, "Potter's parents?"

"Among others, yes."

"I can explain that, Gayle—"

"No need to, Thomas. For now."

"Professor Kenan?" I tried.

"Stephen? Should I be expecting a call from Stephen?"

I shook my head and shut up. Better let him do the talking.

Braithewaite looked at the ceiling for about half a minute—attempting, I supposed, to diffuse his gentle anger. Finally he asked me, "Thomas, do you know a man named Vincent Ciullo?"

Chew-low. The two-syllable, Italianate chorus to my life.

"Slightly, Gayle. He's an acquaintance. What's up?"

"He thinks highly of you . . . a charming man . . . friendly . . ."

"Yes?"

I watched his mind carefully debate some fragile point of etiquette.

". . . wondrously detailed knowledge of Ezra Pound . . ."

"Yes?"

"I don't know precisely how to put this, Thomas. Perhaps ours wasn't a meeting of the minds. On the phone, Mr. Ciullo seemed to suggest that I would be well advised to push your tenure through. He continually referred to 'my best interests.' What do you suppose he meant by that, Thomas?"

"I honestly don't know, Gayle. Mr. Ciullo isn't really familiar with academic protocol. I don't think he intended offense."

"Yes, well, there was something inappropriate . . . something untoward . . . Who is this Mr. Ciullo, Thomas?"

"A local businessman, Gayle."

"Ah," he mused with quiet satisfaction, "business." He regarded me solemnly. "Frankly, Thomas, this question of your tenure is beginning to worry me. You know I've been pulling for you. But it shouldn't be news to you that some on the committee are not entirely swayed by your publications. It's vulgar, I know. What-have-you-done-for-me-lately." Despite his show of concern, I detected a secret note of pleasure in his voice.

"Gayle," I finally said, "would you just tell me what's on your mind?"

"It's no one thing. It's everything together. You're making it more difficult than ever for me to speak with sincerity on your behalf."

"What you're saying," I said, "is that my chances for tenure are slim."

"I can appreciate that you're under a lot of pressure just now. Have you considered seeking professional help? I can recommend a very good man at the Health Services. It might be a good idea for you to talk to him."

"As a matter of fact," I responded seriously, "I just talked to someone at Booker Hills."

"I'm glad of that, Thomas. We shouldn't be embarrassed to seek help over the rough spots. No need to be embarrassed . . ." he said, drifting into silence.

We sat there quietly, until an expression of vague puzzlement came to his eyes, as though I'd been the one to request the interview and had regrettably forgotten my purpose.

I rose with an elaborate sigh and thanked him. Outside, I leaned over Jeanne's desk. "Remember that sentimental bet you placed on me?"

"Yes?"

"Hedge it," I advised.

The Redmont, a resident hotel on the periphery of the Combat Zone, offered refuge to prostitutes as well as the elderly who couldn't afford to move when a 1960s zoning law transformed the neighborhood into a fleshpot. The building dated from the thirties, red brick, a minimum of ornamentation, ten stories. Fire trucks or ambulances were parked out front a lot of the time. Mattress fires, heart attacks, strokes, an occasional arson. Once I'd passed by when the fire trucks were just pulling up, sirens blaring. A false alarm, but I watched as the sirens flushed onto the street an uneasy mob, half in bathrobes or negligees, half in wheelchairs. Some businessmen, too, scurrying off with collars upturned.

The suite number Rachel had given me was on the ninth floor. I knocked, aware of the leap of my pulse rate, aware of a clamminess at the heel of my right palm where I grasped the small white Mug & Muffin sack. She called "Theron?" and I said yes and the door opened and there she was. Rachel stood barefoot, sleepy-eyed, a white terrycloth robe pulled around her, black hair flattened on one side, leaving an ear exposed. A pillowcase wrinkle had left a fresh imprint the length of her cheek. Even so, just out of bed, without makeup, she was more beautiful—and younger—than I would have believed. She reached for the coffee immediately.

"You might want to heat it up," I said.

"Okay."

"There's a bran muffin in there too." Shit, I reminded myself, this isn't a date.

She disappeared into a small kitchen while I paced the living room. The suite was spacious, furnished with matched, cumbrous pieces of a Mediterranean style (E-Z Rental? No credit hassles?). A massive TV console took up most of one corner (Rent-to-Own?). The wall to my

right held three interior doors, only one of which appeared to lead to a
bedroom. I didn't permit myself to contemplate the sleeping arrange-
ments. The perfume of a pine-scented air freshener masked the ripe
odor of cat litter.

I sank down into a heavy armchair that offered a view of Rachel in
the kitchen, reheating the coffee in a saucepan. A small, Formica-
topped breakfast table held a dozen empty cans of Tab, a box of Froot
Loops, a box of Little Friskies. Most of the Tab cans had been used as
ashtrays.

"Is Norma here?" I called.

She frowned. "If she knew you were here, she'd . . ."

The sentence she left hanging might have ended with "kill me" or
"kill you." "She'd what?" I asked.

"She just wouldn't like it. She doesn't trust you. She says you just
want to fuck me."

I winced. "Norma's in a rut. That's how she sees the world."

"And she's right."

"Then why am I here?"

"I have to take a chance."

Rachel carried the coffee through the living room and into the bedroom. A short-haired white cat padded behind her, stopping short
when it spied me. Head cocked warily, it judged its chances of safe passage. I reached to pet it. The animal hissed and sprinted back into the
kitchen.

Ursula's, I thought. Hates men.

In a moment Rachel reappeared, hair brushed, now wearing a man's
white cotton shirt, knotted at the waist, and tight, faded jeans. She sat
on the sofa across from me, her feet curled up under her. She lit a cigarette, silently appraising me.

"You always wear a Tampax on your face?" she asked. Not a challenge, exactly; she was just trying to be tough and friendly at the same
time. I tried too.

"Only four or five days a month," I said.

That got a smile.

"So what do you want to tell me?"

The cat crept back into the room, hugging the far wall. Rachel gathered it into her lap, murmuring, scratching its belly in such a way that the cat's eyes lidded with pleasure. An acrylic-on-velvet painting of a horse hung on the wall above her, looking out into the room with sad, sentimental eyes. Rachel hadn't stayed in college long enough, I guessed, to take a fine-arts course.

"You have to tell me something first," she said.

"Okay. If I can."

"Are Norma and me in trouble?"

"I think you can answer that better than I can. Depends on what you've done, if anything."

"Norma said you kept talking about other people. People that aren't nice, you said. What other people?"

I wondered how much to tell her.

"I checked around at the Lady. There's this guy Alex that's been asking questions about me. A wimp if you ask me, but Norma says he's connected to Mr. Ciullo. Is that who we're talking about?"

"Ciullo is Alex's uncle," I said.

"Did he do that to your nose?"

"Someone who works for him," I lied solemnly. "And Mr. Ciullo *likes* me."

"I just don't want to say anything unless there's a reason," she explained, taking anxious puffs on her cigarette. "Okay, we got to make this fast. Norma's not going to be gone all day. So what does Mr. Ciullo want?"

I couldn't take my eyes off her. Her face remained as impenetrable to me as a face I might see on the cover of a fashion magazine. Large dark eyes, perfect teeth, wide graceful jaw, slender neck. And lips like cherry wine, I teased myself. Her eyes didn't suggest the mind behind them; they merely accepted whatever qualities I cared to imagine there—innocence, experience, or any gradation between. By some intricate operation of chromosomes, her face, her body, her whole being had become an exquisite screen upon which strangers projected desperate fantasies. A face upon which illusions took hold and generated a life of their own. Strangers sought in her image a cure for their own failed lives.

What cure, I wondered, had Kenan found, had Ursula found in that face? And for what disease?

"Mr. Ciullo wants a name," I told her. "He wants a credible assurance that what happened to Adam Feld and—"

"Don't worry," she said, her eyes hard, unreadable. "You can say it. Jacob Bloomberg. I stopped thinking of him as my father a long time ago."

"—that what happened to them had nothing to do with Ciullo's business affairs." I still couldn't say "father" or "murder." Our talk was bothering me a lot more than it seemed to bother her. "If Ciullo's convinced that these events are limited to something personal . . . private . . ."

"He wants to know," she assisted, "if somebody out there is fucking with him."

"More or less," I agreed.

"Otherwise he's willing to live and let live."

I nodded.

"Just a name?" she asked. I sensed that she was feeling me out, trying to satisfy me with the bare minimum.

"Well, not just a name out of the phone book. He wants to know who's responsible."

"Do you work for him? You don't seem the type."

"I'm not. I sort of got in over my head. As a matter of fact, this all began when I bet on the filly your father was training."

"You call that training? You must not like horses."

"I don't know. I like the track."

"One of those," she sighed. "If you ever take the time, you might find out that horses are a lot better than people."

She sat quietly for a while, as though she were making an important business decision. Finally she looked at me and said, "Okay, let's get this over with. Tell him Stephen Kenan."

The name had intruded in my mind from the beginning. Now that I heard her say it, it didn't sound right. Of all the questions I might have asked, I started with the simplest one.

"Why?"

"Wait a minute. You wanted a name, you got it." She glanced nervously at the door. "We don't have time for reasons."

The threat of Ursula's arrival, I hoped, was just part of her bargaining technique. "I'm just asking what Ciullo will ask me," I said. "Why?"

She impatiently lit another cigarette, glancing at her watch. "I dunno. He loves me, I guess."

The possibility of love hadn't really occurred to me. I'd been thinking: suicidal depression, sleep disorder, obsessive-compulsive fixation. You have a subtle mind, I told myself.

"How much does he love you?" I asked.

"A lot, I guess. Enough to kill Jake when he tried to make me go back to New Jersey. Daddy-boy is crazy."

"So that's it?" I said skeptically. "He's crazy in love?"

Silence, then, "He likes for us to hurt him."

"Us? You mean you and Norma?"

"Yeah. He says that if we hurt him, it keeps him from hurting himself."

I put as much disbelief in my face as I could muster.

"Don't look at me," she complained. "That's what he says. I don't know what world you live in, but the one I live in, things are like that. It's everywhere. You just don't see it. Hell, I get a lot of requests weirder than that. That's mild stuff."

"How do you hurt him?"

She stood up angrily. "Norma was right about you," she said. "If you want me to tell you dirty stories, you got to do like everybody else—pay for it. Shit, forget it. Just leave."

"Okay, calm down. What about Feld?"

After a moment of indecision, she hurried into the bedroom. When she came back she handed me a squarish cartridge. "Here. This is self-explanatory. Straight from Adam Feld's film library."

"What is it?"

She looked at me as though I'd confessed an ignorance of indoor plumbing.

"Jesus. It's a video cassette. Norma sneaked it out of Feld's office. He took films of all his customers. If he felt like he could get away with it, he used them. Adam figured a professor—my God, a professor—would dance for him. What he didn't figure on was Daddy-boy being crazy."

"The Quaaludes? The pills?"

"Come on," she urged, "leave. Kenan's got a whole drugstore of pills."

"Okay, one more thing," I delayed as she hustled me toward the door. "Did you tell Adam Feld what your father was doing to the filly?"

She stopped abruptly. "Tell him? For chrissake, Jake was *working* for Feld. My God, don't you read the papers?"

She stared at me, dumbfounded, her mind working to absorb the question I'd posed. The shock in her voice wasn't faked; she really didn't know. She said, "I mean, that's how it happened, right?"

A key turned in the lock. We both stared at the doorknob.

"Shit," Rachel whispered.

The door opened and Ursula backed into the apartment, calling in a husband-home-for-dinner voice, "Sweetheart, I wish you'd come with me today ..." She wore a baggy blue sweatshirt and white gym shorts—soiled on the bottom—pulled over a pair of jeans. Black rubber boots, knee-high. When she turned, her face, raw-looking in the light, slowly absorbed my presence. She smiled tentatively, not recognizing the face behind the bandaged nose.

"Hello," I said, edging toward the door. "Just on my—"

I shouldn't have spoken. My voice sparked recognition.

She glared at Rachel. "What's the freak doing here?"

"Rachel and I were just—"

"Rikki," she hissed at me. "Rikki to johns."

It happened when I tried to slide past her. Norma aimed for my nose—not like a woman, heel of palm first—but with knuckles forward, clenched, putting her shoulder behind the blow. Crouching, half turning, I raised my arms to shield my face. The cassette fell to the floor. My forearm deflected most of the first punch; the second caught me unprepared. What it lacked in power it made up for with accuracy.

Nose, dead center. My vision dimmed for an instant; a firework of nerves blazed before me. I thought I would pass out.

"Fucking freak!" she screamed.

I scrambled blindly out the door, still crouching, a ludicrous simian gait. I took a final, hard blow on my back, near the kidneys. My nose didn't let me feel it. Behind me, I heard her screaming, in the distance it seemed, as though my head were underwater.

Outside the Redmont, I walked half a block, sat on the curb, tilted my head back, and waited for the pain to subside enough for me to drive. Despite the blood on my chin and shirt, I wasn't all that conspicuous in this part of town. Lighting a cigarette, I watched my hands shake like a wino's. My head slowly cleared. I stood up and began the trek down Tremont—a slow-motion stride that wouldn't jar—back to my car. I'd gone about twenty yards when I heard someone call, "Wait."

Rachel was hurrying up behind me. I waited.

"Here," she said, pushing the Mug & Muffin sack toward me.

I looked at her in pain and dumb puzzlement . "Wha . . . ? Keep the goddam bran muffin," I said.

"The cassette," she said. "Take it."

"What for?"

"I don't care. Whatever you want."

Her eyes weren't so hard to read now. They glistened brightly with tears. The pain in her face was so pronounced that it suddenly diminished my own. I put my hand on her shoulder. She didn't resist.

"I'm sorry," I said. "But I don't have to tell you that you're surrounded by crazies. How crazy, I don't know. But if you'd like, maybe I can help somehow. And I'm not talking about Ciullo. You tell me what."

"You want to help," she said, fighting the tears, "just leave us alone. Leave us alone. That would help."

"I have a friend—a woman—who would be good to talk to. I think you'd like her. But anything is better than this. Maybe Norma has been good to you. Cares for you. But God, she's so filled with hate that—"

"Don't say it," she said angrily. "Just don't say it."

Only one thing could account for the emotion that charged her face. "You love her, don't you?"

Lips quivering, her face yielded to the sorrow; a faint sound rose in her throat, a sob strangely muffled, as though she were trying to cry but didn't know how. Her shoulders quaked. I tried to put my arms around her. She moved away.

"Just leave us alone," she said, hardening again.

Not until that night, as I lay back in the warm mud of a hundred-milligram tablet of Demerol, did the details come back to me. No way to be certain, of course, but I couldn't picture Kenan as a target for blackmail. The man I'd visited at Channing College had pushed himself beyond the pale of threats to his reputation. If anything, an extortion attempt would have amused him. Kill Rachel's father out of grotesque jealousy? Territoriality? What made the most sense was that Rachel had made it all up.

Of all the details that might have perplexed me, only one succeeded. The image of Ursula, backing in the door, calling "Hi, honey," or whatever. The white gym shorts, I began to remember, worn over the blue jeans. Gaining weight, probably, and trying to hide that she couldn't get the zipper all the way up. The white shorts soiled at the rear. The knee-high black rubber boots.

The boots, I thought. Riding boots?

=====*NINETEEN*=====

RINGING BETH'S DOORBELL, I tried to remember a question that Thomas Carlyle, the Scottish metaphysician, had posed in a letter to his wife. Carlyle's correspondence revealed two lifelong, intensely personal preoccupations: the first, how to achieve religious salvation; the second, how to cure himself of a case of diarrhea that lasted most of his adult life. I couldn't remember precisely how he formulated the question, but the gist of it was: How can we think about God when we're standing in shit?

"Hi, Thomas," Beth greeted me soberly. She was wearing cutoff jeans and a faded Virginia Woolf T-shirt. "God, your nose looks like it's getting worse."

"I don't heal," I said, "I atrophy. You mind if I come in?"

"You should've called," she said, stepping outside and closing the door behind her. "Why don't we just sit out here for a while?"

"Sugar Boy Breck's here, I take it."

She nodded. "He'll be calling you to apologize."

"Tell him not to bother."

"Breck and I have to sort some things out. We really needed to talk."

"I hope that's all you're doing."

We sat on the brick steps, hips touching, shoulders touching, looking out at Marlboro Street, the dogwoods newly budded with pale green leaves and white blossoms. Beth rested her hand on my arm. A breeze caught her hair and blew a wisp of it across my face. Telling her would be even harder than I'd thought. For the briefest moment my mind cast about for options. Keep quiet now; later, if need be, blame it on Breck? No, Thomas. No.

Mustering my courage, I told her what Jeanne had told me. "Chances are it's a false alarm," I observed cheerfully. I was looking on the bright side; why couldn't she?

Silence at first. She removed her hand from my arm. She shifted her rear on the steps and put a space between our hips and shoulders.

"Are you sure?" she asked.

"Nobody has symptoms yet, except this friend of a friend of a friend. Maybe she just has a yeast infection. Ha."

"I don't know how well informed you are about these things"— softly spoken, a strong undertone of martyrdom—"but not everyone gets symptoms."

"Okay, shit. Then I'll hang a sign around my neck. Maybe wear a Scarlet *H.* This isn't easy to say. Don't milk it."

"Okay, Thomas, you're right. It's not just that."

"Then what is it?"

"The other night. I can't help remembering you say how lonely you were, how you're not seeing anyone."

"Christ, I'm sorry. I said I was lonely. I never said I was chaste. You're one to talk."

"So now I have to tell Breck," she said, shifting, edging farther away from me.

"You don't have to tell him anything. Why not just stay out of bed with him for a few days. Until we know."

"Too late."

"Already! Jesus. How do you find time to eat?"

Suddenly she jumped up, shouting, pacing down, then up the brick steps like a small caged animal. "You fucking men and your fucking

egos. As a matter of fact, Breck is proving himself to be as big an asshole as you are. He knew I slept with you, so he had to make this big
point of my showing I cared. You know what *that* means."

I did, but I didn't want to think about it.

"Couple of babies. You'd figure I could find one man in this world
who had an emotional age of more than ten."

She stopped abruptly on the top step and stared down, as though she
were on a ledge from which she planned to jump. But her anger subsided and she sagged down onto the step. "I just need a little room to
breathe. I'm going to sit here a minute. I'm going back inside. Get rid
of Breck. Then take a bath."

"I know," I said. "Men. A mouth to bullshit you with, two fists to
hit you with, a cock to fuck you with, etcetera. I know, I know."

A sharp laugh, more like a cough, erupted in her throat. She regarded me with wonder in her eyes. "Thomas, I think that's the first
smart thing I ever heard you say."

"Thanks, but it's not mine. I'm quoting."

"Yo, Ed," a salesman in the Mister Video shop on Commonwealth
Avenue called to the store manager. "This guy wants to rent a VCR.
Get this. He wants to hook it up to an old black-and-white Philco, fif-
teen years old."

I smiled patiently while they enjoyed a knowing, low-tech laugh.

The salesman turned back to me and said, "I wish you'd told me that
fifteen minutes ago. You could've saved us the trouble of filling out
these rental forms. Unless you want to rent a TV too."

I told him no. The cassette Rachel had given me lay on the counter
between us ("Need Beta for that," he'd said).

"Tell you what," I offered. "No rental forms. I give you twenty-five
dollars and you let me use one of the machines here. Just give me a little privacy."

He looked down at the cassette with fresh eyes. "That must be some
movie."

Recognizing a seller's market, he held out for thirty-five dollars, then
led me to an office in the rear. He showed me how to work the Sony

Betamax that sat on top of a twenty-five-inch Sony Trinitron. "I'll give you an hour," he said before he closed the door behind him. "And so help me God, if I come back and find the carpet messed up, you're gonna buy a new one."

I didn't need fifteen minutes, much less the full hour. And it took even less time than that for me to understand that Kenan hadn't lied. If I kept peeping into his life, he'd warned, I wouldn't like what I saw.

The perspective suggested a camera hidden above—behind a ceiling mirror? a light fixture?—positioned to aim directly down upon a platform bed. The film frame didn't permit a view beyond the bed itself. The design of the bed—blond wood, clean Scandinavian lines—was in keeping with the modern decor I'd seen at Feld's brothel.

If I hadn't been expecting him, I wouldn't have identified the figure on the screen. Kenan lay bound on the bed, spread-eagled, leather straps on his wrists, ankles, and neck, blindfolded with what might have been swimmer's goggles with the lenses blacked out. If his goal had been to make a beast of himself, he had succeeded.

The sharpness of the focus, the heightened realism of the videotape shocked me.

His torso, surprisingly lean, was pale and shorn of body hair; beneath his belly, still another leather strap—a miniature belt and buckle—noosed the base of his penis. A final device contrived to distend his testicles. Together, the equipment achieved a kind of gross nakedness, a radical exposure of his privates.

My God, the picture was clear!

His mouth moved as though he were talking, but the film did not record the sound. His head turned from side to side on the bedsheet, like that of a blind singer. Whether he was pleading for mercy or for more, I couldn't tell. Sado-masochists, I'd read, paradoxically enjoyed a sense of power. They manipulated their torturers by provoking them to inflict pain. The dominatrix was simply the instrument of their self-loathing.

From the left, a woman's arm intruded into the frame, manipulating a leather prod, dragging the point of it teasingly along his stomach. Kenan's penis, torturously confined, gave an involuntary twitch.

So real was the grotesque image that I found myself leaning toward the screen, as if to peer beyond the edge of the frame to glimpse the face of his mistress.

The cassette, as it turned out, was a compilation of scenes, apparently taken at different times, all featuring Kenan, all monotonously consistent in theme: humiliation, debasement, degradation. Though I never saw more than the woman's arm—indeed, couldn't swear I had seen the same arm throughout—I did identify the prod, the slender, leather-covered stick she wielded. A gad, Cleve had called it. A jockey's whip.

On my way out of Mister Video, the salesman leered at me. "Good movie?"

Numb, rendered mute by what I'd seen, I couldn't respond. I could only think of the question Thomas Carlyle had asked his wife over a century ago. I thought I knew the answer. You can't think about God when you're standing in shit. You can only make jokes.

I turned back toward the salesman. "That Sony gets a helluva picture."

"You're telling me," he agreed.

Stepping outside into the bright light, I wondered if Kenan had been truthful, too, about the second part of his warning.

The object of my peeping might turn on me, he'd said. Might bite me on the ass.

PART III
BLOODLINES

═══TWENTY═══

THE MORNING BETTING LINE listed the filly Raggedy And—formerly raced under the name Jesus Saves—as the longshot of the sixth race, an $8,000 starter allowance for fillies and colts. When the betting began at fifteen minutes to post, the odds shot up to 60–1. Over the next five minutes, each time the toteboard flashed, the odds dropped. 50–1. Flash. 40–1. Flash. 25–1. Flash. 15–1. At ten minutes to post, the odds stabilized at 12–1.

"Word gets around," Cleve said. "Everybody's a sucker for a hard-luck story."

I nodded. "What does Bud Spina think of her chances?"

Though Cleve wouldn't admit it, I knew the race excited him; he had raised only a perfunctory complaint when I asked him to forsake the Paddock Bar and join me outside on the spectators' grounds to watch the post parade. The temperature was in the low seventies, the air dry and comfortable. I wanted to see the filly up close.

"Even if Bud knew something, he wouldn't blab it," Cleve said, removing the tan jacket of his new summer-weight suit, adjusting a pointed shirt collar that might have kept a small plane airborne. "He's paying Hector Gutierrez to ride her, and I don't think he'd do that unless she had a chance. She turned a couple of good times in workouts. Three furlongs at thirty-five-and-four, breezing. Four at forty-seven flat. She's only carrying a hundred and nine pounds. But who knows if she can carry herself over a mile and three-eights. When Bloomberg had her, she never ran more'n six furlongs."

"So what do you think she'll do?"

His eyes twinkled. "I think she'll get about halfway through the race and decide she oughta be home cooking dinner. Spring ain't the best time to run a filly. They get too distracted. Think about love."

"That's what you said before her last race. Look what happened."

"Them was cheap horses, T.T. Didn't care who passed 'em. Today's race's got some young stallions in it. They ain't heard about women's lib yet."

The previous week, Bud Spina had petitioned the Jockey Club for permission to change Jesus Saves's name. Requests for name changes were usually made by new owners who wish to honor themselves or tease their wives (Mac's Pride, Joanne's Folly, and so forth). In the case of Jesus Saves, the Jockey Club had complied immediately, eager, I supposed, to obliterate any reminders to the betting public of the filly's larcenous past. The name Raggedy And had been devised according to the traditional formula, conflating the names of the filly's sire and dam. Sire, Raggedy Fella. Dam, And The Wind. Offspring, Raggedy And.

Bloodlines. A centuries-old obsession with conserving and propagating superior equine genes resulted in a circumstance that always struck me as incredible. Of the hundreds of thousands of thoroughbreds running today, at any track in the world, the pedigree of every one of them could be traced back through the male line to one of three stallions at stud in late-seventeenth-century England. Unschooled in eugenics, I sometimes wondered why the restricted gene pool hadn't produced animals—very fast animals—with pinheads and webbed feet.

"Cleveland!" someone called. "Tommy!" We turned and saw Petey, maneuvering his wheelchair in close quarters, parting the spectators lined up three and four deep against the fence.

"What'd I tell you, teach?" Cleve said when Petey parked himself next to us at the fence. "Everybody wants to get a look at the hard-luck filly."

"Well, listen to this," Petey grinned up at me. "I heard your friend here's getting softhearted in his old age. Softheaded too. A friend of mine behind the windows said Cleve bent the rules, sneaked himself a second-party bet on the filly."

At first I thought Petey was kidding, but when I looked at Cleve, he studiously avoided my eyes. "People that's full of shit," he said evenly, still not looking at either of us, "shouldn't be opening their mouths."

The toteboard flashed again; Raggedy And dropped to 8–1.

A procession of nine thoroughbreds, now saddled, jockeys up, circled the walking ring, preparing for the post parade. Suzy, the stable girl who'd displayed the filly for Cleve that morning two weeks ago, was leading Raggedy And, Hector Guttierrez aboard in yellow-and-blue silks. The filly bore little resemblance to the quaking animal I'd last seen—smallish next to the colts, yes, but spunky and full of animal spirit. She tossed her head briskly, ears erect and forward, jauntily toe-dancing, nipping willfully at Suzy whenever the opportunity presented itself. The scars still decorated the hide of her muscled rump; otherwise her coat was sleek and shining like gunmetal. Her tail had been groomed and bobbed—a "bangtail" Cleve had once called it.

The filly looked good, I thought. Ready. But that was one reason I usually stuck to the TV monitors inside. Studying horses in the post parade only confused me. Live horses all looked good to me.

Flash. 4–1.

Somebody knew something, I thought. Or maybe just hoped something. If Cleve had sneaked a bet on her, had succumbed to a sentimental tug, it wasn't hard to understand why. Who could resist the deep myth beneath her drama? The rise of the oppressed. Brutalized and diminished by Evil, Good endures and prevails. Versions of the story thrived everywhere: just open a book, turn on the TV, go to a movie. Of course, the track wasn't a stage. Then again, it wasn't life either.

Passing from the walking ring to the track, the thoroughbreds joined their stable ponies in the post parade. "How's she look to you?" I asked Petey.

"Outside, pretty fair," he replied without enthusiasm. "If I had money on her"—a look at Cleve—"it'd be her brain I'd worry about. Them scars don't show."

The 2–1 favorite, a big roan colt named Tee It Up, passed us, taking frenetic little hops, turned sideways, looking very much like pure energy confined. He held his head high, and white showed all around his pupils.

"Looks good," I said.

Cleve shook his head. "A little washy. Too keyed up. Gonna use himself up before the race."

"You're the one too keyed up," Petey needled him. "Too much in love with . . . what they calling her now? Raggedy Ass?"

I pointed to another likely animal, a lanky chestnut that appeared more relaxed than Tee It Up.

This time Petey objected. "Easing off his left rear. Looks a little ouchy."

"Petey," Cleve said, "I knew about your legs. When your eyes go bad?"

The horses, now accompanied by stable ponies, made a final circle in front of the grandstand. All healthy-looking horses, I thought. All fast. I refrained from further comment while my companions argued awhile longer, punctuating their judgments with insults and curses, speaking in a language I only vaguely comprehended. One colt was "spitting its bit," another was "pig-eyed," another "goose-rumped," another had a reputation as a "cribber" (was that good or bad? I wondered).

As I left for the betting windows, Petey asked me to place a bet for him on a colt named All Smiles. He handed me ten dollars, adding diffidently, "None of 'em are money in the bank."

I paused and stared at All Smiles, watching him try to plant his yellow teeth into the rump of the pony beside him. I searched for some quality of physique or presence or temperament that set him apart from the other eight horses in the field. By four minutes to post, I still hadn't found one. I hurried off to get my bets down.

"Mr. Theron," Gus greeted me at his window, "where you been? I thought we'd be seeing you every day. Giving us all that money back."

"Well," I said, smiling, "here's two hundred fifty dollars of it right now. Put it on Raggedy And to win."

"That filly's getting real popular all of a sudden. I got twenty on her myself." He winked. "What's the word from the toilets?"

"I heard she can't miss," I said. "I also heard she doesn't have a chance. And I heard everything in between."

"That's why they call it gambling."

"Move it!" a man behind me shouted. "Shake your ass."

I got Petey's bet down, then hustled out of the grandstand toward the homestretch fence. My stomach felt light. I didn't look for Cleve; I wanted to watch the race alone. By the time I pushed my way through to the fence, the track announcer had already shouted, "They're *off!*" And by the time I composed myself and trained my eyes on the thoroughbreds taking the first turn, Jesus Saves—Raggedy And—had opened up five lengths on the colts. She was flying. Flying.

Less than a week had passed since I'd viewed the cassette. The following day I'd appeared in Vincent Ciullo's office at the rear of the Pink Lady. My visit didn't surprise him; the thought never crossed his mind, I'm sure, that I wouldn't attempt to gather the information he'd requested. He inquired politely about my nose. Out of pride—or some lurking desire to impress him—I adjusted the narration of the two punches to cast my own role in a more heroic light. The revisions might have been a mistake. Was there quiet satisfaction in his eyes as he listened? Did he see in my bruises a symbol of a burgeoning commitment to passionate involvements?

Later he accepted my revelations about Kenan, Ursula, and Rachel with perfect equanimity, befitting a man who had been a life-long beneficiary of the darker cravings of the human spirit. I offered to show him the videotape.

"Oh, that won't be necessary," he declined with a slight flutter of his fingers. "Professor Kenan is not the first man to achieve profound insight at the expense of his mental health. I sometimes wonder," he mused solemnly, making a sweeping gesture toward the bookshelves, "if we really appreciate at what price these words are purchased."

Fifteen bucks, hardcover, I thought, stubbornly resisting his solemnity.

One detail momentarily punctured Ciullo's reserve: my portrait of Jacob Bloomberg, wife-beater and child molester. The trainer's family history angered Ciullo, hardened his face with a brittle scowl. But all he said was, "I wish I'd been aware of that . . ."

Watching his anger, I began to suspect that beneath—or more likely, coexisting with—his love of exotic ideas was a homespun belief in the sanctity of the family unit. I remembered the Beacon Hill townhouse strewn with children's toys, the air heavy with the smell of cooking. Try as I might, I still couldn't imagine him fondly patting the rear of a plump wife, moored to a stove. Would she bring him a cup of tea while he labored on his poems? Straighten his bow tie, hand him his attaché case, and with a kiss send him off to the Zone to sell flesh?

"So, Thomas," he finally asked, "have you drawn any conclusions? Should any of this be of particular concern to me?"

"In a business sense," I replied, "no. Unless I misread her, I don't think Rachel ever knew, still doesn't know, that her father was working for you. So she didn't tell Adam Feld anything. No guarantees, of course. But as far as I can tell, whatever happened had nothing to do with you or your business interests."

"I see," he replied simply.

"Beyond that, I'm a little confused. I talked to three very screwed-up people, any one of whom might have committed two murders."

"Kenan?" he prompted. "Mightn't this young girl have told you the truth?"

"I suppose it's possible. He's obviously suffering a spiritual crisis of gigantic proportions. But I can't see that a threat of blackmail would have impressed him. Whether he was worried that Jake would take Rachel away from him, who knows? Stranger things have happened in the name of love."

"I have the impression, Thomas, that you don't believe it."

"I believe that Kenan hates himself. That's clear enough. Whether

he loves Rachel Bloomberg, or developed some psychological depen-
dence on her, whatever, is another question. With Kenan, it's the flip-
side of narcissism. Just substitute self-loathing for self-love. Either way,
the preoccupation with self is identical. If you ask me, that doesn't
leave much room for sentimental attachments."

"That's an interesting way of looking at it."

"That's about all I have. Interesting ways of looking at it."

Which bothered me. I was long on subtlety, short on the obvious.
Whatever it was that provoked a person to commit murder, God
knows it wasn't subtle. Like everyone else, I'd read the numberless reports of murders triggered by ludicrously trivial incidents (man blud-
geons wife when she buys unsalted peanuts; woman stabs lover when
he makes fun of her favorite TV heroine), but there was nothing subtle
about the subterranean rage that such incidents tapped. The rage was
always there, existing beneath humdrum lives like a complacent monster unacquainted with its own power. Sooner or later, the unwitting
provocation, the monster unleashed—stabber and stabbee, no doubt,
equally surprised by its fury—a body falls to the floor, a free-with-ten-
dollars-worth-of-groceries steak knife piercing the ribcage.

Forget the subtle, I told myself. Give the obvious a chance. Think
less about love—masochistic, homosexual, narcissistic, or otherwise—
and think more about rage. Think hate.

"What do you know about Ursula Undress?" I asked Ciullo.

He paused thoughtfully. "Very little, really. Unless there's a special
problem, I don't get reports on lower-echelon employees. I do know
that she's unique for length of service. But for a showgirl, endurance is
a marginal virtue at best. Most of our patrons prefer to view youth;
they can see age at home. Is something bothering you?"

"Well, it could be a coincidence. But I think she rides horses." And,
I thought, if Bloomberg planned to whisk his daughter away to New
Jersey, Ursula had as much reason as anyone to be upset about it. "You
think I could get a picture of her?"

"Mr. DeVito should be able to provide you with one." He studied
me for a few seconds. "So what do you plan to do?"

I knew the question was coming sooner or later; I still wasn't sure how I would answer it. On the bright side, Ciullo didn't seem particularly anxious about anything I'd told him.

"I don't know. First I ought to return the cassette to Kenan, no questions asked. Then . . . hell . . . maybe I should just write everything down, nice lurid prose, and submit it to the *National Enquirer.*"

Ciullo's face soured. At first, I thought, because of the suggestion—even in jest—that I might betray his confidence. But then he said, "For a moment, Thomas, I believed that these events had cured you of your joking reflex. Perhaps given you a new sense of responsibility."

"Responsibility?" I began irritably. "All this time I've been thinking it was nausea. Jesus, I may need a few jokes." I'd become more reckless, but I couldn't stop. "If Braithewaite keeps getting phone calls, I'm going to be unemployed."

"Professor Braithewaite mentioned my call?" The question was matter-of-fact; he ignored my anger as he would have a child's.

"I know you're trying to help," I retreated, "but someone like Braithewaite just doesn't understand these things."

"Oh, I think he understands."

"You mind if I ask what you said to him?"

"Not at all. I merely suggested to him that you, in my opinion, are especially deserving of consideration."

"That's not the impression he got."

"Well, you're correct to some extent. Professor Braithewaite is perhaps slow to comprehend the more practical aspects of life. I think—in time—the merits of my recommendation will sink in on him." Ciullo looked at me. "You're not worried that I've jeopardized your tenure prospects?"

"To tell you the truth, I'm looking forward to some time off. I'm a little soured on academic life just now. Tenure never was a sure thing."

"I see," he said, "I see," closing the subject.

We talked a few minutes longer, Ciullo eventually bringing the conversation around to a German poet I'd never heard of. For once the topic, though of his own choosing, failed to rouse him. We exchanged a few desultory remarks before falling silent.

Feeling I was about to be dismissed, I made a final request: "When I visit Kenan this week, I'd like for Gerald to come with me."

"Yes?" A faint smile. "I thought you'd labeled Professor Kenan a narcissist, not a murderer."

"I did. But so far I've been wrong every step of the way."

"Let's hope you haven't missed the mark altogether. Understand, I'm prepared to take steps based on your judgment."

"Steps?" Not the word so much as the way he pronounced it. A surreal image appeared in my mind: a stairway, the tiers of which were corpses.

"I'm satisfied—owing in part to your assurances—that these crimes have more to do with passion than with economics. What variety of passion? in consort with what motivation?" His hands blossomed in a delicate, questioning gesture, like a priest's. "I'm left with three people, two of whom are my employees, all of whom are, in your phrase, 'screwed up.' I won't deny that I'm intrigued. Given the time, it's a knot I might enjoy unraveling. Still"—here a trace of regret—"the simplest solution, the most obvious solution, is not to understand these people, but to rid myself of them."

"You're not serious."

"Does that bother you?"

"You're damn right," I said hotly. "First of all, I'm just guessing. Second, if you're saying you want to kill all three just to cover the bases—"

Ciullo was smiling. "Ah, professor," he interrupted. "For someone who claims not to confuse life with books, you certainly have a fevered imagination. Who said anything about killing?"

"You did . . . I thought."

"I referred to a simple relocation. Why should it surprise you that I have sympathy for the young girl? Alex will speak with this woman— Norma? Tell her that it would be to her advantage, to Rachel's advantage, to relocate. Similar employment could be found for them in another city. Whatever ties Professor Kenan has to this club would be severed."

"Oh," I said. "That's all fine. Except Norma will feed Alex his lunch."

"Yes, so you say. From your description, she does have strident views. Perhaps I'll speak with her myself."

That, I thought, was a conversation I'd like to hear.

Raggedy And hit the three-quarter pole in a minute ten, a stakes-race clip. She'd opened up a good seven lengths on the colts. Still flying.

"Come on," I urged, snapping my fingers, trying to attune myself to some ineffable equine rhythm. "Come on." I slapped the *Racing Form* on my thigh, hard. I half squatted. I stood on my tiptoes. I spun around. "Come on."

Nearby, a swarthy man performed a similar ritual for the benefit of another horse.

"Filly gone die," he shouted in an accent I didn't recognize. "Filly gone back up."

"Come on."

"Filly gone die!"

"Come on."

At the far turn, Raggedy And still in control, the colts fighting for positions from which to mount a final rush. All Smiles, the horse Petey had bet, surged under a whip and made up three lengths. Tee It Up showed signs of life, veering from the middle of the pack to the outside.

"Filly gone die!" the man shouted with new vigor, beginning to smell blood.

When the thoroughbreds turned for home, it looked more and more as if the man beside me might have a point. The gap between the filly and the colts slowly disappeared. A crescendo rose behind me in the grandstand. Everyone screaming. Screaming for the filly to hang on. Screaming for her to die.

"Come on."

A quarter-mile to the wire, Raggedy And held a length over All Smiles. Gutierrez pumped his hands at her neck, trying to keep her on rhythm. She lugged in, beginning to fade.

"Filly backing up." This time not a shouted hope, but a statement.

Helplessly I watched the classsic illusion of racing: a horse from the rear of the pack, suddenly igniting, gaining speed to overtake and pass a front-runner. Well, that was what it looked like. But that sudden jolt of speed was an illusion. Over the course of a race, all horses ran progressively slower. Or as Cleve explained it, some horses, at race's end, "just run more slower than others."

Raggedy And was running more slower than them all. All Smiles passed her at the eighth pole. Three strides later, Tee It Up shot by. Next came the animals that Petey and Cleve had ridiculed: the pig-eyed colt, the goose-rumped colt, the cribber. The filly reached the wire, exhausted, off stride, head down, eighth in a field of nine; one of the colts had broken down. There was little doubt what the official line would read: "Used up."

Later, in the Paddock Bar, Cleve said, "I fucking knew it. Filly in with colts. Somebody ought to goddam kick me in the ass."

=====TWENTY-ONE=====

THE FOLLOWING AFTERNOON I stopped by the Pink Lady and asked Frank DeVito for a photograph of Ursula Undress.

He shook his head. "Don't think we got one. The girls don't go in for promo shots anymore."

"What about out front, the tease photos? I thought I saw one out there."

"Shit," he said, "didn't think of that. We haven't touched those cases in years."

Frank took a large ring of keys from a bartender, then led me out to the front of the club. Bolted to the walls on either side of the main entrance were long glass display cases. Inside each case, under a line of vanity lights, was a series of glamour photos that, in theory at least, served to entice passersby into the bar. Frank was right. The photos hadn't been disturbed in years. Compared with what went on inside the bar, the poses seemed modest, even prudish.

"Sonofabitch," he said. "Funny how you don't notice something right under your nose." He opened the lock on the case and handed me an eight-by-ten black-and-white with a glossy finish.

Miss Ursula Undress it read at the bottom. *Courtesy Patriot Productions.*

A much younger version of Norma assumed a standard Marilyn Monroe pose, bent slightly from the waist, hugging herself, shoving lots of cleavage near the camera, lips parted. Spangled costume, unsensuous, rigid as a truss; old hairstyle, teased on top, girlish bangs in front. An antique, but the face was unmistakably Norma's—and remarkably pretty.

"Not bad," Frank whistled, peering over my shoulder. "Not bad at all." Then his face suddenly turned solemn, his voice confidential. "You knew Norma had TB, didn't you?"

"What?"

He slapped me on the back. "Two Beauties."

Halfway down the block, I could still hear him laughing.

"If this guy's a professor," Gerald said, "you mind telling me what you want me for?" We were in Ciullo's Mercedes, working our way along Brattle Street toward Kenan's home in Belmont, a quiet suburb adjacent to Cambridge and west of Boston. It was Sunday morning, a little past nine.

"Gerald," I confessed, "I wish I knew. He's a little weird. He sometimes plays with guns. As far as I know, unloaded guns."

"What kind of gun this guy like to play with?"

"Shit, a gun. I don't know." I held my forefingers about six inches apart. "About so big. Has a barrel, a trigger, a handle, a place to put the bullets. A gun."

Gerald glanced over at me without apparent concern. "He plays with one in front of me," he said, just getting the rules straight, "I have to take it away from him."

"I understand that. Just don't use unnecessary force. Don't hurt him."

He shrugged. "No difference to me. It's up to him."

"Well, it probably won't matter," I said. "I don't even know if he'll be home. If he's home, he may not be sober enough to answer the door."

Dipsomaniacs—if that's what Kenan was—didn't observe bourgeois drinking hours; but if there were ever a time I might find him sober, I

figured Sunday morning was it. I peered through the tinted glass of the
Mercedes, thinking, I could have left the cassette with Kenan's secretary at Channing College. Or simply mailed it to him, explanatory note
attached. But what would the note say? Please find one Betamax video
cassette, suitable for blackmail? No, I wanted to put it in his hand.
Offer assurances, if necessary; leave no room for ambiguity. Then make
a graceful exit.

Yesterday, when I'd asked Jeanne for the professor's home number,
she'd smiled and told me not to bother. "You'll just get frustrated. He
has an answering machine; at least he did when I worked for him.
Thing is, he uses a recording that sounds like the phone company. You
dial his number, the machine comes on, and an operator says the number you've reached is no longer in service. That's how he deflects calls
from students, colleagues, whomever."

"Damn," I said, "wish I'd thought of that."

Following Brattle Street past Mount Auburn Cemetery, we crossed
the boundary between Cambridge and Belmont. A right turn put us on
Trapelo, a winding two-lane road shaded by oaks and lined with small,
well-maintained houses on quarter-acre lots. The dwellings once would
have been judged modest; the last decade had watched them rapidly appreciate into affluence. Why here? I wondered. Why had Kenan squir-
reled himself away in this sunny, innocuous suburb? A resident for
almost twenty years, Jeanne had said. Had he moved here before the
demons rose up within him? Or had he sensed their presence even
then, and sought to calm them, defuse them in the cozy tranquility of
Belmont, Mass?

I looked at Gerald and asked the question that was beginning to pre-
occupy me. "Do you know anything about Ursula Undress?"

"Who?"

"A dancer at the club."

"I don't pay much attention," he said.

"You must at least have seen her. She's a little hard to miss. Her ci-
vilian name is Norma."

"Her? Yeah. Been around a long time."

"So, what do you know about her?"

He shrugged. "She takes her clothes off for money. Puts her clothes back on, takes a seat at the bar. Guy buys her a drink, she talks. No takers, she twiddles her thumbs. Then she gets back on stage—"

"I mean, have you ever talked to her?"

He thought for a minute. "Couple of times. Way back, when she first started working, she'd come on to me. She thought I was a customer, something. I told her no."

"Did you know she's gay?"

"Now wait a minute," Gerald said quickly, adjusting his fists on the steering wheel, glancing over at me with mild pain, as though I'd tricked him. "I just said she come on to me." His tone was defensive, as if Ursula's sexual preference somehow reflected badly on him. "She comes on to everybody. That's her job. I never had nothing to do with her."

"Just asking," I said, adding diplomatically, "She gave me her pitch, too."

We turned off Trapelo Road onto a shaded cul-de-sac that held perhaps a dozen houses of similiar design: two-story garrison, gambrel roof, a large bay window on the first floor, two dormers on the second. I spotted Kenan's house without benefit of the house number; conspicuously unkempt, white clapboards peeling, a small yard choked with weeds and, like Kenan himself, going to seed.

Two houses down, a slim man of roughly my age, wearing a rugby shirt, worked in his yard. When we parked and got out of the car, I sensed him pausing, watchful, leaning on the aluminum bar of his lawnmower. I felt his curiosity as we passed through the miniature wilderness that comprised Kenan's front yard. Were we about to contribute, I asked myself uneasily, to the neighborhood legend?

I knocked twice, then stepped back, looking for the mailbox or some likely place to leave the cassette if he didn't answer.

"You want," Gerald offered, "I can open it."

But the door opened—a surprise in itself—and Kenan appeared, unshaven, cigarette at his lip. His blue-gray eyes held me with an unblinking stare. He wore a white T-shirt, khaki pants, deck shoes on his bare feet, laces missing. The skin sagged on his bare arms, but a surprisingly hard core of sinew and muscle lay beneath. I don't think he recognized me at first. Finally a wry smile came to his lips. "The Good Samaritan returns."

I apologized for disturbing him, and held out the cassette. "I thought you ought to have this . . ."

Not so much as a glance at the cassette. Kenan stared past my face, his features enlivened with an odd emotion, either fascination or dread. He was looking at Gerald.

"So," he said, hawking his throat clear as if he hadn't yet uttered a word that morning, even to himself. "Is this the Angel of Death about whom you made such a fuss?" An expectant pause. "Well? Come in."

The second surprise: Kenan wasn't drunk. And, as far as I could tell, not hung over either. He ushered us inside, moving easily, his body relaxed, every part of him under control—except his eyes. An intense, unblinking gaze, eyeballs almost reptilian, bulging as though at any moment they might become unmoored from their sockets. Only a pharmacologist, I was thinking, could tell me what made them that way.

Kenan sat on the sofa. I placed the cassette on the coffee table in front of him and remained standing. As always, Gerald hovered in the vicinity of the door. "After you look at that," I said, "we'll leave."

His living room, and what I could see of the small dining room, was not the bedlam I'd expected. Recently cleaned or, more likely, rarely used, sparsely furnished with an old sofa and chair, a coffee table, a bare desk near the bay window, two bookcases empty of books. On the walls, sooty outlines, geometrical vacancies where pictures had once hung. On the coffee table, two ashtrays, each bearing a lit cigarette, the cassette, and a small square of tinfoil.

"Bearing tribute?" he asked, picking up the cassette with an elaborate show of disappointment. "A bottle of Scotch would curry more favor."

"Do you know what it is?" I asked him.

"Offhand, I'd say it's an amateur production, one in which I'm featured. The *auteur* sacrificed polish, to my mind, for a certain immediacy of effect. I trust my performance didn't disappoint you."

"Listen to me," I said. "Keep the cassette. It's none of my business. Nobody will hear about it from me." That's what I'd planned to say; but I hadn't planned it to sound imbecilic. Kenan wasn't paying attention anyway; he kept glancing at Gerald.

"Have the executioner stand nearer," he smiled sardonically. "Let me stare Death in the face."

Gerald stood impassively; knowing him better, I now imagined nobility in his imperviousness.

"Instead of the traditional cigarette," Kenan said, "I think I'll have a pick-me-up." He unfolded the square of tinfoil on the coffee table. "Join me?"

"No thanks."

I watched him touch his moistened fingertip to a white powder, then touch his finger to his tongue. "No?" he said. "I promise, this is not a bland condiment imported from South America. This is a beast. A steel cable that fixes you to a freight train. It will drag you through every backyard in the neighborhood."

"No thanks," I declined again, lighting a cigarette.

"Ah, I remember now," he said. "You're the amateur who drinks and smokes cigarettes." Leaning back luxuriously on the sofa, he closed his eyes, apparently waiting for someone to call out, "All aboard." Whatever he was thinking, it wasn't about the cassette.

I sat in the armchair and waited. In a minute he opened his eyes. "One question," he said.

"Yes?"

"What do you suppose?"

I waited for him to finish the question. He didn't. I said, "Beg pardon?"

"What do you suppose?" he repeated.

Time to leave, I thought, watching him. Could the drug have already taken him in its grip? But then his deep voice sounded, theatrical, yes, but with enough of a cigarette rasp to give it credibility.

"Do you suppose me a jealous lover of a young girl?" he began. "Do you suppose me the frightened victim of a ruthless blackmailer? A paranoiac protector of an unblemished reputation? Or helplessly adrift, caught in the undertow of a prodigious sexual desire?" His eyes pierced me. "I wish you'd tell me, professor. It intrigues me. What keeps you coming back offering help? Your goodwill visits are trying my patience. So let's settle it now. What do you suppose?"

At one time or another, I thought, I had supposed it all. "I didn't just make this up. Rachel told me that you love her. She said that you were afraid her father would take her away."

"Love her?" he laughed. "Yes, she's right. When her prices please me, when I find her service courteous, when I hanker for her familiar product, then I love her with all my heart. Ours is a durable love. We've put it to the rigorous test of the marketplace."

"In your office," I countered, "you implied . . . well . . . that she had impaled your brain. Before that, you said you depended on her. I didn't invent it," I repeated. "I heard you say it."

"Where did you hear that?"

"At the Pink Lady. You were buying her a drink. I overheard."

"Good! You're right again. I do depend on her. It's only fair to add: I also depend on the proprietor of the liquor store on Trapelo Road. If you ask him, he will tell you that my brain is impaled there too."

"Well," I said, my resolve waning, "there's the cassette. Blackmail."

"My reputation?" he smiled. "Do you seriously believe that I care? Adam Feld—whoremaster!—couldn't understand that. I honestly miss him. His ignorance was touching. He was like a puppy rushing my leg. Distribute your film, I told him. I'll appear at a gala premiere. All the world loves a sinner. It's saints that make them uneasy. And I am nothing if I'm not willing to please."

I looked at him. "All right. You tell me. What should I suppose?"

"Shall I make it easy for you? You're looking right at it, but you still don't see. You're stumbling."

"See what?"

"A triangle," he said simply.

"You mean a lovers' triangle?" I asked. "You, Rachel, Norma?"

He shook his head impatiently. "Forget me," he said. "That's what I've been telling you. And forget about lovers. That's why you're stumbling. You reduce everything to libido. You see everything through spectacles tinted with sex."

I couldn't decide whether he were merely babbling or really trying to tell me something. I couldn't take a chance. "Okay, I'll forget you and sex. What am I missing?"

"It's very simple. The triangle I have in mind, some say, generates all of our pleasure and all of our pain. It can be fraught with psychic danger. No, not a lovers' triangle. Not a triangle we enter into willingly. I speak of the triangle to which we are all born. Every one of us."

I sat quietly, wondering what the hell he was talking about. Okay, I thought, a triangle. Potentially dangerous. We're born to it.

Kenan's body suddenly jolted upright, his eyes wide and glassy.

"WHOOSH!" he said.

I stared at him. "What?"

"WHOOOOOSH!" he repeated, his head sweeping left to right, as though his eyes were fixed on a racing car. There was no mistaking it. The drug—some kind of amphetamine?—had kicked in. He shivered like a Labrador coming out of the sea.

"Gregory Peck!" he shouted.

No question now. It was time to leave.

Kenan, a steel trap sprung, leaped off the sofa and circled the room, shouting as he went.

"Ahab! Splayed prostrate on the hump of the leviathan. Strapped to the beast among fouled harpoon lines. WHOOOOSH! The whale sounds. WHOOOOSH! Ahab is sucked down, borne to horrible depths at a horrible speed. He knows the bliss and terror of surrender."

Suddenly he stopped in front of Gerald. His eyes bugged. "Good Christ!" he whispered. "There are sharks in these waters."

We left him there, landlocked, whaling, in Belmont, Mass.

In the car Gerald said, "Guy's fucking crazy."

I didn't respond. I was thinking: triangles. By the time he dropped me off in Cambridge, I'd only come up with one. Father, mother, child.

═══*TWENTY-TWO*═══

THE SLIGHTEST SHIFT OF A PRISM, a minute re-angling toward the sun, will refract the light and cast a spectrum of color. So, too, the addition of a single fact, sometimes, will refract the light of our minds. A single fact is sufficient to reshape one's entire point of view. The world is round, you say? Well, hold on. That changes everything.

So it happened with me. I felt as though I'd been staring at a pyramid of cubes—the classic puzzle of perspective—and I could see it only one way. But now, suddenly, the points of the cubes became recesses, the recesses points. And I couldn't see the pyramid any other way. My eyes and mind caught by a particular way of seeing, as inexorably trapped in my new vision as I had been in my old. It all seemed so clear now, so obvious. How had I ever seen it otherwise?

Father, mother, child.

"Thanks," Petey said when I handed him the pari-mutuel ticket on All Smiles. "I thought you forgot."

"No, I left right after the race. Wasn't in a mood to talk."

"Well, I wouldn't waste any tears on the filly. I'd say Bud Spina is feeling pretty good right now."

"What are you talking about? She got killed."

"I'm talking about speed. What'd you expect? The filly never had a chance to run before. Gutierrez couldn't rate her, so she blew it out early. But damn, she's fast. Couple more races, shit. Put her in with other fillies, maybe drop her down in class, stick to six furlongs. Shit, she'll burn their ass up."

It was good to hear, and I'd have to think about it later. But here goes, I thought, pulling out an eight-by-ten glossy from the folder in my hand.

"Petey, I'd like for you to look at something," I said, handing him the photograph.

"No thanks," he said after a quick appraisal. "If you're selling dirty pictures, you ought to get you some better merchandise. They show more'n this in *Playboy.*"

"Don't you recognize her?" I asked impatiently. Shit, did I have it wrong?

He grinned. "Your sister?"

"Come on. This is important." Maybe Kenan had been joking. Maybe I'd misunderstood him. Or just maybe it was the amphetamines talking.

Petey looked at the photograph again, studying the old-fashioned pose. Ursula Undress leaning slightly forward, hugging herself, breasts thrust front and center, enlarged by their nearness to the camera lens.

"Nice tits," he said. "Don't see many that size anymore. All the girls want to be skinny now."

"Forget the boobs. Just look at the face."

"I'm looking," he complained. "I don't get around to the strip clubs as much as you."

"Don't think about strippers. Think about New Jersey. Think about Jacob Bloomberg."

The import of the question I'd posed gradually dawned on him. His eyes began to glow. "You shittin' me?" he said, not moving his eyes from the photograph. "I don't know ... been a long time."

"Well, could it be? I mean, is there some chance?"

He whistled. "Well, I wouldn't swear to it, but yeah, could be. I

only saw her a few times. She wasn't around all that long after he
started beating up on her. You want, I can send this to a friend of mine
at Hopworth. He can tell you for sure."

"No. Just give me your opinion."

He thought for a few seconds more. "Well, yeah, I'd say it could be
. . . Norma, I think they called her. Jake's wife."

And Rachel's mother, I thought.

"I never noticed her all that much. Always a lot of young girls
hanging around the stables. I guess that's how Jake met her. Pretty
good with animals, as I remember, a lot better'n Jake. Which ain't saying much."

"She liked horses?"

"Like 'em? Love 'em, I'd say. Otherwise what's the point of mucking
stalls for minimum wage? Lot of young girls like to be around the stables. You know what I heard this shrink say about young girls and
horses?"

"Yes," I said, cutting him off.

Petey looked at me. "Wait . . . you think . . . is Norma still around?"

"Yes."

"You saying she's the person I should thank?"

"Could be," I said, beginning to wonder just how much Norma
loved horses. Enough to kill? Enough to give her ex-husband Butazolidin, let him have a taste of his own medicine? Then go looking for the
man she thought was giving the orders?

Father, mother, child. The fact didn't answer every question I had,
but it answered enough so that I got a chill thinking about it.

I spent the next two days at my desk, phone off the hook, vaguely
shirking vague responsibilities. Should I call Ciullo? The police? Or
was now the time to write the letter to "60 Minutes"? The academic
term was coming to an end; my tenure interview was less than two
weeks away. But all I could think was: Norma. Rachel. The bedroom
scenes I'd imagined earlier now embarrassed me.

The first day, I tried to lose myself in *Helpless Laughter;* after a morning, afternoon, and night at the typewriter, I delivered a single page, each word stillborn.

The second day, I picked up a Dickens novel—what better place to numb the mind? I stopped reading on page 384, when I came upon a character who solemnly observed: "Accidents will happen in the most well-regulated families."

Well, the Philco wouldn't fail me, I thought. I lay in bed, reached for the pliers, gripped the on-off spur with the needlenose, and gave it a turn. Eleven P.M., "Eyewitness News." A report from the suburbs. A young woman had attacked her husband of six months with a baseball bat. He'd put the garbage on the curb, it seemed, a day early. A friend of the woman, in an exclusive interview, mentioned pre-menstrual syndrome.

A report from the city: a customer at a gas station had pummeled the attendant after being shortchanged.

The monstrous rage lurking just beneath the surface, I thought. Kenan had summed it up nicely: There are sharks in these waters. While I listened to the newscast, I imagined the anchorman offering the following report: wife murders husband who had brutalized her, brutalized her daughter, and brutalized a racehorse. I couldn't help but think that my imagined scenario had as much logic—more logic—than the real reports of violence I'd just heard.

On the third morning, after a deep, dreamless sleep, I rose early, showered, and stared for a long time at my image in the bathroom mirror. A knock on the door interrupted my private moment of self-scrutiny. At first I didn't move. But the knocking continued until I pulled on a robe and opened the door.

Rachel Bloomberg stood before me, tears and anger in her eyes.

"They'll kill her," she said.

=TWENTY-THREE=

GET DRESSED," Rachel said, pushing past me. She headed for the living room, looked around, saw the telephone receiver off its cradle, and said, "Shit." She turned back to me. "Come on, hurry." Whatever emotion had filled her eyes with tears, she now suppressed in favor of purpose and speed.

I still hadn't moved from the door. "Wait a minute. Who'll kill whom?"

"Mr. Ciullo will kill Norma."

"Why would he want to do that?"

"You coming or not? I got a cab waiting downstairs. You're the only one I could think of. You said Ciullo likes you."

I still didn't move. "I know what I said. But that doesn't mean—"

She came near me, reached down into the folds of my robe, and put her hand on my penis. "You come with me now," she said, "later I'll give you anything you want. You hear me? Anything. Okay?"

Flushed with anger, I wanted to say something bad to her. I got as far as "What the fuck makes you think—" and discovered that my anger was diluted with shame. Was it her fault that's what she thought of me? I shut my mouth, threw on a shirt, jeans, and sneakers, and followed her downstairs, calling after her, "Okay, but you better tell me what the hell's going on. And you better understand, whatever it is, I probably can't do a damn thing about it."

Outside on the street, Rachel started cursing. The cabbie hadn't waited. "You got a car?"

I pointed to the Volkswagen. "It runs," I said. "Whether it's a car . . ."

We jumped in, and when I pulled out of the space, I got a piece of the rear bumper of the Volvo in front of me. Keeping the wheel hard left, I made a U-turn and—goddammit!—grazed the door of a Celica parked on the opposite side of the street.

"You got a license?" she said.

We turned down Mass Ave in rush-hour traffic and missed the first light we came to. Rachel yelled, "Run it."

"First," I said, "tell me. Why would Ciullo want to hurt Norma?"

"Come on!" she pleaded. I kept my foot on the brake, and she said, "The young guy—Alex—came up to her after work last night. He said Mr. Ciullo wanted to see her this morning in his office."

"I just hit a car for that?" Not asking her, asking myself. "For crissakes, I already know about that. Ciullo just wants to talk to her."

"Maybe. It doesn't matter. Norma doesn't want to talk. She's supposed to meet him at nine-thirty. She'll be early. She took a gun."

The light had turned green, and the cars behind us were zipping past. "She what?"

"She figures Jake was working for Ciullo, that Ciullo was paying him to do that to the filly. That won't make sense to you, but it makes sense to her."

Unfortunately, I corrected her mentally, it made sense.

Ten minutes later we were no farther than Central Square, still fighting traffic. I didn't bother with the horn; a horn in Boston didn't impress anyone. Rachel kept ordering me to weave this way and that, to veer out into oncoming traffic, to squeeze through openings suitable only for a bicycle. I was having trouble changing the driving habits of a lifetime. A delivery truck in front of us double-parked. I jerked the wheel, then hit the brake when a bus on the left stopped to unload, trapping us against the curb.

Maybe thirty seconds had passed when Rachel cursed, flung open the door, and jumped out. "Leave it!" she shouted. I watched her run through traffic to a cab idling in front of the delivery truck. To tell the truth, even now I was mostly watching the action of her rear end. A bizzare image popped into my mind: myself, lying on a hospital death-bed, tubes in my nose, arms. A nurse rushing to tell the doctor, no vital signs. My final breath passes while I leer at the nurse's buttocks as she hurries out of the room.

Now me. Out of the Volkswagen and on the street, dodging traffic, my eyes crazed, no doubt, by the deathbed image in my brain. Then I was in the back seat of a Yellow Cab, hearing Rachel tell the driver the Pink Lady, Washington Street, and what was in it for him if he made good time. The cab shot off the curb defiantly, knifing past cars not so much by driving skill as by sheer willpower. Glancing over my shoul-der, out the rear window, I watched the VW disappear from view, abandoned in the middle of Central Square, both doors gaping. I thought: My keys.

On the Mass Ave Bridge, crossing into the city, I turned to Rachel. "Who told Norma that? About Ciullo?"

"Who do you think?" she replied impatiently. "Listen, you come around out of the blue, asking her about two dead men. Then you tell her watch out, the boogey man is going to get her. What did you ex-pect her to think? There's only one boogey man in our part of town. It doesn't take a genius to figure it out. I mean, Ciullo was behind the fix from the start, right? You kept asking these questions—like Feld wasn't supposed to know anything about it. Like the newspapers had it wrong."

I sat quietly for a moment, hoping the slip wouldn't come back to haunt me. As we neared the Combat Zone, the strain began to affect my thinking. If Norma succeeded at what she planned, I wondered, would tomorrow's headlines use the word "murder" or "assassina-tion"?

Rachel brought me back when she softly asked, "You think she's crazy, don't you?" There was a quiet despair in her voice that was painful to hear.

"That's not a word that means much to me."

"There's a lot you don't understand," she went on, suddenly wanting to talk. "She has reasons. Maybe they're crazy reasons—"

"I know more than you think," I said. Then I told her what I'd learned about triangles, about her father, her mother, and her; she seemed more relieved than surprised. "I guess it doesn't matter," I said. "But I can't help wondering if you, well . . . when she was—"

"Did I know?" she asked. "God, I guess I did, part of me. But I wouldn't let myself know. I hoped that . . . you must think I'm crazy too." Now, in the final moments, as the cab turned down Washington Street and crossed the invisible boundary of the Zone, she began to talk, urgently, as if she might never have another chance. "You know how long I tried to find her? I didn't even think she was alive until I was fourteen. Well, I found her and then I saw how she was. But we did fine for a while. Things weren't so bad until Jake found us. Jesus, Jake. She had a lot of reasons to do it. But when she heard about the filly, that was the thing. After all the other shit, that's what really got to her. You heard her. She has all these ideas. All she could talk about was that poor dumb animal. Every time she thought about the filly, it was like she was thinking about herself. Like she couldn't see any difference. She's say, 'There's always a man standing there with a whip. You ever try to do anything for yourself, sooner or later, you'll feel the whip.' Stuff like that. She'd say it over and over. 'The man with the whip. That's the only thing in life you can count on.' " Rachel paused and looked at me. "You know what's the craziest thing of all?"

I shook my head.

"I know this sounds sick," she said. "Maybe it is sick. But killing them was good for her. That's why she didn't just stop with Jake. I think it made her feel better. I think she liked it."

With a reckless flourish, the cabbie swerved past one last car, then braked heavily at the curb in front of the Pink Lady Club. Ten minutes past nine. I gave him double fare. On the sidewalk, businessmen strode briskly to work, passers-through, immune to the lurid images that surrounded them. A few derelicts inhabited the doorways, sleeping in bands of threes and fours—prides? gaggles?—acknowledging some primitive instinct for community.

A steel bar and padlock secured the street entrance to the club. Without speaking, we circled the building and entered the alley that ran behind it. A few yards from the back door, an old man in a tattered sweater leaned against a green dumpster. I tried the doorknob and it turned.

"Spare some change?" the old man asked me, rising, displaying a single brown tooth as he spoke.

"Have you been in this alley long?"

"Off and on," he said, "about six years."

"Come on, this morning?"

He stuck out his hand, palm up. "Seems like I ast you something first," he said.

I reached in my wallet and gave him the first thing I pulled out, a twenty. "Did a Mercedes come through here, drop anybody off?"

"Not bad," he said, smoothing the bill. "Mr. Ciullo"—he said Chew-ler—"only gives me a five now and again."

"You know Mr. Ciullo?"

"I told you. I worked this alley for years. Mornings, I wait to see if Mr. Ciullo comes in. About ten o'clock I move over to out back of the Bradford. Mr. Gatto, the manager, gets there about—"

"Jesus, save it! Has he been in?"

He rubbed his mouth. "No."

"Anybody been through that door?"

"Mr. Ciullo's man. Big guy. On days the boss is due, the big guy gets here 'round eight, eighty-thirty. That's how I know whether to stick around. The kid drives the Mercedes in the mornings. The kid's sometimes good for a couple of bucks. I never get a dime out of the big guy."

"Anybody else?"

The old man started eyeing me, his look saying that twenty dollars would only buy so much. Rachel brushed past me and grabbed his collar. "Listen, you piece of shit, we don't have time. Did a woman go in there?"

"All right, lady," he said, cowering. "Just testing the water. Yeah, about twenty minutes ago. A blond. Had makeup on. I think she works here."

When Rachel put her hand on the doorknob, I held her back. "You stay here," I said. "When Ciullo shows up, tell him anything. Just keep him out."

"I'm going in," she said.

"I know Gerald," I said, striving for an optimism that I really didn't feel. "If he's in there, maybe it will be okay. He might listen to me."

She hesitated, still suspicious. "Shit," I cursed, "you dragged me here. Okay, I'm here. I might as well do something."

Alone in the pitch dark of the inner hallway, I wished I hadn't been so persuasive. Feeling my way along, taking baby steps, right hand sliding against the wall, left hand extended, searching the blackness as I moved into it. Wrong, I thought; the yogi I'd heard claim he could hear his own heartbeat was wrong. If such a thing were possible, I would've heard mine right then. I reached a corner, turned it, and saw a thin line of light maybe fifteen feet away, at the bottom of Ciullo's door. A quicker step now. I put my ear to the door. Silence.

Open it? Kick it in and shout, Freeze? Following the procedure universally adopted by TV cops, I stepped off to the side and knocked. Nothing. I reached down, turned the knob slowly, pulled, and looked in. I breathed again. Ciullo's office was empty. Hell, I thought, relaxing a little, surveying the room. Maybe Gerald had already hustled Norma outside. Maybe took her for a cup of coffee and told her things couldn't be as bad as all that. But then I looked at the oriental rug and saw the gun lying there. And next to the gun a dark oval, damp-looking, the size and roughly the shape of an artist's palette. Either someone had recently lost blood there, I decided, closing the door, or lost control of his bladder.

Next, around another corner, which brought me into a larger hallway, filled with a dim bluish light coming from the bar. I passed two pay phones and the men's-room door, stopping short at the bar entrance, listening, calling to mind an image of what lay beyond the threshold: the stage, just inside and to the right. The long runway of polished oak extending from the apron of the stage into the room. Bars on both sides of the runway; out from that, tables and chairs, and finally, booths against the walls. I peered into the mirrors on the side walls, trying to see inside the bar. The mirrors held only an image of a blue spotlight, carving a cone of light into the darkness. The spotlight was aimed toward the stage, where it usually zeroed in on the strippers. I couldn't see the stage without stepping into the room, into the light.

If I'd heard a sound I wouldn't have moved. I took two steps forward and looked to my right. In the middle of the stage Gerald stood motionless, coat off, shoulder holster empty. With his right hand he gripped his left shirtsleeve above the elbow, and I saw blood seeping through his spread fingers. He turned toward me and put a funny look in his eyes. A warning, I realized too late.

A metallic *cha-klunk*. The spot shifted full force on me. I raised a hand to my eyes. "Wha—?"

"Far enough, freak." Norma's voice, weighted with venom, rose out of the blackness behind the spotlight, saying, "Right there, freak. Don't move."

Frozen, I squinted into the blue orb of light.

"Okay now, slow. I want you to join your friend on the stage." I couldn't move. "Come on now. Up those steps. Your friend didn't want to go up there either. He didn't think a woman would shoot him. I think I cured him of his stage fright."

Slowly I mounted the three steps—the spotlight following me—and stood on the stage next to Gerald.

"Good," she said, "we got a big freak and a little freak." She laughed. "Looks like I got lucky. All the freaks are out this morning. Now we just wait here for the old freak with the bow tie."

"You okay?" I whispered to Gerald.

"No talking, professor," she warned menacingly. "You bored?"

I said no.

"Since you're bored, tell you what. While we wait for the head freak, let's have a little entertainment. Just to pass the time. So nobody gets bored."

There was a pause, and from the blackness I heard her say, "Yeah," as if the idea suddenly took hold, appealing to her. "Big freak, you first. You've seen enough strippers, you know how it goes. Come on," she hooted, mimicking the catcall of a man, "show me that gut. Show me that nasty little worm. Yeah, Miss Geraldine. Yeah. Show it or I'll shoot it off."

Gerald slowly dropped his hand from where it gripped his wound, clenched his fists at his sides, and assumed an intractable pose of defiance. I watched him anxiously, knowing that he would rather die than take off his clothes. I knew, too, that if Ursula started shooting, she might not stop with Gerald. She might go for the whole chorus line.

"Wait," I called into the barrel of light. "I'll go first. I know the routine better."

"Shut your mouth, freak," she snapped. Then she laughed, reconsidering. "You an exhibitionist? Okay, no difference. Everybody gets a chance in the all-freak revue."

Well, I'd asked for it. My fingers at my shirt buttons, I slowly moved my feet, executing an awkward, spastic dance. Even under romantic lights and in loving arms, I wasn't much on the dance floor. Now, with both a spotlight and a gun trained on me, my sneakers sticking to the floor, I deteriorated into a horrible jerkiness, bereft of rhythm, a performance that in other circumstances might have indicated brain damage.

"The fuck is that, freak?" she hissed. "Put some hip in it. Get into it."

I quit moving. "Norma, listen. Why don't we stop this before things get worse."

"Ursula," she spat, "Ursula to—"

Several things happened at once.

The ceiling lights came on, filling the room with light. To my left, Rachel ran into the bar, shouting, wailing, "Mother! Noooo!" I felt Gerald pushing me off the stage, shoving me down onto my belly, then bolting past me in a crouch. Rachel running toward Norma, screaming, "Mother!" Gerald charging behind her, using her as a shield.

When Norma aimed the gun at them, I ducked. Not out of fear; I was beyond that. I just couldn't make myself watch. But I didn't hear shots. I heard bodies clash and the *oomph* of breath knocked out of lungs.

I looked. Norma lay pinned to the floor on her stomach, Gerald on top of her, expressionless. He forced her arms behind her, pressing a knee into her back. She tried to talk; her lips, thrust against the floor, misshapen, would permit only an inarticulate blubber.

Rachel knelt beside them, quietly reaching out to stroke her mother's hair, whispering "It's okay" over and over. The scene was oddly familiar. I couldn't place it at first. Then I remembered: television. "Wild Kingdom." Rachel comforted her mother as one comforts a wild animal similarly pinned, that is about to have its ear tagged.

It was just now ten o'clock. Leaving the club in a daze, I found a police officer in the first coffee shop I came to, a half-block away. I told him just enough so that he spoke into a walkie-talkie and followed me back down the street.

Fifty yards away, heading in our direction, Ciullo's Mercedes cruised slowly down Washington Street, Alex driving, his uncle in the rear seat. Alex slowed as he passed, catching my eye with a quizzical expression.

I shook my head, a barely perceptible signal of warning.

The Mercedes kept going. In the rear seat, Ciullo's eyes, disinterested and aloof, never veered right or left. His affect reminded me of something I'd once read in a liberal Boston tour guide. Should you get lost in a bad section of town, the pamphlet advised, don't gawk. Show respect to all citizens. Don't make other people's lives your experience.

EPILOGUE
ME

AT THE END OF THE SECOND WEEK in June, on a morning that portended an afternoon of oppressive urban mugginess, I found in my mailbox the letter from the Department of American Civilization informing me of the tenure committee's decision. One of those many letters I'd received in my life that required only a single word, yea or nay. But the letters were always longer.

Memories of the interview itself sometimes popped into my mind without warning, causing me to wince; it hadn't been a disaster, really, but close enough. Braithewaite had chaired a committee of four antique scholars, all sitting opposite me at a dark mahogany table in a small room on the first floor of Talbot House. Professors Millsap and Lutcavage to the extreme right and left, dozing. Nearer, Professors Donleavy and Gurney: the former bubbling with an indiscriminate friendliness, the latter regarding me with an expression of such austere displeasure that I was tempted to check the bottoms of my shoes. Professor Braithewaite sat in the center of the happy clique, directly across from me, peculiarly discomfited, even fidgety. Stephen Kenan had been true to his word; he didn't show up. Frail health, Braithewaite explained solemnly, nodding toward the vacant chair.

To be fair, my own attitude might have put them off; Beth had referred to it, without irony, as "passive-aggressive." I chain-smoked; I neglected to remove my sunglasses. I kept the glasses on—this is what I told myself, at least—for cosmetic purposes. A few brusies, rapidly fading, still discolored my eye sockets. The strip of gauze across my nose was the size of a Band-Aid. Except for the smoking, I looked the part of a boxer at a post-fight press conference.

Braithewaite, though surprisingly congenial, didn't say one word more than he had to. He emphasized the informality of the gathering and his hope that we should all enjoy a fruitful exchange of views. The interview must have lasted forty-five minutes, but now, looking back, I could remember only one question. Professor Gurney—like Braithewaite, a medievalist—roused himself to a fine rhetorical pitch. "Nineteenth-century America," he said, mildly contemptuous, as though he were pronouncing the name of a passing fad. "How far back does one go, do you suppose, how many years back into the history of literature, to understand"—strong emphasis—"to comprehend nineteenth-century America?"

Quietly reflecting behind my sunglasses, I asked innocently, "Eighteen hundred?"

If it were possible, the interview went downhill from there. We didn't exchange views so much as mutual stares of reproach and disappointment.

"Uh . . . thank you, Professor Theron," Braithewaite concluded the proceeding uneasily. "We'll be in touch. Expect a letter in about a week or ten days."

Now I lay on the floor of my apartment, in my undershorts, a small fan nearby rotating back and forth, sending a blast of air the length of my body. "Drumroll," I said aloud, opening the letter. Beneath the elegant Am. Civ. letterhead, two paragraphs, the first beginning: Dear Professor Theron: We are pleased to inform you that your request for tenure has been granted . . ." Some terms of the contract followed, some "I look forward to . . ." sentences.

The second paragraph startled me even more than the first. "The committee has decided to grant you a year's sabbatical, beginning September of this year, so that you may complete your work on the biography of Edmund Lowell. ..." At full pay, of course, it continued. Research grants were available, and so forth and so on.

Gayle Braithewaite's spidery signature graced the salutation. A brief, handwritten postscript lay beneath his signature. "Dear Thomas: Congratulations. Please inform your friend, Mr. V.C., of the committee's recommendation. Good luck."

I folded the letter and returned it to the envelope. My hands didn't shake. My pulse didn't increase. Somewhere in the back of my mind, I must have expected it.

The following afternoon, I placed the tenure letter on Vincent Ciullo's desk.

"Congratulations," he said simply.

"Thanks. What's the postscript mean?"

"Usual procedure, I'd say. Informing someone who has made a recommendation of the outcome."

I was almost afraid to ask. "Run it past me again. What kind of recommendation did you make?"

"I simply told Professor Braithewaite that you had my full confidence and support." Ciullo smiled. "The sabbatical idea, I don't mind saying, was just a stroke of genius. You'd mentioned a desire for time off."

I looked at him. "You're not going to tell me, are you?"

"Ah, Thomas." He smiled. "We've been through this before. Do you really want to know?"

"No, I don't want to know. You know I don't. But it's like everything else. I ought to know."

"Ought to know," he repeated. "The desire to know, Aristotle once said, subsumes all other desires. Well, Thomas, as you wish. There's nothing magical here. If the past two months have taught anything, they have taught that every man clutches to his heart a secret of some kind. In Mr. Braithewaite's case ... how to say this ..."

"Stop," I interrupted. "Enough."

After a moment's silence he continued, "Why not look at it this way: in the process of helping me, you damaged your chances for tenure. I'm just helping to set things straight. To my mind, you deserve something more . . ."

"I promise, we're even. I'm not out anything." Then I remembered myself in the cab with Rachel, looking back, watching the Volkswagen fade from view. "Well, almost anything," I smiled. "I haven't seen my car since I left it in the middle of Central Square."

"I didn't realize," he said.

"Not that it's a problem," I said quickly. "Whoever took it did me a favor."

Before I left, Ciullo mentioned again the sheaf of poems he'd wanted me to read. "They're resisting me a bit," he said sadly. "They're not just yet what I want them to be."

"It's a hard thing to do," I agreed, wondering for the first time if I would ever see them. Would his poems ever be what he wanted them to be? Not that I minded.

"By the way," I said, "how's Gerald?"

"Just fine. I gave him some time off. I offered to send him anywhere, actually, anywhere in the world. He wanted to visit his brother in Worcester."

On the subway, heading to Back Bay—Elizabeth had asked to hear as soon as I got the letter—I studied the Boston newspapers for the second time that day. A month had passed since that morning at the Pink Lady Club, but the furor over Norma, Rachel, and Jacob Bloomberg showed no signs of dying down. I had watched with profound fascination as the media portrayed Norma as, in turn, a demented murderess, a victim of sexual exploitation, and lately, more or less, a heroine and martyr. Her story gradually took hold of the public heart. One photograph in particular seemed to distill the episode and imprint it on the public psyche: mother and daughter, arm in arm, leaving the courthouse, their eyes crystallized with fear and pain. What made the photograph memorable, of course, was the composition; on either side of Rachel and Norma stood two huge state troopers, their faces caught in attitudes of masculine malevolence.

Few words were offered on behalf of Jacob Bloomberg or Adam Feld; a range of opinions were voiced that could all be reduced to "They got what they deserved." Norma's prospects, if not bright, were not nearly as bleak as I would have expected.

The drama was not restricted to the media. A "Take Back the Night" demonstration was organized. The Daughters of Sappho kept a vigil in front of the courthouse. A national organization of prostitutes began collecting a legal fund. A local talk show featured representatives from a group called Protect Our Children. The ASPCA called for an investigation of racetrack veterinarians. College radio stations, following news reports, played "When the Whip Comes Down."

Despite extensive coverage, one glaring omission remained. My own name never made the papers. Neither did Gerald Valentin's—no account of his wound, much less of charges being filed or dropped. Certainly no mention of it from Norma or her lawyers. Why disclose that she'd gone to the Pink Lady that morning, trying for the hat trick? There were, of course, the usual rumors about Vincent Ciullo. Actually, more than usual.

I found Beth packing for a weekend in Martha's Vineyard. White shorts and a light blue tank top, already tan, Californian.

"That's great," Beth said when I handed her the letter. Then puzzlement. "I can't figure it. The way you described the interview . . . you weren't just making it seem worse than it was? You do that, you know."

"It was that bad. I didn't even tell you, whenever they stumped me, I took off my shoes and chewed my toenails."

"Okay. Spare me. Well, it's great news anyway. You're on a roll. First, no herpes. Now tenure."

I ignored the dig. "Who knows what lurks in the hearts of medievalists?"

While I helped her stow her bags in the trunk of the Granada, we didn't speak.

"So," I finally said. "Martha's Vineyard."

"That's right."

"Good weather for it."

She nodded.

"Good time to go."

She slung a brown canvas bag over her shoulder, set the police lock in place, and shut the door. Then she turned the key for the deadbolt, then the door lock. "If you're asking, Thomas," she said, "I'm not spending the weekend alone. I'm going with a friend from the clinic. A woman."

"I was just thinking about that raincheck we talked about. You remember?"

She said yes.

"Well?"

"Thomas, I'm a little off men right now. Maybe after a while. But right now I think I should spend some time by myself. Some time with women friends. None of this hopping from one man to the next."

"Are you seeing Breck?"

She shook her head. "I'm telling you the same thing I told him."

When she got in the car, she rolled down the window and sat there a minute, looking at me. She said, "It's a shitty business, isn't it?"

"What is?"

"All of it. Just getting by."

"That's what I've been telling you for a couple of years now. Maybe not in so many words . . ."

"I know. I'm just tired. Very tired.'"

"That's what living does to you," I said as she put the engine in gear. "It wears your ass out."

Before the end of June, I found another item of special interest in the *Boston Globe*. This time on the sports page. The day before, Raggedy And had dropped in class to a $12,000 claiming race restricted to fillies and mares. Leaving the gate at 4–1, she'd won by six lengths.

I put the *Globe* down and returned to my desk, glancing at the wall where I'd formerly kept the Three Boxes. There was only one box now, the box with *Helpless Laughter.* The pages were coming, slowly, painfully, but coming. Somehow, somewhere in the back of my mind, I'd expected the writing to be easier. I'd convinced myself that my time with Ciullo and Rachel and Norma and Kenan had, well, rejuvenated me, hardened me. Maybe tempered me in some passional fire of life itself—something like that. Of course, it hadn't done anything of the kind.

I sat there another hour, smoking, restless, the manuscript spread on the desk before me. Then I rose and paced nervously around my apartment, suddenly feeling claustrophobic. I checked my watch and thought: Screw it. A quarter to noon. I picked up the keys to Ciullo's Mercedes—impossible to think "my Mercedes," even though he'd given it to me—and headed for the door.

With any luck, I could make it to Suffolk Downs in time for the daily double.